SEVEN AGAINST SEYMUS

The Last Shadow Epic, Book Four

by

AJ Cooper

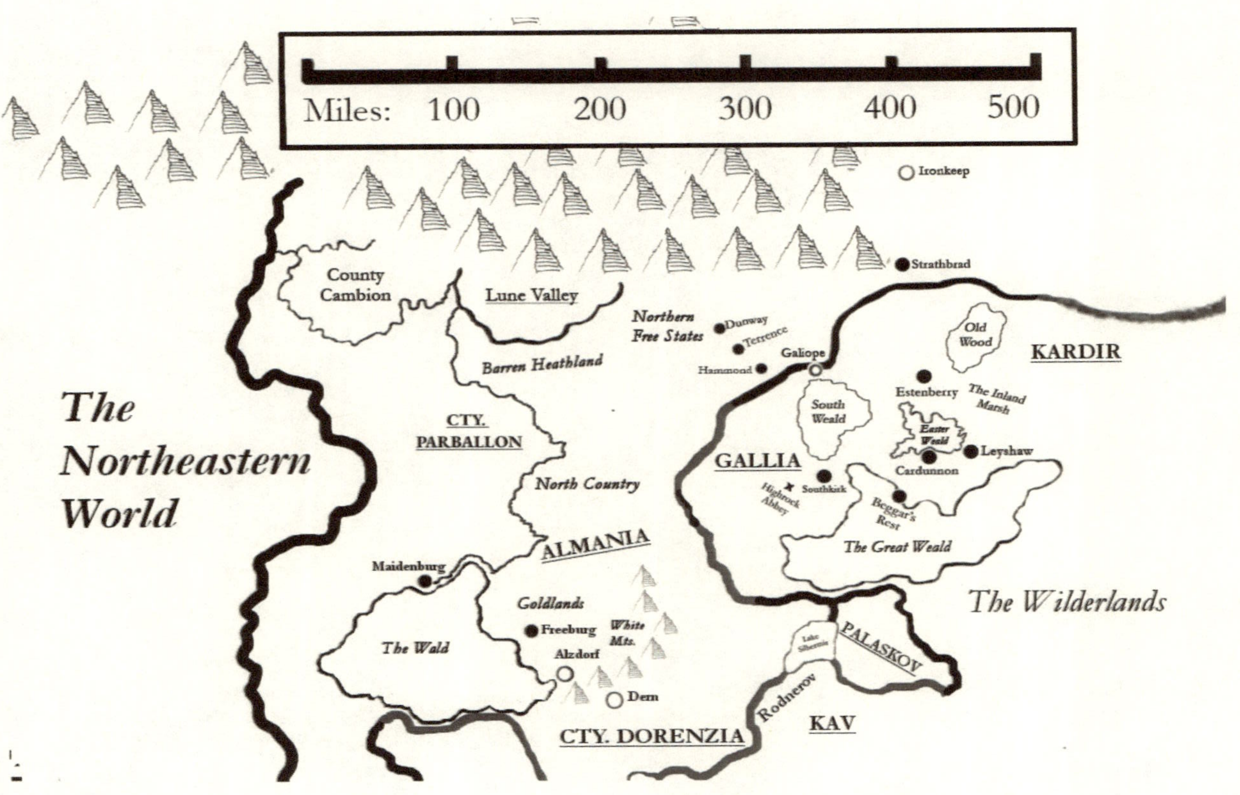
The Northeastern World
Miles: 100 200 300 400 500
County Cambion
Lune Valley
Barren Heathland
CTY. PARBALLON
North Country
ALMANIA
Maidenburg
The Wald
Goldlands
Freeburg
White Mts.
Alzdorf
Dern
CTY. DORENZIA
Northern Free States
Dunway
Terrence
Hammond
Galiope
Ironkeep
Strathbrad
Old Wood
KARDIR
Estenberry
The Inland Marsh
South Weald
Easter Weald
Leyshaw
Cardunnon
GALLIA
Highrock Abbey
Southkirk
Beggar's Rest
The Great Weald
The Wilderlands
Lake Silvermist
PALASKOV
Rodnerov
KAV

GALIOPE

Garrick's Gate
THE ELVEN QUARTER
MARKET DISTRICT
SELWYN'S PARISH
Hawk's Keep
Strathbrad Gate
Tower of Pythor
Horn Keep
MIDDLETOWN
WODENSCROSS COURT
LONEN TOWN
GREENWATER
Bridge O'er Galios
RIVERSIDE
CATHEDRAL DISTRICT
Godsgate

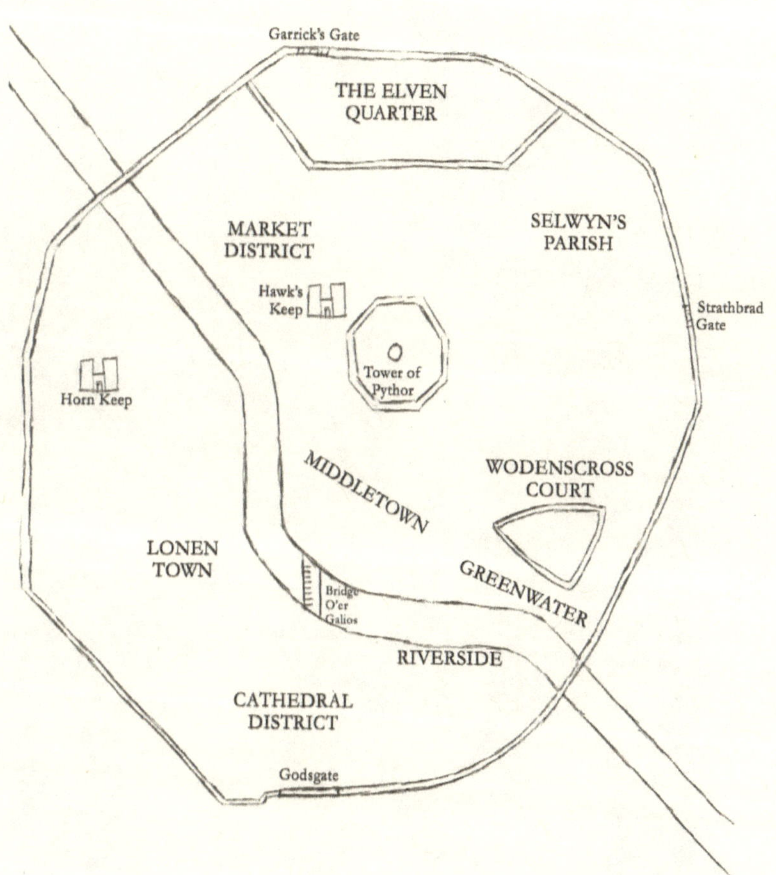

The Fox and the Hound

Brenua 11, 1153 Y.E.
26th of Rial, 1469 of the Age of Humanity

The abbey at Highrock was said by the people of the North to represent heaven — an abode of the gods, fallen from the sky — but to Sergio, leader of the Empire's 19th cohort, it seemed the opposite. A monstrous thing of spires and towers, it was, without care for symmetry or the whole, crowding out the sky in the summer sun, bell towers and chambers built up throughout the centuries without a grand design.

Yet in the Empire's conquest of Gallia, the abbot had offered his help. When the eye of the emperor was fixed on a new place, traitors innumerable appeared, weak men wishing to take advantage of an assured defeat. The Empire lost battles, but not wars.

And so, what did Abbot Bailock want? It was for Sergio to discover. He made a signal for his men to secure the perimeter.

And like cogs in a grand machine the soldiers began to span out, covering lost ground. The monks working in the fields gave no resistance, nor did the common people in the town of Dog's Head.

And with a force of a hundred men, Sergio personally made his way down the road, toward the great doors of the monstrous abbey, where wealth there was in abundance, gold that could buy mercenaries and fund the construction of ballasts and ballistae, silver that could bribe the Gallian elite… theirs for the taking.

When the Empire came, the weak men and the cowards profited. When the Empire arrived at a nation's door, the least in character did best.

~

If the outside of Highrock Abbey was monstrous, the inside was abyssal — caverns of rooms and hallways, cluttered chambers filled with gold and silver relics, crammed without care in the darkness. Worst of all was the incense which filled the air like smog, choking in its omnipresence, causing Sergio's eyes to water, and his mouth to strain to breathe. To those symptoms was added a headache as the chamberlain guided them through the rabbit's warren of chambers, past statuaries and tapestries, in the light of candles and torches and chandeliers. Sergio was not greedy like the great families of the Empire, who drove its conquests, but as he passed the rooms filled with precious objects, reliquaries made of gold, doves made of silver and statues in whose eyes were set emerald and sapphire and ruby, he knew the men who followed behind him were thinking of loot. Legionaries were paid a salary, but with each sack of a town, with each conquest, there were opportunities to steal and rob, chances to stow away valuables and run off with them in the night.

Yet Highrock Abbey had offered their assistance. They wished to be allies. Therefore, their wealth was safe for now, for as long as the Lornodorises or Kerii, the Maiadores or Verruses did not know about it.

At last, through the choking incense, Sergio found himself passing through a set of oaken doors, and past those doors a vast chamber, lit through a rooftop window by the sun above, a marble floor that reminded him of home, tapestries and paintings of stories from the priest's book, and ahead of Sergio a chair, on which sat a portly man with a ruddy face, his hair cut in that silly way monks had it — a tonsure.

On the abbot's face was a scowl. His plump fingers clutched the armrests of his makeshift throne. His cloudy blue eyes met Sergio's, and as they stood, transfixed in their gazes, more monks appeared from the shadows of the room, five, ten, twelve — a dozen, and then dozens.

"Sergio Baris," said the abbot, "centurion. Leader of the 19th cohort. Welcome to Highrock Abbey, the seat of our god Heron in the north, or rather *my* seat — his vicar."

Sergio hailed him.

"Will you bow?" the abbot said.

"The Empire bows to no one," said Sergio.

The abbot seemed to stiffen, and with each passing moment more monks were emerging from the darkness. Dozens there were, and a hundred, perfectly veiled by the light of the candles, dark inscrutable shadows to Sergio and not much more.

"The god of justice and just war demands honor from his followers," the abbot said. "His demands for upright conduct are absolute. We shall not prostrate ourselves before man; or any of mankind's kingdoms."

The air in the room seemed to change, and Sergio's hand was moving of its own accord to his sword.

"We shall not call anything a god which is not a god… and that, according to our reports, is what some subjects of the emperor do to him."

"Only in the east," Sergio tried to say, but what emerged from his mouth was an inaudible squeak.

"In fact," the abbot said, "the god of justice and just war demands we struggle against such blasphemers and such blasphemy. In fact, we must not leave such blasphemers alive — who call the emperor a god."

Sergio drew his sword, and the hundred men with him did the same. The metal of those swords gleamed in the candlelight. "You are monks!" Sergio cried. His heart was pounding in his chest. "You are sworn not to shed blood."

"Aye, we may not shed blood," the abbot said, "but we can break bones."

And he drew from his side, from the folds of his robe, a mace of iron, and the two hundred monks in the vast chamber did the same, at once, in unison.

They charged in a mob, two hundred against one hundred, and more monks were pouring from Highrock Abbey's doors and tunnels by the second.

A soldier sank to the ground, pummeled, beside Sergio; in the dark they were at a disadvantage, for the monks could fight blind in this place, in this abbey they knew every inch of, wherein they had spent their lives.

More cries issued — more soldiers fell, and panic fell on Sergio — panic, the pipes of Brecko. He turned and fled in the dark, into the maze of rooms that composed Highrock Abbey.

The leader of the 19th cohort, its highest-ranking centurion, had abandoned his men unto death.

~

Sergio charged through the darkness, past corridors and hallways, through rooms, pursued at all moments by the sound of approaching footsteps and shouts.

But the abbey at Highrock was a maze, and he did not know where to go — panic drove him and only panic. He had not died a soldier's death; he had turned, and he had run.

Through the darkness his run became a sprint — light appeared through some inscrutable doorway, and Sergio under his breath uttered prayers to whatever god would hear him. He bolted through the light, down a hall, through a door…

And he was in a chapel, not outside. The light was emanating from a great window of stained glass — depicting Antheleon treading the serpent, as it was in the priests' book. Each pane of glass was lit, fire-like, by the sun outside, celestial blues and emerald greens and ruby reds.

Sergio thought of death, and saw flame.

He turned in view of his pursuers, monks by the dozen, wielding iron maces and wooden war clubs. He cast his sword clattering to the ground and raised his hands.

"Mercy!" Sergio cried. "Mercy!

"You are monks… you will not kill a man who has surrendered."

The faces in the light of the stained glass window gave no disagreement. One made a signal with his hands, and a monk walked up to Sergio from among the masses, bearing a length of cord.

They tied the cord around his wrist, so tight that Sergio thought it might bleed. They tossed a sack of horsehair over his head, and all went dark.

~

Sergio was being led outside, through the summer air. Each halting step was full of danger. He was being led outside — and how long had he been captive? It had to be longer than an hour.

A switch struck him, slicing the fabric of his cloak, cutting his skin. He felt blood running down his back as he was kicked to the grass, to his knees.

A hand roughly jerked the sack from his head. His eyes only slowly began to adjust to the light. Grass there was, and farmers' fields — a flowing stream, and a face… yes, a face, looming above him.

It was a face he knew.

"Fortunato?" Sergio cried. "It can't be you…"

***

"Shall we kill him, commander?" one of the monks said to Fortunato.

And all Fortunato could do was stare, stare at his childhood friend… Sergio Barus from Straight Street — from Caro's Wharf. "Sergio," Fortunato uttered, and he was in disbelief.

"Shall we kill him, commander?" the monk said again.

Sergio's blue eyes were looking at him in astonishment, in incredulity. And Fortunato did not know what to say.

His childhood friend had surely swiftly moved through the ranks, becoming the leader of a cohort. Fortunato would have said, "Kill him," but could he kill Sergio Barus from Straight Street, Sergio from his boyhood home — Ríva?

"It's been a while since we stole those apples from Farmer Gaspare's orchard," Sergio said — and the disbelief in his eyes was beginning to fade.

The incident at the orchard was not one that Fortunato was proud of. Indeed, it brought him shame. "Sergio," Fortunato said, and the soldiers behind him drew their swords, "I am not the boy you knew. I am field marshal of this battalion. You shall not speak so informally to me."

"Will you kill the boy who introduced you to poppy's milk?" Sergio went on. "Will you murder the boy who taught you how to woo?"

"You are not he, not anymore," said Fortunato, "and I am not the boy you knew."

Sergio's familiarity, the slight smile that had appeared on his lips, vanished. Fear was beginning to dawn in those dull blue eyes of his.

"Nevertheless," Fortunato said, "enough blood has been spilled this afternoon. Free him… let him go."

And Sergio would tell all — he would tell everyone he knew. Fortunato of Ríva had joined the enemy; Fortunato had betrayed his country — Fortunato had betrayed the Empire's cause.

Chapter One:
As Through A Mirror

From the high window on Rosetree Manor's topmost story, Reev looked down to the city streets. Galiope, a city in peril, a city in danger of extinction, was not the safe haven it once had been, not the secure bulwark for the exile. The Empire threatened Gallia on its borders, yes, but what Reev feared most was the danger within.

"Reev!" Gastreel's voice called out from some room.

Reev turned from his high perch to see the Green Wizard walking through the door. "Reev!" Gastreel said again, and for the first time in weeks there was a smile on his face. "A victory at long last… the Empire's forces were defeated at Highrock Abbey. And your friend Fortunato led the charge…"

Reev could not bring himself to smile. A ray of good news was not much to celebrate in a world of so much darkness and peril. A defeat for the Empire, Reev supposed, was welcome news, if only for the safety of those he loved best. A defeat for the Empire — but what of the Lord Eventide and his dark counsel, what of the ship of burial on which he had burned the body of his son? What of the meetings held in secret groves? What of the heathen prayers now uttered at the Council of War?

"Good news," Reev said, "and it is good to hear of Fortunato."

He had not seen his friend in a long while; it seemed an age. He was fighting for the Gallian people, for his adopted homeland. He had left behind the country of his birth, now, for once — forever.

"Good news," Reev said, but the victory, far away, did not bring him any joy.

Perhaps, Gastreel could sense it, for as he stood there the light in his eyes faded, his smile vanished, and he seemed to shrink, to darken.

"Well, Reev," Gastreel said softly, "the Lord Eventide has summoned me. Be on your guard.

"The Empire has sympathizers in the city."

"It is not the Empire I fear," Reev said.

"I know," Gastreel replied, and turned, into the darkness.

Reev watched Gastreel's green-garbed form walking out onto the street, dispersing into the crowds.

Be on your guard, he had said; stay safe. No doubt Gastreel would like Reev to cower within Rosetree Manor all his days.

Observing from such a height, Reev watched the crowds pass to and fro, here on Galiope's high flattop hill, where the rich and well connected lived.

He spied, walking by, his Aunt Ramona, dressed in an unseasonable fur coat. Even from so great a distance he could see the gold rings on her fingers and the diamond necklace about her neck.

Beside her was his cousin Ash — Asher Nax Bensange, garbed all in black. The summer light was casting him in shadow.

~

Gastreel pushed through the swarming crowds of Wodenscross Court, at times sliding past the passersby and at times even pushing them roughly aside with his staff. The Lord Eventide, chancellor of the League and mayor of Galiope, had sent him a summons not long ago. He expected timeliness and punctuality of the Green Wizard.

At last, Gastreeel raced through the gate, through streets that were even more crowded, a mélange of smells and scents, of colors and a variety of tongues.

In the center of the street someone had erected a Brenua pole, and children, boys and girls, were prancing around it. They were celebrating the coming of summer, even now, when the Empire, and certain destruction, was at the door.

Past the crowds Gastreel pushed, past horses and dogs and even pigs running free, across hole-pocked roads and streaks of mud, from Wodenscross Court into Middletown.

A burly man was at a street corner, patting a tambourine. A woman was beside him, singing.

Summer is a-coming in
Loudly sing, yes, you!
Summer is a-coming in
And the pipers too!

Markets had been set up in the squares — peas and asparagus for the taking, spices to sell, barnyard animals at auction. And it seemed that if destruction and fire lurked just a little distance away, no one in the City of Galiope knew.

Yet Gastreel began to make headway, past markets and crowded streets, across the river bridge, through Lonen Town. And before he knew it, the spires and stone towers of Horn Keep were before him. Here in this gloomy wonderwork, the Lord Chancellor had set up his headquarters. Here, amid shadow, the commander-in-chief undertook his work.

The candles in Lord Eventide's office offered scant illumination, and the face that greeted Gastreel was one wreathed in darkness.

"Your Honor," Gastreel said, and his voice had grown faint.

In this chamber at the height of one of Horn Keep's towers,

the leader of the war effort ruminated. On his desk was a drinking cup made from a rokahn's skull, in which was a black liquid. Also on the desk was his dagger, on which he had embossed a dragon's eye in gold. Eventide claimed the spirits of his ancestors would help him, but there was little evidence thus far.

"Green Wizard," said the Lord Eventide, "you came here swiftly, as I have learned to expect. Few can I trust in Galiope, but you are an exception."

"I am glad to be of service," Gastreel said, "to the city I love."

"And to this city, you are indispensable," said Eventide.

"How may I be of service to it this day?" Gastreel said.

"Our treasurer has made an accounting of all our supplies — swords and axes and shields, money in gold and silver bullion. We have taken note of something being pilfered — our stores of pipeweed."

Gastreel could not imagine such a thing being integral to the war effort. Yet the nobility of Gallia could scarcely do without it.

"Our agents have kept watch on the stores," Eventide said, "the warehouses and otherwise. They are so vast, so well supplied, that they are difficult to keep track of. But last night one of those agents saw the thief running away."

"What does this have to do with me?" Gastreel said.

"Our guard followed him, as fast as he could run — down the street," Eventide continued. "And he saw the thief sprinting into that den of villainy, the Dragonpaw Inn."

"Wrinn Finnis," Gastreel said, "Wrinn — that rascal. I shall have a word with him, or worse."

"So you know the thief — as I thought," Eventide said. "He owes the Gallian state some ten marks."

"A price he shall not easily be able to pay," Gastreel said, "but I have an idea for him.

"He shall work his way through it. He shall be a slave – "

"There is no slavery in Gallia," Eventide said.

"He shall be a servant — a specialized servant — of the state… a bondservant for the Council of War. He will repay his debts… I will see to it."

"First," Eventide said, "we must have proof."

Gastreel spent his afternoon at the Dragonpaw, in the company of Glenda and Bala, and in view of Wrinn, who it seemed had fallen in with bad characters. From morning until dusk, Wrinn played dice, between sips of ale, with a group of young Mountain Folk men. And Gastreel pretended all was well, that he was none the wiser, sitting in his booth, only occasionally stealing glances at Wrinn, until night fell, and darkness was over the land. At that time Wrinn retreated to his room, returned with a bag, and stepped outside.

Gastreel found him smoking with the Mountain Folk men, at a dock, in the district of Riverside. The pipes in their mouths flared, and in Wrinn's bag was plenty of pipeweed.

"Wrinn Finnis!" Gastreel called out.

And Wrinn looked up, and shuddered — guilt appeared in his eyes, guilt and the realization that Gastreel knew everything.

Gastreel grabbed him, pulled him to his feet.

And the guilt in Wrinn's eyes turned to indignation. "Don't touch me," he said.

The young Mountain Folk men were continuing to smoke; the light of their pipes was glistening in their eyes as they looked up at Wrinn and Gastreel.

"I have news for you," Gastreel said, "news you will not much like.

"The Gallian government knows what you did. And so do I. You've been pilfering from the warehouses. Admit it!"

Wrinn's indignation seemed to grow twofold; an insult, it seemed, hovered on the edge of his tongue. Then his gaze softened; his shoulders began to relax.

And as the Mountain Folk men grumbled and stood up, speaking amongst themselves, and then walked off, into the darkness, Wrinn at last spoke. "I've been a little stressed," Wrinn said.

"As have we all," Gastreel said. "Wrinn, dark things are at work. Powers, greater than Gallia, greater even than the Empire.

"The war we face is the least of our dangers. And you have a part to a play, Wrinn. You are the Sage's dear friend…"

"*Adari*," Wrinn said.

"What?" Gastreel couldn't make sense of the boy.

"*Adari*," Wrinn said again, "I am his helper."

"Yes, you are… and for the cost of the ten marks worth of pipeweed you stole, you will be my helper, too.

"A bondservant… a bondservant of Galiope's Council of War, until such time as the debt is paid."

Wrinn's indignation returned a hundredfold; he pitched back his hands, as if to strike.

"Wrinn," Gastreel snarled, "be glad I made such an offer to Eventide.

"The Gallian elite are allowed to kill a servant who breaks a crystal cup. What would they do to you if I had not intervened, you, not a Gallian…"

"I am a Gallian," Wrinn snapped.

"No," Gastreel said, "no, no… you are not. Nor is Reev. Nor is your friend Fortunato.

"Sometime soon, we will have to leave."

The ambient night noises were rising above the wind — far away was the sound of music, a street festival even at a time of such peril.

"Gallia is not safe," Gastreel said. "We will see the war through.

"But you and I, Reev and Fortunato… we… we will not be long for here."

"And where will we go?" Wrinn said.

Gastreel did not have the answer.

"Be ready… tomorrow, at dawn, the council sits. Dress for war, and bring your quarterstaff, bondservant. Until such time as your debt is paid, you are not your own."

~

The night was inky dark outside the windows of Rosetree Manor. Reev had fashioned himself a small meal of bread and leftover roast duck, but as always Reev had been left alone, to his own devices; as always, he had been instructed to go neither in nor out — to remain in Gastreel's mansion, which had become a fortress.

Now from his perch he was watching the streets below, watching Greenwater to the south and the sparkling waters of the River Galios. Riverboats were passing through the way, even now, this late — even now, at a time of war.

A noise rose above the ambient night sounds… rustling, the tearing of branches. And a bush was being tossed this way and that in the front yard below. A shadowy shape was in the darkness, a humanoid figure, not Gastreel — and Reev wondered if this had been the moment that Gastreel had been worried about. On and on, he had talked of Imperial sympathizers, of the Dark One's minions, even his Servants… and gods help them all if they had returned.

In such a circumstance, Reev was to find a place to hide. But at his side, even now, was Doomblade, his father's sword, and Reev was not a coward, nor would he ever be.

And the dim-dark shadow was peering through windows now, rummaging through the yard.

In the art of the sword, Reev was not of the caliber of Fortunato or even Gastreel to that fact, but whatever evil had been brought to Gastreel's doorstep he intended to drive away.

He hurried downstairs, to the hearth which had turned to dull embers. He grabbed a torch and set it alight. With Doomblade in his right hand and the flaming torch in his left, he stormed down the corridor, kicking open the front door, and leaping outside.

The dark shadow which had been peeping through windows and tearing through the bushes stiffened and even seemed to wither in size. It — or rather, he — was not even as tall as Reev.

"Ash?" Reev said to his cousin, the slight form in whose eyes his torch was reflecting.

It was the middle of the night; it had to be eleven hours after noon.

"What is the meaning of this?" Gastreel's voice was a storm as he pushed through the gate, down the yard, up to the front door. The light on Gastreel's staff brightened into existence, a soft blue.

And Asher Nax Bensange, for his part, seemed unbowed, unafraid, even defiant.

"What have we here?" said Gastreel. "A demoniac? A servant of the Enemy?"

"My cousin" was Reev's reply, and his heart was no longer racing. He smiled at the sight of Asher Nax Bensange.

"What are you doing here, Ash?" Gastreel said.

Reev's cousin, just a few years younger than him, was acting perfectly calm, as if it were normal to snoop around in the garden past eleven o'clock.

And Reev for his part was relieved it was not an Imperial sympathizer or one of the Dark One's minions, sent to do harm.

"My mother," Ash said, his Zarube accent faint but noticeable, "sent me to check on you... to make sure you were all right,

Reev…"

"At half-past eleven o'clock?" Gastreel said.

"She said," Ash continued, "that you have been leaving him alone, unattended, Mr. Wizard… all day, all night."

"That is not her concern," Gastreel said. Any fear in his eyes had evaporated, and now in them was confusion, bordering on suspicion. "And a mansion with only one entrance is a safe place for him to stay… a perfectly reasonable place to remain alone — just as it is unreasonable for a boy of fourteen to wander outdoors, after dark.

"Hurry home, Asher… tell your mother all is well, and that her prying eyes and ears are unneeded."

Gastreel had spoken sooth, but he was wrong in one regard. The mansion was not safe; last summer, Ivan Xandrast had broken in, and injured Reev.

Ivan Xandrast… he had not heard from that man, or seen his face, in almost a year.

"Strange tidings," said Gastreel, and the look he was giving Ash's disappearing form was suspicion, full and true. "Strange tidings indeed… a strange boy, a strange mother.

"I wonder why he really was here."

Chapter Two:
A Hired Staff

The rosy light of dawn was filtering through the Galiopean Townhall's high windows. Gastreel was at his stone lectern, and in the dark corners of the room was Wrinn Finnis, dressed in a leather jerkin as if for war — holding his quarterstaff in both hands.

The faces in the Gallian Townhall were not ones Gastreel wished to see, not even in good times. The Lady Llewyn of Leyshaw, an aristocrat to her innermost sinew, heaping scorn on the common and never associating with them… The Lord Alden with the flame-red hair, who spoke at the queerest times, and offered the strangest of advice… the Lord Eventide, chancellor, who had foresworn the gods of Gallia and now wore a folknut necklace about his neck… and the newest addition, a member merely for her last name and the good memories it brought — Ramona Nax.

This was the Council of War, in which Galiope had vested its powers. Each member, save Ramona and a few others, had been elected by the guildmasters of Galiope's great guilds and the patriarchs of the noble families.

There was no invocation; Bartholem, the rector of St. Sigmund's Cathedral, had as good as excommunicated the Lord Eventide, and the priests and monks and abbots in Cathedral District considered him and all who worked for him anathema. Their threats of rebellion had not yet come to fruition; it was a time of war, and whatever they thought of Eventide, they despised the Empire more.

And so it was Gastreel who initiated the Council of War, without the blessing of the gods, without the invocation uttered by Bartholem.

"Friends," Gastreel said, "partners… nobles all.

"You may see in that dark corner our council's newest member… a member, of a kind, whose quarterstaff we collectively own — in a manner of speaking. Whose hands will be put to good use. Wrinn Finnis."

"A thief," said the Lady Llewyn of Leyshaw.

"But our thief," said the Lord Alden, red-haired and gray-eyed. "Our thief… a skilled warrior, one who fought in the Battle of Galiope — a battle we won."

"And not the last we won," said the Lord Eventide. "Good tidings, good tidings at last… a victory at Highrock Abbey, after the disasters in Dark Harrow and Nieville-by-the-Sea."

"A victory won by treachery," Gastreel said, "when the abbot lured the Imperials into the halls and tunnels of that abbey, and then turned on them in an instant."

"Silence, wizard!" Eventide said. "Our ancestors smile on us. Three thousand Imperials dead, and only a hundred of ours were lost, and two dozen monks."

Eventide's ancestors were dead, buried in the ground — those he was descended from, of which he spoke, were dry dust now, or lying under peat bogs. Every time he spoke of his "ancestors" Gastreel wanted to strike him, to try whatever way he could to break him free of this delusion of heathenry he had been nursing after the death of his son.

"They shall not dare strike us now," Ramona Nax offered from the dark shadows of the room.

"They will," Gastreel replied, "they are gathering up their strength… an adder, a poisonous viper, coiling itself about, preparing to strike.

"We will hear from the Empire soon. Of that, you can be sure."

For a while there was silence. And then Eventide spoke. "Aldermen, alderwomen, people of the council, we must make our next move. Wars are not won by reacting; they are won by acting."

And we will not win this war. Gastreel kept his thought to himself. They were only delaying, only nipping at the Empire's heels, only making small cuts and abrasions upon a monstrous enemy, one who had felled far greater foes than Gallia.

I shall not be so pessimistic, he vowed.

"The Empire's forces have not dared approach the city directly," the Lord Eventide said. "Their legions are camped a hundred miles to our north and to our west. They have not crossed the River Siecle. They dare not cross the Pale of Wettin."

And yet they outnumber us, Gastreel wanted to say. *You fool, you fool.* But again he remained silent, and allowed the Council of War to bicker, to plot and to plan.

"We must act," the Lord Eventide said, "we must take full advantage of the victory that Fortunato of Ríva delivered us. They are stunned, bruised, bleeding… in shock, but for a moment."

"They are distracted," Ramona Nax offered, and the light of the Townhall's windows was glinting in the whites of her eyes.

"Distracted, stunned — but for a moment," Eventide said. "An opportunity we cannot waste.

"Our situation may seem good…"

It does not, Gastreel thought.

"But the way to Almania is clear. The Imperial patrols will not be looking so thoroughly. Their forces have just taken a battering… and Gastreel Osiris, wizard — " Eventide's dark eyes were fixed directly at him. " — he of all people can visit the grand duke, and by sword or spell ensure that he gives us his due."

All the eyes of the council were fixed on Gastreel, even its bondservant, Wrinn Finnis, an elf, aged eighteen. They were so demanding — they expected the impossible of him.

The grand duchy of Almania lay some two hundred miles south and west, beyond a war zone. The duke had promised his help in the event of an Imperial attack, but that help had not come.

"You expect the impossible of me," Gastreel said, aloud.

And a smile appeared on the Lord Eventide's face, the leader of the war effort, the chancellor of the League. It was a dark smile, lit by the high windows' dim light. "An impossible task, perhaps, convincing a selfish nation to hold up its end of a bargain…

"But who better to accomplish an impossible task than a wizard?"

Gastreel's power was not over the mind, but over lightning and the storm. Nevertheless, they were right; there was no one better to send. Gastreel's reputation would be intimidating to the grand duke, and against the might of a powerful wizard, a small army was required to defeat him.

"I have pledged my utmost to the city of Galiope," Gastreel said, "and if this council requires of me impossible things, I will nonetheless do them.

"And yet I request help… a baggage boy and guard — this council's bondservant."

Wrinn's blue eyes sparkled, and for the first time this morning, there were rumblings of a smile on his young face.

"Take him!" the Lady Llewyn of Leyshaw cried. "We have no use of a thief."

The vote was unanimous; Gastreel and Wrinn were sent. They left swiftly out of Godsgate, Gastreel on Ivy, Wrinn on Noble, just after dawn.

Chapter Three: Family

Reev had been left with the sparest of explanations, a frenzied Gastreel hurriedly procuring his horse, with Wrinn by his side — sad eyes, and then worries… "Do not go in or out," he had said, "much depends on you… in fact, all; the Sage."

And Reev was now in the parlor in the light of early afternoon. He did not know what to do with himself; Gastreel was gone, who knew for how long, and for what? And Wrinn, who entertained him and dragged him along on his misadventures, was gone, too. Bala was at the Dragonpaw Inn, and would be up for a game — but the Dragonpaw had changed. It was different, now. In the past few weeks, there had been more strangers than faces that Reev recognized… Mountain Folk, rough men, the kinds of people Reev did not feel safe around… men and women speaking foreign tongues, and others who would stare at Reev from afar with their dark eyes, eyes in which Reev sensed evil — evil, and a cunning malice.

No, the Dragonpaw was not safe, and he was glad to be here in this sanctuary.

But in the parlor there was only backgammon, a game not easily played by one, a spinning top with which he had already grown bored. There was Gastreel's library, but most of it was elven texts which Reev could not read, or otherwise treatises on magic and thick codices that only wizards would be interested in.

There was a knock on the front door, and Reev snapped to his feet. His heart began to race in the long shadows of the afternoon, but surely a devotee of the Dark One would strike in the night, in the dark.

And so Reev didn't bother fetching Doomblade. He hurried to

the door and cracked it open to find his aunt, yes, his aunt, Ramona Nax — once *Bensange*.

The early afternoon light was reflecting on her neatly parted black hair. Her grayish eyes twinkled.

Her scarlet gown was made of pressed satin. A rope of gold fabric bound her waist. Around her neck was a diamond necklace, and she seemed to epitomize wealth and high status, between her gold and silver rings and the way she posed, her lips tucked into the slightest of smiles.

"Reev," she said, "nephew."

"Hello, Aunt Ramona," Reev said. "May I help you?"

"No," Aunt Ramona said, "but I thought you might help yourself.

"I heard the Green Wizard abandoned you."

Abandoned was too strong a word… and Reev had sensed that Aunt Ramona didn't much like Gastreel. "He's on an important mission," Reev said.

"Yes, yes," said Aunt Ramona. "Terribly important, I'm sure." Her smile became noticeable, large. "It is so good to see you, nephew."

"And you as well," Reev replied.

The smile vanished, and in her eyes a stormy look appeared. "You are home alone. And Wodenscross Court is not as safe as it appears. The guards aren't supposed to let the riffraff in, but my neighbor Marjorie spotted some hoodlums from Greenwater who got past them. They were peeping in windows, ready to rob…" The smile returned. "There are many spare rooms in Sunstone Manor. You should stay with us, Reev."

"Us?" Reev said.

"Me, and Ash, of course…" Her dark eyes twinkled in the sunlight. "Families, after all, stick together. That's what they are supposed to do."

Gastreel's instruction had been firm: go neither in or out. But

Gastreel had left; and he *had* abandoned Reev in some small sense.

Reev was starved for company… and he could feel himself beginning to smile. "Yes, yes, Aunt Ramona," he at last said. "Let me pack a few things."

~

Where Galiope as a whole was a city of squalor, with people living beside and on top of each other, with precious little space, the streets of Wodenscross Court were wide open, not to mention swept clean. Reev, hauling his bags down the street, had plenty of room to trip about and fumble.

"It's about time the Naxes acted like a proper family," Ramona said. "Between your grandfather Kal and your nanna Trita, it was always difficult. Not to mention your great uncles and great aunts, rest their souls."

Reev had gone to the Nax stead… he had buried his grandfather, high up in the mountains — mountains now conquered and overrun by rokahn. And yet he felt he shouldn't tell his aunt, though he didn't know why.

Down the streets they walked, past manicured gardens, past yards tended to by servants, and homes that took up entire blocks… it was difficult to imagine that just a short walk away, there was squalor and poverty.

Reev had not grown up in such magnificence; in the town of Norwood, in the Empire, where he had been raised, he and Gastreel had lived in a small house, little better than a hovel. After Gastreel left him for the first time, his lodgings had improved at the Buckhorn Inn, but it had never been so luxurious as this — and Reev felt a bit guilty partaking.

And yet the long, lonely days and the dark nights had been wearing on Reev, loneliness and fear at Rosetree Manor, living by himself. It had seemed things had all come undone in Galiope ever since the war began.

In numbers, there was safety… it would be good to stay with family, even Aunt Ramona, at least until Gastreel returned.

The red stone of Aunt Ramona's mansion greeted Reev, the crystalline blue windows, the mounting levels and sandstone towers… and memories returned to him. He had been here only a few times before.

"Amée!" Ramona cried out.

A red-headed servant girl was trimming the rose bushes.

"Tell Guy that our dinner plans have changed. He shall be serving three, not two."

And the shadows of the afternoon were turning to dusk as Reev entered Sunstone Manor, to find opulence and wealth — and by the parlor, a hearth. His cousin Ash was standing there, staring into the flames.

~

Dinner was served at dusk. On platters of silver were roast pheasants with their feathers decoratively returned to them, river trout upon a bed of groats, baked wood pigeons and bowls of fruit and custard… far more than was necessary for a small group of three, and Reev doubted they would eat it all, but perhaps the servants would be hungry later.

As the servants doted on him and Aunt Ramona and Ash, in the veranda which had been transformed into a dining room, Reev was growing uncomfortable, and he wished to get up and help, to ensure they knew he didn't think he was better than them — no, not at all.

"Summer at last," Ramona said. "After last winter, I thought it would never come."

Reev had spent the winter in the mountains, and under the earth — the details of an adventure he was sure his Aunt Ramona would like to hear, but again something inexplicable told him not to inform her.

He had removed the coin necklace he had found in his grandfather's house; it was tucked away in one of his suits of luggage, upstairs, in his quarters… quarters far too princely for his taste.

"Summer," Ramona drolled on, and with her knife and fork began to carve up the river trout, of which she'd taken a helping.

Amée the servant girl came by with glasses and set them down, one, two, three. She uncorked a bottle and poured Ash, Reev, and Ramona a generous amount of wine.

"It was summer when I met your father, Ash, for the first time." Aunt Ramona's eyes grew darker. "Summer when Simeon and I left the High Country." She looked up at Reev, and smiled. "Summer when I met you, my nephew… a long-lost scion of the Nax family.

"Such goodness, all in summer… and yet now, the terrors that I left in the west have followed me here. The Empire at Galiope's doorstep, threatening to lay it waste."

Reev took a small sip of the wine. It was rich and fine, unlike the cheap fare that Wrinn used to buy, tangy and smoky, with a note of berry. It was worth probably many weeks of labor at the Dragonpaw Inn… but that life was gone to Reev now. No more Glenda, no more Bala, no more Ambrass — but Reev had not seen Ambrass in many months.

"Are you worried the Empire will win?" Reev asked his aunt, and helped himself to a dollop of custard.

"Worried? No," Aunt Ramona said. "I shall keep my head up. I shall hope the Gallian fighting spirit will see us through the day.

"But I am not worried. The rich always manage… it is the poor and the lowly born that should fear the red and gold standards — not Ash, not I."

It was probably true. If the city fell, Ramona could artfully negotiate a peace. The Empire left power structures in place, and in place of kings they left puppets, and in place of nobles they left pawns. The common could be sold as slaves, but the gentlemen and fair ladies of Wodenscross Court would survive.

"You'd think it would be hopeless," Ramona said, "after all, in the west our efforts against the Empire were led by the bluest of blue blood... kings and princes whose bloodlines go back millennia. Noblemen whose pedigree was unlike anything we have here, in Gallia.

"The best of noblemen here are descended from a king's steward. There has not been a king in Gallia for more than a thousand years.

"And the west fell. The best of the best could not save it. What hope is there for Gallia? And yet I have hope."

Noble descent to Reev meant little; an accident of birth did not grant intelligence or insight. And Fortunato of Ríva, no man of noble descent, had by his wit delivered Galiope its first victory in this war, a victory that had stunned the Empire, that surely had sent shockwaves through the Imperial world.

"Ash here has some relation to Cordeleon," Ramona said, and smiled at her son, who seemed totally focused on his food. "The bluest of blue blood. Perhaps, he shall save Gallia."

"Perhaps," Reev said.

Ash was picking at his wood pigeon in a way that resembled dissection. He had not yet touched his wine.

"In the west, I had to hide my origins," Ramona said, "though there was rumor that the Nax family had royalty in their blood, far back.

"And your mother, Reev, was a chambermaid, but she would tell everyone she knew that she was related to an emperor — which emperor, she could not tell me."

"May I be excused?" Ash said.

Ramona looked to her son. "You've barely touched your food," she said.

"I'm not hungry," Ash said.

"Very well," Ramona said. "But don't go sneaking about. If I catch you wandering around after dark again, I'll lose my mind."

It had been last night that Reev caught Ash staring into the windows of Rosetree Manor… and he looked at his cousin suspiciously as he wiped his mouth with his napkin, stood up and walked off.

"A smart boy," Ramona said, "intelligent and wise and full of wit. A politician, he will be. I daresay he will rule the world one day.

"But with such brilliance comes trouble." Ramona seemed to be talking to herself and no one else, and her eyes had grown dark and dim. "Such trouble there has been…"

Chapter Four:
The Omen

The thousand men in Fortunato's battalion were behind him in the dark. They had just arrived at Emmet's Bluff, and from a great height they could survey the Pale of Wettin below.

The night air was kissing Fortunato's clean-shaven cheeks. He had continued to shave his beard… though he was fighting with the Gallians, he was not one of them, and he had to remember.

"Marshal!" a man cried, and the voice Fortunato thought he recognized as Thingel, the cook.

"One moment," Fortunato said, not bothering to raise his voice above the din of camp.

The Pale was below them, a border region of farmland and marsh, little inhabited, bound by the River Siecle to the far west. The night was deep and dark, but the darkness provided an advantage — the lights of the Imperial camp were visible, and if the enemy made their move, Fortunato would know.

"Marshal!" that voice cried again, louder, bolder, with great volume.

And Fortunato at last abandoned his watchmanship to focus on his men.

No fires were burning, as he'd demanded, yet his men were huddled in circles anyway. In their hands they had bowls and horn spoons, and were feasting on slop — for the seventh day in a row.

"Marshal!" In the light of the moon, eyes gleamed. It was not Thingel the cook, but one of the sergeants. Stenn was his name, Stenn from Sauer's Brook in full.

He was standing in a mass of soldiers, most of whom were still wearing their helmets and quilted jack armor.

"Tell us… we are wondering. Who tied that white cord about

your wrist? Who fastened it to your skin?"

It was not their concern.

"Was she fair? Eyes blue as the sea?"

Yes.

"Hair red as an autumn leaf?"

Right again.

Yanenré, the daughter of the elvenking, had departed from Gallia almost a year ago, before it fell into this darkness. "You shall not speak to your marshal that way," Fortunato said, "or you'll see yourself discharged, without honor — sent to the gallows, or the headsman's block."

But Stenn was smiling, brightly, and his men for the first time since the victory at Highrock Abbey seemed jovial. The long hard days of marching in the rain, through mud and field and trackless swamp, had at last ended — here, their destination, Emmet's Bluff, from which they could surveil the movements of the enemy.

The enemy… the country of Fortunato's birth — once his home. And what would his father Petro of Ríva think? Worst of all was the thought of his mother Alessa being disappointed in him.

A traitor to his country, maybe, but a man loyal to the things that mattered… the defense of his friends. The cause against Seymus and his servants in the mortal world. A higher duty called than the duty of nation or family… a duty that mattered most of all.

"Did you love her?" Stenn seemed unbowed by Fortunato's threat. "Did you love her in return?"

He would not dismiss Stenn or have him punished. Stenn would not be made an example of.

"Did you love her?" Stenn said.

Had he? There was another one he loved… one who had returned to her people and spurned Gallian society, one whom he would give anything to have and to hold. But she was gone, forever.

Ambrass… he had loved her. Ambrass was the one he had

loved.

He peered into Stenn's eyes, tried to think of a cutting insult, but instead turned back, walked over to the cliff's edge, to this high place that surveyed the Pale of Wettin. Campfires were on the far edge of the River Siecle, camps, hundreds in number. Fortunato estimated the Empire's number at four thousand, and in pitched battle Fortunato's men would quickly crumble.

Victories could only be had by subterfuge, like at Highrock… but Highrock had been the Empire's greatest disaster in years, one of the worst ever, and against a numerically inferior foe… Gallia had bruised and battered the greatest power in the world, the greatest power that Varda had ever seen.

"Marshal!" Stenn's voice called out in the darkness, but instead of hearing another of his deluded rants, Fortunato climbed down, beyond the cliff, to some unsteady ground below, keeping his eyes always on the Imperial camp, for any sign that they intended to breach the border.

Not far from here was Thelamar Fortress, where once he had slain the glyrn Drayfin. Not far from here, Jerek had been defeated… Jerek, who had claimed to be the Dark One's Hand. But a greater foe now was here.

That foe was here: the world he had known, the world in which he had been born, which was in his blood — now at Gallia's doorstep. That foe — the world from whence he had come.

"Marshal! Marshal!"

Fortunato turned back in irritation. He supposed there was no solace, no privacy, to be had when he had been appointed the leader of his men. He would endure their taunts — he would endure their insulting words, until he could endure them no more.

He imagined Danenhir cutting those wiley cheeks of Stenn, and drawing blood, and he smiled — the first time in days.

"Marshal! Marshal!" The shout had become a howl, and more commotion could be heard, the shuffling of feet, cries of alarm.

And for the first time, Fortunato thought something might be wrong, truly wrong.

He leapt back up to face his men.

~

Stenn was on the ground; others were surrounding him. His eyes had turned pale, his skin white and bloodless. He was trembling, looking at something that wasn't there, but which was greatly vexing him.

Fortunato walked over and stooped at his side.

"Stenn," he said to the one who had taunted him, and knelt down, touching his hand, then his wrist. "Stenn! Can you hear me?"

He was chattering, muttering words that seemed indistinguishable to Fortunato's ears, but as he listened, he began to discern the contours of vowels and consonants — a language of a kind, but one ineffable.

There were scattered screams in the distance — cold gasps. And a terrible air seemed to fall over camp.

Fortunato looked down to the Pale of Wettin and could see some of the lights moving about. But the Imperials were not yet making their move; they were not yet broaching camp.

"Fortunato," a voice was saying, "of Ríva."

Who was talking? Stenn!

"You do not love her. You never did."

The face of Ambrass flashed in his mind.

He looked to Stenn, still on the ground, and others in the camp were backing away. In the distance, he saw Thingel the cook, now shouting at a man he recognized as Carolus.

Stenn's eyes were pale and growing paler; his skin was wrinkling, turning a grayish hue.

The air of the night was dark and full of terror.

And terror Fortunato sensed — and he also sensed a presence, one he had felt long ago.

What was that presence? He did not know. A name did not come to mind.

He looked at Stenn, overcome suddenly with this sickness. He ignored the racing of his heart. He recalled the words that Gastreel had used in dealing with such dangers.

"*Illunaddori vadila!*" he shouted. *The lord of light guard you.*

And Stenn hissed, and the paleness of his eyes seemed to wane, all but for a moment.

Shadow had fallen over Stenn, and dark powers.

"*Illune!*" he shouted. *The light.* "*Solardi!*" The elvenking's standard.

Stenn seemed to laugh in the darkness, and in the darkness he said, "Silence, Fortunato of Ríva. The gods are not with you. You abandoned the gods of your fathers! You betrayed your nation. Your ancestors despise you and, from the realm of the dead, curse your name!"

From the darkness emerged another, Ulrich, the battalion's priest. In his left hand he held a vial of holy water; in his right, a rod on which was forged Heron's mark. In Old Imperial he began to chant, and the darkness and terror was met with resistance at last.

As Fortunato fell backward, Ulrich screamed, "Out of him!"

Stenn shrieked, and the paleness began to fade from his eyes. The dark air began to lift, but a stain remained.

"What was that?" Fortunato said. "What happened?"

He thought he knew — somewhere, deep in his memory, the answer lurked. Somewhere, in his life, the question of what had happened could be laid bare. The air of terror and despair was so familiar; the feeling of darkness was like an old friend.

"What happened?" Fortunato said again.

But Ulrich, staring at Stenn, said nothing; and his silence told Fortunato that he did not know.

Stenn sat up, and his eyes sparkled; he remembered nothing.

And memories returned to Fortunato, half-formed. A scepter forged of dark iron. A mask crafted of metal. A name: Gogg.

Stenn was smiling. He remembered none of it. "Was she fair, Fortunato? You didn't answer me. Hair red as an autumn leaf? Eyes blue as the sea?"

Dissensions in camp were growing; Thingel and Carolus were continuing to argue. Fergus, leader of one of the hundreds, told Fortunato later that night that Stenn had accused him of all manner of things, Severn a common footsoldier that he'd brought up an old offense of his against his wife. Everyone seemed to hear something different from Stenn as his mouth babbled in that senseless tongue.

The power of the gods, working through Ulrich, had driven the darkness out.

As Fortunato's men went to bed, one by one, it was not the incident that plagued his thoughts, but instead Stenn's words when he had been in his fullness. *Eyes blue as the sea… hair red as an autumn leaf.*

And in his bedroll he quietly stroked the elvencloth. It hung about his left wrist, a constant reminder of Yanenré Iradahir. The daughter of the elvenking — a bearer of light. And wouldn't light be of great use, in the darkness they had found themselves in?

Chapter Five:
Good Days

Light was dawning over the hills, glorious light. On Ivy, Gastreel galloped on, and Wrinn, ever eager, was just behind him on Noble. Across the grass their beasts swiftly bore them, and there was no sign of the Imperials thus far, no red-gold standard nor any sighting of an outrider. It was the second day of their journey to Almania, and thanks to the actions of Fortunato of Ríva their enemy was scattered and disoriented.

"*An!*" he said. "Go," in the Elven tongue.

Gastreel was no fool; he knew the victory at Highrock Abbey meant little. He knew the war effort, if it was not doomed imminently, it was doomed eventually.

Yet he had pledged himself to Gallia; he had pledged his utmost. He would do all in his power for her.

Yet he remembered his true task, one that mattered more than Gallia, one that mattered more than his own life or the lives of Wrinn and the people of the Galiope.

Reev Nax, the Prince of the Dawn.

"*An!*" They were not traveling the roads, riding west by southwest, toward a land far away, which spoke a foreign tongue.

"*An!*" And Ivy galloped, and the wind was picking up, when through a veil of rain, a forest appeared, a perfect place to cloak their movements. Thunder was rolling, and lightning flashing, when the pines and elms swallowed them whole.

~

Ivy was struggling, straining to breathe. In the darkness of the forest, Gastreel strained to find the sun, but the sky was obscured by the boughs of the pines.

The waters of a black stream were up ahead.

"Let's stop!" Gastreel said. "Have something to eat..."

He'd grown weak, and he'd grown hungry. It had to be about noon.

Wrinn, young, in the prime of his life, could likely ride for many hours yet without complaint. But he seemed happy to take a rest.

The road-bread, only edible with a little soaking in the black waters, and the water of their waterskins, filled at some bitter stream, only seemed to upset their stomachs more. In the forest, exposed, they quietly ate their meal, as birds chirped and the wind rustled the branches of the trees above-head.

Ivy, tied to a tree, was bucking slightly against her restraints. Noble's eyes had a mad look, but that was nothing new.

"How long would you say is the journey to Almania?" Wrinn said.

"Ah, Wrinn," he uttered quietly, "I am sure you would like to know, and to divine the future; but many factors are at work. The movements of the Imperials. The rain, the wind. The will of the gods."

Did he think he would get an easy answer from a wizard?

"In good times, the journey could be made in less than a week," Gastreel said, "but these are not good times, as I am sure you know."

Wrinn's sullen blue eyes were dull in the dim light.

"Not good times," he mumbled, softly, under his breath. "No — they are not. But there have never been good times for me."

The elf had spent his life a slave — freed, now, as the world came undone, and peril fell over the land.

"Good times will come to you," Gastreel said, "if you have the grit to continue on. If you do not give up."

"How are you to know that?" Wrinn said.

Gastreel did not know it. But he believed it for Wrinn — for everyone, in fact.

"Soon, for you," Gastreel said, "the clouds will part. The sun will shine. And you will see good days."

"At a time like this?" Wrinn said.

"Yes, at a time like this — especially," Gastreel said.

They were almost finished with their road-bread, and Gastreel had had about his fill of bitter water.

"The sun clear up," Wrinn said, "the skies — part. A bondservant of the Council of War. I don't believe it."

As they sat by the banks of the stream, the rain was dwindling, and the winsome light of the sun was seeming to grow more visible.

"Perhaps," Gastreel said, "even in Almania — you'll find that good fortune."

"I don't think so," Wrinn said.

But Gastreel had a feeling the gods would someday smile on Wrinn, on Wrinn — born a slave.

~

As they rode through the silent forests, under clearings where the sunny skies could be seen, past rosebushes and spring flowers blooming, and white spring blossoms dancing in the tall grass, Wrinn thought on Gastreel's words.

The gods had not smiled on Wrinn since his birth, Wrinn — who had never known his family, who had labored from his earliest days. He had been freed from bondage by his friend, Reev Nax, and now, the habit of pipe-smoking he'd picked up from the Mountain Folk had placed him in bondage again. From travail to travail he had gone, from slavery to servitude.

And the gods did not smile on him, nor would they ever — but perhaps he could part his own clouds. Perhaps, at an opportune moment, when he wasn't under Gastreel's watchful eye… perhaps, amid the crowds in Almania's capital, he would endeavor to find his own sunshine. At the right instant, when no one was looking, he'd wrest what he deserved from the vagaries of life. In dark of night, in the cover of the crowd, in the chaos of some perfect moment, he'd slip away.

Reev Nax would understand. Reev Nax after all had freed him. If Reev Nax knew what had happened to him, and how he felt, he'd help create that perfect moment when Wrinn Finnis ran away, and seized a life for himself on his own terms.

At the perfect moment, Wrinn would run away.

Chapter Six:
Suspicion

At the House Bensange, there was no set time for rising, no labors to attend to at dawn, no cooking breakfast — that was Amée's job, no watering of the plants — that was the task of Horace, the gardener. In his bed in his private room, Reev laid awake under the sheets, waiting for the toll of the church bells in Cathedral District, for some sign he should at last lumber onto the ground, and start his day.

At Gastreel's house, Rosetree Manor, he had lived amid fine furnishings and elaborate spaces, but not among a staff of servants attending to his every whim. Compared to Sunstone Manor, Aunt Ramona's house, he had been roughing it.

Yet he was not happier here, not even the slightest bit.

The bells began to chime, one, two, three.

It was five hours after dawn, eleven o'clock, and though Reev was by himself, alone, he felt himself begin to blush. What an embarrassment, sleeping so late. What would Gastreel think?

But Gastreel was gone, and with him, Wrinn.

He hurried out of bed and got to his feet, and in a frenzy began to dress for the day.

The gleam of his grandfather's amulet flickered in the light of the window, the coin necklace he'd found in his house. It was sitting in one of the cases. He ruffled through the belongings and donned his tunic, his trousers — and someone was at the door.

"Master Reev?" Amée said. "Would you have some breakfast? Eggs on toast, a tipple of tea…"

"Don't call me master," Reev said, perhaps more curtly than was needed, as he struggled through his sleeves and at last pulled the tunic over his head. In a softer, more gentle tone, he said, "Reev is fine — just call me Reev."

Amée's bright eyes sparkled, and the brilliance of her smile was like the sun rising over a hill. It was as if she had been treated like a human for the first time in her life, though as far as Reev knew she was not a slave but a servant, paid — a free woman, choosing to stay in the House Bensange of her own free will.

"Breakfast," he said to her. "That sounds good. Although, it's a little late."

"Madame Bensange is not up yet," Amée said, and a look of humor appeared on her face amid the brightness of that smile. "You are not the latest riser in the House Bensange."

He imagined his Aunt Ramona sleeping and snoring on those fine sheets, a woman full grown — not a boy of sixteen who needed his rest, prone to stay up late and rise late.

He followed Amée and thought he heard her giggle as he followed her down the halls. He wondered if she fancied him, though she was far too old.

~

Eggs, toast, a bit of tea — and Amée was turning away from Reev when he said to her, "Why don't you eat with me, Amée?"

She turned, and there was a trace of fear in her brown eyes. "I'm not allowed, *Maste*— ehrm, Reev."

"My aunt is snoring," Reev said. "She won't know... I won't tell her."

"I do not *zink*—" Amée began, her Zarube accent slipping through. "I do not think it is appropriate."

"But it's an order," Reev said to her. "Sit down! Have breakfast with me... this breakfast that *you* made."

The fear in her eyes faded; her lips twisted into the slightest of smiles. And she walked over, and took from the silver platter a bit of toasted bread. She sat down, and as she did, wind was beginning to gently blow. Reev feared it would rain.

"How long have you been in my aunt's service, Amée?" he said to her.

As she nibbled the bread, she seemed to be calculating the number in her head. She began to count with her fingers. "Seven years," she said. "Seven years at the House Bensange."

At each moment, her hands would tremble, and she seemed to be resisting the urge to look into the window and discern if her master, Aunt Ramona, had arisen.

Yet the more time went on, she seemed to be caught up in thought and pondering. "Seven years," she said, "and when I first began to work at Castle White, a storm, yes, a storm — a terrible storm, there was."

Her gaze now seemed distant; she was more and more caught up in the moment, a moment long ago.

"I took it as a bad sign," she said, "the lightning, the thunder…" She looked up, met Reev's gaze, and then looked away, unable to sustain the exchange of glances for long. "But I was wrong. Lord Elfraine was just in his dealings, pious to a fault — a reverer of the gods. Upright, and he paid me promptly."

She said nothing of Aunt Ramona.

"And what of him?" Reev said. "Why did my aunt leave?"

The marriage, it was said, had been annulled — dissolved as if it had never existed… that was what Gastreel had told him "annulment" meant. It was granted when a marriage was undertaken by false pretenses. But what had those false pretenses been?

"I — I *zink* I must be going," Amée said, and her Zarube accent had returned stronger than before, a sign perhaps of her nervousness.

There was the sound of creaking footsteps — someone descending the grand staircase. And in a panic Amée was gone, but Reev sensed that Amée knew why the marriage had been annulled, and that the secret was dark indeed.

He heard chatter from inside Sunstone Manor — Amée's faint voice, and the far-off sound of Aunt Ramona's harsh tone.

He nibbled at his bread and eggs, and sipped at his tea, and stirred in his seat, wondering if he'd caused some discontent in Sunstone Manor and among the House Bensange.

But a question had now arisen, one that wouldn't easily be answered. His aunt and his uncle had parted ways — his uncle, whom he'd never met. Their marriage had been dissolved in a country, Zarubain, where — Gastreel had told him — divorce was almost impossible.

So why, and how? Did the answer lie somewhere in Sunstone Manor?

~

At the base of the grand staircase, before a mirror, Aunt Ramona was dabbing at her cheeks with red powder and lining her lips with ointment. She was wearing a brocade dress of sapphire blue, and a diamond necklace. "Nephew!" she said to him without looking at him, aware of his presence, perhaps aware of the outrageous thing that had been done, sharing a breakfast with a servant. "I am headed to the Council of War. I shall not be back until dusk. If you have need of anything, Guy is in the kitchen. Our butler Lionel is somewhere about. Amée will not be available; she's being punished, and she's been given time to think on her insolence."

"It was my idea — eating breakfast with me!" Reev said, desperately. "You shouldn't punish her for it."

Ramona stopped her dabbing. She turned to Reev and smiled. "She ate breakfast with you? How quaint.

"No, that is not her offense, Reev. It is something else entirely. I told her to change the drapes in the foyer, and she forgot... like she always seems to."

"And where is Ash?" Reev said.

"At school," Ramona said, "the cathedral school at St. Sigmund's. He won't be back for a few hours.

"So tiresome… in the west, I could just find the best pedagogue, and have him educated at home. Now he must walk through those filth strewn streets through Middletown — even with my guards, I don't feel it's safe.

"A few hours and you'll have your cousin back! You'll be able to spend the evening together."

A few hours, all alone… plentiful time to investigate.

She turned and walked off; in the distance, Reev caught sight of a servant scurrying in the way, through some darkened doorway.

A marriage… annulled. And the secret was dark — he could read it on Amée's face.

~

Where to look, Reev wondered, to uncover the truth? How would he find out? Amée, sequestered somewhere for her "punishment," had made it clear she was unwilling to tell Reev.

He passed the grand staircase through a corridor. Paintings had recently been hung on the wooden walls, portraits of a younger Ash with a dog, and a younger Ramona with an infant, probably Ash — the picture cut away to hide another subject — Count Elfraine, likely.

Above all, Reev got the sense in the cluttered rooms that their move had been hasty, and that though they'd gotten to Galiope more than a year ago, their belongings were not fully unloaded, and in places baggage was piled toward the ceiling, still in its cases.

The dark wood-paneled hallway opened up into a vast space on which was set marble tiles — beyond, clear windows that bathed Reev in sunlight, potted plants, a fruiting shrub on whose branches were growing orange drupes.

And Reev wondered what he was doing, just how he would be able to uncover the secret of Ramona and Elfraine's annulment.

"You," a voice startled him from his thoughts, and he whipped around, seeing Amée, her curly auburn hair hanging in locks down her neck, her silvery brown eyes bright despite Aunt Ramona's "punishment" of her.

"Life has been hard since it was just Naxes," Amée said, "but you — there is something different about you."

"My aunt Ramona means well," Reev told her. "She only has a tough outer shell."

But who was he to say that to Amée? He barely knew his aunt, and had only just begun to spend any length of time with her.

"I thought you were being punished," Reev said.

"Your aunt tells a thirty-three-year-old woman that she must 'stay in her room and keep silent,'" Amée said. "Who does she think I am? Her little child? As soon as I saw that shrew leave, I was out of there. I won't go back until I hear the *tridium* bell ring."

Tridium — midday, when Ash could be expected home from school.

Reev didn't blame Amée but against the fury of that "shrew," his aunt, even Reev was afraid. He would never dare cross her.

He wouldn't cross her… but what exactly was he doing now?

"You are looking for something," Amée said. "What?"

She did not seem as afraid as before, when they had eaten breakfast. So perhaps, the truth would now emerge from her lips. "My aunt and uncle… their annulment. I wanted to know what happened. I know it's not my business; I know it's a private matter. But I'm curious."

"Oh, the dark trails we wander," Amée said, softly. "Your aunt and your uncle were peculiar people. And your cousin… your cousin…"

The air in the room seemed to grow cold. Something was on

the tip of her tongue, something she dared not say.

"I am sure you can tell I am not fond of your aunt. But I am in her service. I am a professional, and lips are sealed shut.

"But I can tell you that whatever your aunt endeavors to hide, she'll keep it in the cellar. She's stuffed many suits of luggage down there."

For a moment, Reev only peered into Amée's silvery brown eyes.

"Now, I think I'll go find myself a pipe. Have a smoke with Guy. You're welcome to join us on the upper balcony."

That did not seem the best of ideas… but the cellar. Amée said the darkest of secrets would be buried there.

Amée turned and walked off, disappearing through some dark doorway.

The cellar, Reev would have to find it. He grabbed an unlit candle from a shelf, and headed off toward the hearth in the main hall to light it.

As he walked through the network of hallways and corridors, he kept watch for any sound of the main doors opening or shutting, any sound of his Aunt Ramona's voice, any sign she'd changed her plans and wouldn't be going to the Council of War, after all. His heart began to race in his chest until it was thundering, and a cold sweat was beginning to cover his hands, for in a way what he was doing felt like a betrayal.

Yet he had to know… he had to. He had not known his aunt, or his cousin, but he had an inexplicable sense that whatever had gone on, had something to do with him.

At last, down a golden hall, behind a door, he saw the cellar, and he questioned himself not for the first time, certainly not for the last. He didn't want to lose his image of Aunt Ramona, cold and calculating yet concerned for her kin — he didn't want to make that image worse.

But something inexplicable drew him on, and he stepped forward, at last laying hold of the door and jerking it open. He began to descend downwards, into inky darkness, past cobwebs, to coolness and the smell of must.

~

The splendor of Sunstone Manor was gone here, here, under the earth — flagstone floors and rough rock walls, a rack of wine bottles covered in a film of dust… and in the distance, in the flickering candlelight, cases and bags from Aunt Ramona's move.

For a moment, he was again assailed with hesitance — what he was doing felt like a betrayal. But something not at all was right in the House Bensange, and he wanted to know why, nephew or no, aunt or not.

So, with his candle in hand, he approached, and as he did, the thundering of his heart was so strong he felt he might heave, and his hair was beginning to be lathed in sweat.

He unsealed one case and opened it — there was a portrait there, lined in gold.

It depicted a woman, young, in her twenties perhaps, with bright green eyes and curly light hair, dressed in a floral gown. Her eyes were tantalizing, teasing… an enchanting air.

Beneath the portrait was a name: Madame Ballens.

Only a portrait, Reev thought, only a portrait — and he felt himself exhale.

Yet another case was on top of the others, larger than the rest, colored black. It was lined with silver markings in geometric patterns Reev could not discern, and it beckoned him — it beckoned him, and his trembling heart.

He walked over and took the case, and set it on the floor. He unlatched it on its hinges and it fell open.

There were books inside, books of many sizes and shapes, thick codexes bound in parchment. On one of the books' covers were the words "House of Sighs: My Life As A Lady of Pleasure."

It was scandalous material, in truth, but in the homes of the fair ladies and gentlemen of Wodenscross Court, weren't there far darker secrets?

He continued through the books, seeing the rest were written in the Zarube language, which Reev could not read.

On one book's spine were words, what he guessed said "Dictionary Infernal."

A dark topic for sure, but many delved into such matters didn't they, for the protection of the gods, for the safety of their lives and souls?

Yet as he held that book, he felt a pain in his arm flare — the pain, a wound, the imprint of a scar, where many months ago Ivan Xandrast had cut him. He had been cut with *Serpentax*, the Dark One's own sword, and the pain was returning… it was unbearable. He cried out and cast the book down. Luggage spilled over, bags and cases emptying their contents before him.

There in the candlelight was a rod, on which was an inverted Heron's mark, black candles all in a row, a statuette of some fork-tongued horned monster, and worst of all, worst of all by far, a Black Book.

Had Aunt Ramona pledged herself to the Dark One? It couldn't be, it couldn't be.

He seized on the Black Book, in the light of his candle, and the pain in his arm was like searing fire poured onto him. He read, and saw in red ink many names, which he scanned exactingly despite his agony.

"*Madame Flourons,*" he read a name, "*Messeur Tireau.*"

"*Eloise Sanchion.*"

"*Jourmande vis Abernis.*"

He saw no sign of Aunt Ramona's name, nor that of her husband Elfraine.

As the pain in his arm reached his apogee, he read them again, panting, sweating, making sure he did not miss anything. But as he paged through it, he confirmed — Aunt Ramona had not signed this Black Book.

He cast it to the floor, now dazed, in a panic.

Her name was missing… but why had she brought it with her?

Her name was missing… but why did she have black candles, and a rod with an inverted Heron's mark?

He did not trust his aunt, no, not at all, and he would have to put everything back in the exact way that he had found it.

Aunt Ramona could not know that he'd snooped about her secret room.

"Hail, Reev!" The voice he heard sent him from panic to mad terror. He turned and saw a small lithe figure on the stairs, far away.

"Hail, Reev! My cousin… what exactly are you doing?"

Chapter Seven: Beyond the Pale

In the light of the sun, Fortunato was back on the cliff, observing the Imperial camp on the far side of the Pale of Wettin. The memories of the night before had not left him, nor the sense of danger those memories had brought. Stenn, afflicted by some dark power, had brought the morale of Fortunato's battalion to the precipice.

They had signed up to fight the Empire, not the powers of shadow.

Stenn, for his part, remembered nothing.

A trumpet pealed in the midday light; there was the sound of marching feet and chanting.

He drew Danenhir, and hurried up the cliff, back to camp.

~

Gallian soldiers were pushing through the trees and brush, Gallian soldiers from a different regiment. There were about a hundred that Fortunato could see, and these were only a hub in a much longer train.

At the fore was a marshal of their own, dressed in an iron breastplate unlike the quilted jack armor of the others, and wearing on his head a helmet from which a horsehair crest protruded.

"Fortunato, commander," he said, "we are your reinforcements. Hail!"

"Hail," Fortunato said softly.

He wondered why they had come.

"Why have you come?" he said, aloud.

"You didn't hear?" said the marshal. "After your victory at

Highrock, you've been promoted to General of the Army. Did not Eventide's outriders tell you?"

They hadn't… but perhaps they'd been intercepted by Imperials, killed to a man.

General of the Army… it was an honor that Fortunato did not want.

"Our two thousand men of the Sun Brigade are at your command," said the marshal.

"Hail," Fortunato said, "thank you," and he gave him a small salute.

Yet a force of three thousand men could not contend with the army that lay across the Pale of Wettin.

He turned and went back to his post on the cliffs.

Through the farms and marshland, he could see a lone Imperial riding in their direction, in the direction of Emmet's Bluff.

Again, he drew his sword; again, he drew Danenhir.

~

He watched as the Imperial rider ascended the hills and mountainous outcroppings below. He did not call on his archers to shoot, or his men to strike. It was against the laws of proper war to kill outriders. Now, he was the General of the Army, as much as he didn't want it to be so. He watched, and he waited; he stood by the cliff's edge, and as the outrider made his way up and down switchbacks, he made his approach.

As the rider galloped and then trotted into camp, what Fortunato thought first was how splendidly arrayed and well equipped the outrider was, compared to the hastily mustered army of yeomen that the Gallians employed. On his chest was a suit of scale-mail armor, glittering in the sun and embossed on its edges with a gold material. In his hand was a spear with a sturdy shaft and a finely-forged steel head. His helmet was glossy with a white crest, glittering in the day's light.

Fortunato realized he was among the only people in camp that could speak the Imperial tongue proficiently. "Hail," he said.

The rider's horse reared up. Bits of black hair escaped his helmet. He was pale, yet his skin had a healthful luster. Across his eye was a long scar.

"I am here to speak with one man and one man alone," the rider said. "The leader of your efforts. Fortunato of Ríva."

"I am he," Fortunato replied, in the Imperial tongue.

At the sight of Fortunato, the rider's eyes seemed to harden; his lips puckered with pugilistic scorn. Perhaps, at that moment, he realized who Fortunato was — an Imperial, or at least an Imperial by birth, now leading the fight against his own country.

"His Honor the Proconsul of Cambionia and Gallia wishes to request of you a meeting, tonight, at sundown," the rider said.

"Nicollo is not the proconsul of Gallia," Fortunato said, "Gallia is a free state."

"Careful with your words, traitor," said the rider. "Nicollo on behalf of His Undying Glory the emperor is offering the people of Gallia a deal, one which they do not deserve. I hope you will listen carefully, and act wisely, Fortunato of Ríva, traitor… offers are made only once."

Fortunato peered beyond him, to the Pale of Wettin below. The news that he had become the General of the Army had reached Nicollo before it had reached him; Fortunato imagined Eventide's messenger assailed on some lonely road by an Imperial soldier, and the news drawn out by threat of a knife.

"At the midway point, between Emmet's Bluff and Camp Castevanus, you will meet him, tonight, at dusk," the rider said, "else, our forces will begin their march, and Gallia will be razed to the ground."

Fortunato peered into the rider's dark eyes. The Imperials did not bluff; their word was their bond. He would meet with Nicollo as they said… but only to buy time. There would be no surrender under Fortunato's watch.

"Tonight, at dusk," Fortunato said to the rider, "I will meet Nicollo, as you said."

Chapter Eight:
The Promise

"Don't tell your mother," Reev said to Ash's dark form, standing in the stairway. "Don't tell your mother, please… I… I…"

His voice was trembling, his hands were covered in sweat, and the searing pain of the wound in his left forearm had retreated not at all.

"What are you doing?" Ash repeated himself.

"Snooping around," Reev said. "Not knowing what I'd find. I'm sorry… I'm sorry."

"It is quite all right," Ash said softly. "Has Amée told you things?"

"No, no," Reev said, "she hasn't…"

For a while, there was only silence. "I will not tell her," Ash said. "Don't worry, cousin. What did you expect to find?"

Reev wondered if he could see the Black Book in the flickering candlelight, or if Aunt Ramona had hidden all this from him, too. "I don't know," Reev said. "I don't know…"

"You'd better put everything back the way you found it," Ash said.

"I will… I will…" Reev was only just beginning to catch his breath. "Say, Ash… I thought you were supposed to be at school."

"My teacher is a dumb oaf," Ash said, "he knows not whether I'm there or absent. My mother's guards know not to cross me.

"My secret is safe… and your secret — your secret is safe with me, as well. Promise not to tell?"

"I promise," Reev said.

"Then I promise, too," Ash replied.

~

It had begun to rain when Aunt Ramona returned home, and the sun setting through the windows painted the grand staircase in orange light.

Amée's secret was not safe with Ash, the fact that she'd escaped "sitting in silence in her room." Reev hoped his secret would be safer.

Far off he heard Aunt Ramona's wild screaming, her verbal lashing. From the conservatory he thought it might come to blows.

At dinner, a rich feast of lamb shanks and wine-braised chicken, he learned that Amée had been dismissed. Among such elaborate food and expensive wines, a new sense of discontent was in the air, discontent and fear — fear that Ash's lips would be loose, and Aunt Ramona would discover what Reev had done, that she would learn what he now knew.

Chapter Nine:
A Deal

In the sunlight, which was waning, Fortunato rode — by horse, not by wolf, for he did not want to distract or by his stunning appearance provoke a conflict. In the sunlight, which was waning, he traveled alone as was agreed, to meet the leader of the Empire's forces in Gallia, Nicollo.

He only knew the name, rumors of his bright blue yet wolf-dark eyes, the knowledge that not long ago Nicollo had been in the Lune Valley, and had kept Reev Nax captive. He only knew the name, and rumor, and now he would meet Nicollo, who called himself proconsul of Gallia, in the flesh.

The gold and red light was reflecting over the grass; to Fortunato's side were mountains, and in front of him, scattered marshland and cattle-farms. He rode in the waning light, as the day began to pass into another, dreading what might be said, wondering what he should do. He supposed he would meet the moment with all due bravery — make the most of it… serve Gallia.

As the sun sank beneath the horizon, beyond a stand of oaks and elms, Fortunato could see a rider approaching.

That rider rode astride a white horse, a mighty thing half again the height of Fortunato's mare, whose steel barding was glistening in the soft twilight. On the horse's head, protruding from its armor, were feathers of red and gold.

The one riding on the horse was not a man he had seen before, but it was the man as he had imagined him. His hair was a pale blond, his eyes a bright blue with a shark-like vacancy seeming to lurk behind him. The armor on his chest was embossed in gold with pictures of the gods as Imperials saw them — Amara the Mother, a cornucopia in hand; Alabastrus the king, wielding a spear;

Seladora on the half-shell.

And like his visage was as Fortunato imagined it, Nicollo's voice was as he imagined it too — deep, resonant, carrying far even from where he rode.

"Fortunato of Ríva," said Nicollo, and as he came to a halt, his horse reared up. "General of the Army for Gallia… a traitor to your people."

Fortunato would not argue with him.

"It seems, in war, only an Imperial is good enough for Gallia," Nicollo said. "An Imperial will deliver them from Nicollo; that is what they think. An Imperial can match the Imperials… how foolish the Gallians are, in all."

"That is not what happened," Fortunato said.

The burden lay heavy about him — the guilt, the fear. He had betrayed his nation in a sense but in a cause that would eventually benefit them and all… the cause against Seymus and his servants in the mortal world. The burden lay heavy about him — but he would stand firm.

"It is a good day for Gallia," said Nicollo as darkness was beginning to fall over the land. "His Undying Glory, Emperor Khandaraeus, has given Gallians a way out of their imminent destruction.

"We will consider your declaration of war no crime if you agree to end this war, under certain terms," Nicollo said.

"What terms?" Fortunato said, and looked beyond Nicollo, hoping to gain some intelligence about the Empire's movements, but they were too far, not in sight.

He was only barely listening when Nicollo spoke.

"Your leader Eventide will pledge loyalty to the Eagle, and not wage war against it. Red and gold standards shall fly above your walls, and above the walls of every walled town. Your army will be disbanded. Eventide will receive his crown from a representative of His Undying Glory, and will bow before an image of Khandaraeus.

He may govern the affairs of Gallia, but a garrison of Imperial soldiers will be stationed in Horn Keep."

Fortunato was continuing to look past him, continuing to plot, to think, to plan. There would be no acquiescence to the Empire, no submission. Yet how long would Fortunato remain in Galiope, when the true cause — the cause against Seymus — took him elsewhere?

"Answer me, traitor," said Nicollo.

And at last Fortunato listened, and he peered into Nicollo's shark-like blue eyes. "The Gallians are a free people. No deal will be made. We will not bend… even if we break."

"You will break, then," said Nicollo, "and you, Fortunato of Ríva, will die a traitor's death."

Against such a foe, so much mightier than Galiope, Fortunato thought of breaking the laws of war, of waylaying Nicollo here, while no one watched, driving Danenhir into his chest and further scattering the Imperial forces.

But it would do no good. Another would arise, perhaps an enemy wiser and less hot-headed than Nicollo. Nicollo… his nemesis. Fortunato would prevail, he vowed, though he knew not how.

"Tomorrow, at dawn, Gallia's doom shall come," Nicollo said. "Consider yourself forewarned."

His white horse reared up and he galloped away, as twilight turned to night.

~

At dawn, on Emmet's Bluff, Fortunato was awake, watching, and as Nicollo had said, the troops in the Imperial camp began to move. The masses of dark shapes began to move across the fields, through the farmland and forest of the Pale of Wettin. The invasion of Gallia had begun.

"Shall we fight?" said Thingel with a croak in his throat.

"We can beat them!" said Stenn.

And Fortunato said, "No."

"No," he continued, "we flee. Grab your things. Retreat. We will live to fight another day."

Fortunato sent a messenger on a horse to Galiope proper; with all due speed he would inform Eventide of what had happened, and what was soon to come.

War, fire, destruction, death… maybe slavery for those who resisted. Fortunato would stand in the gap. Fortunato would walk toward the fire. Fortunato would fight for the Gallian people — but wisely, and on another day.

In the morning light the thousands of troops retreated, preparing to strike at the best possible moment. They were outmatched, outnumbered… but Fortunato felt that the gods, and the gods of his ancestors, were with him.

Chapter Ten:
Landswehr

Many days of hard riding and the gently rolling fields and mixed farmland were giving way to high rocky hills and crags. Gastreel could feel the ground beginning to ascend, and the air taking on a cooler character, though still the summer was sweltering. He estimated he and Wrinn had crossed into Almania proper, though its capital, Alzdorf, and the grand duke, were still a good distance away.

It was the place Gastreel where had grown up, though his childhood was a faint image, and one that did not often come to mind… his mother doting yet often preoccupied, his father a shoemaker who had been disappointed at the discovery of his son's magical talent.

But Gastreel was not an Almanian, no, at least, not anymore. Did he belong to Gallia? He served it — and he had, with all his heart. Yet it seemed to him that he belonged to no nation in truth, only a higher cause… the cause against Seymus. Reev Nax. *The Prince of the Dawn.*

"*An!*" he shouted and kicked Ivy's flanks, and she took off at a gallop up the ascending rocky roads. He could hear Wrinn thundering ahead on Noble, behind him.

~

It was afternoon when the rolling fields had become mountainous hills, as memories returned — of a life Gastreel had long put behind him, which he no longer dwelled upon. Amid the tree cover and ponds and small farms, signs of civilization began to appear… hamlets and lone houses, high gables and thatch roofs the color of gold… brightly painted window frames and spacious yards… walking among them, tall and plump men and women, well fed and lacking in fears — the people of Almania, the people of his youth.

"How much farther?" Wrinn said behind him as the long shadows of the afternoon grew.

They were in the White Mountains, compared to the Dragonteeth mere hills. Alzdorf was not far off. But Gastreel wouldn't reward Wrinn's impatience. "Wait, and see," Gastreel said.

To the hamlets and scattered homes were added walled towns, and Wrinn and Gastreel at last began to be noticed. The tall and strongly built people of Almania remarked at their passing, at the doors of the houses and the gates of the towns.

Dusk was setting in, daylight was waning, and Gastreel was not surprised when he heard the peal of a trumpet… a sound that brought back half-formed memories of a life he had long ago left behind.

Ivy began to slow her gait until at last, in the wan light, she came to a stop. Noble nickered in the distance.

Standing in the road were a group of dark figures — tall, like the Almanians, made taller by the armor that they wore. Over their heads were iron greathelms. Their dark full-plate covered every inch of their bodies. Over their pauldrons were green half-capes. The symbol of the Heron's hammer, burnished onto their breastplates, marked them as landswehr — the Almanian grand duke's fiercest fighters.

They did not ride on horses; it was not their method. Pledged to Heron, god of justice and just war, they were a religious order, but their taste for violence was legendary — even in Gallia.

From their sides they drew spiked morningstars. In a guttural tongue, they began to babble, bits of language now returning to Gastreel.

"Gallians," one said, "you are Gallians."

And they began to speak the Gallian tongue. "Intruders," the chief of them said, "the Grand Duke does not take kindly to trespassing."

Gastreel lifted his staff, and the chief of the landswehr took a step back.

"We are emissaries," Gastreel said, "from your ally, the Lord Eventide. And I am Gastreel Osiris."

"The Green Wizard," said the chief of the landswehr.

"The Grand Duchy of Almania has given Gallia promises of aid," Gastreel said, "aid which has not come. You and your men should be fighting with us… fighting the Empire."

"Almania is for the Almanians," the landswehr chief continued. "The Grand Duke has only duties to his people, and we to Heron god of justice."

Gastreel did not wish to strike the landswehr dead, but he would not allow them to hinder these efforts. There was a reason Eventide had sent him here, stealth combined with power — and against a wizard of Gastreel's caliber, many more soldiers would be required to resist.

"You may know, good sir, that I was born in Alzdorf," Gastreel said. "The Grand Dukes pride themselves on their oaths… their word is binding. He promised help and I will hold him to it. Would the god of justice smile on anything less?"

"Almania for the Almanians," the landswehr continued, "the lord of justice for justice.

"Nevertheless, we will not stop you. Yet you will not travel through His Honor Martin's lands unaccompanied — nor will you travel through them armed.

"We will escort you. But you must give us your weapons… you your staff — this elf, his quarterstaff."

Gastreel could rain lightning down on the landswehr; he could smite them by his powers of magic. What then would the Grand Duke say, if he had brought harm to these, the soldiers in his employ? Would he offer his help? No, the cause would be lost.

"So be it," Gastreel said, "Almania for the Almanians. The lord of justice for justice… and let justice be done."

He handed over to the landswehr his staff, and his sword, Maderias.

Wrinn, grumbling, allowed them to take his quarterstaff, and a dagger he had on his person.

The landswehr began to lead them down the road, and Gastreel followed, walking, leading Ivy by the reins.

~

In the morning, up a hill, a mountain appeared… walls of stone, many mounting terraces. Alzdorf, the White City, was before them, and memories returned, memories, unbidden.

In his mind's eye, he saw a shadowy face, and two red eyes.

Chapter Eleven:
The White City

The gates to the White City were open, and the road pierced it, north to south. Houses crowded out the sky, houses with thatch roofs and high gables, like those of the Almanian hamlets. But at the base of these houses were shops and as Gastreel walked, those hints of memories were swirling, returning, stronger than before. His father a shoemaker, his mother doting yet distant, and another presence, scarcely remembered. A shadowy face… two red eyes.

The men of the city were dressed in kirtles, the women in dresses of ivy green and chestnut brown and cherry red. They were tall, thickly built — well fed, and without fear. Through the streets they walked, laughing, talking, doing business, as if a war was not raging on their northern border.

Gastreel tried not to glare, tried to keep his dark thoughts in check. Happy, they were, and when he saw a man in hose and a green hat guzzling a tall glass of beer, he thought — *they should not be happy. They broke their bond. They betrayed their word. They did not fight for Gallia, as they had promised.*

Throughout the streets, clogged with people, music was rising on the harp and clavier, and the sound of laughter irked Gastreel, and the pouring of the drink. The landswehr led him and Wrinn, pushing past the winebibbers and beer-drinkers, and as he saw the tall glasses and the girls in country dress, more memories half-formed returned to him, and it dawned on him that they were in the midst of Almania's greatest festival, the Day of Andern.

Bells began to ring as they broached the central square, and the streets, once crowded with people, were now packed to a person. Rising above the city streets and the towering houses were the spires of a cathedral, the Greatminster, half again as large as St.

Sigmund's back in Galiope — and beyond it, the crenellated towers of the Great Hoff, where the grand duke resided.

The chief of the landswehr turned to Gastreel. "Your presence will be announced to the Grand Duke. If he will hear you, we will tell you. Until then, you will be kept in the House of Guard."

He pointed to a great tower near the edge of the city square, carved of stone. It was half as tall as the spires of the Greatminster, yet much wider, and its crossbar windows made it seem a prison — and a prison it likely was.

"I have endured much already," said Gastreel, "will you dare try a wizard's patience?"

But his voice was swallowed up by the sound of the crowd, the laughter, the clinking glasses, the music to which maidens in country dress were dancing.

"Will you dare try a wizard's patience?" Gastreel said, and with magic caused his voice to carry louder, but even that could not match the sound of the festival's revel.

He looked to Wrinn, to the elf's sullen blue eyes. Then he looked back to the landswehr. In truth, there wasn't much of a choice.

"Very well," he said, and his words were swallowed up.

As he made his way to the tower, a peasant in hose and a straw hat said to his wife, "Have you heard? The Imperials have crossed the Pale of Wettin!"

And time now was of the essence, time… time Gastreel did not have. He walked toward the tower, called the House of Guard, and looked to Wrinn. He plotted, and he planned, and he thought of his best next move.

Chapter Twelve: Gamesmen

For days, Fortunato and his men had fled, and for days, they had been pursued, or so it seemed, as they marched from dawn until dusk and warned everyone in their way that the Imperials were coming. From dawn until dusk, they hurried, and he was at the fore of them, joined now by the creature he loved best in the world, his black wolf Tyra Jade. As they moved from the wilderness around Emmet's Bluff to places of civilization, Fortunato sent more outriders, north, south, east, west, warning everyone who would hear that the invasion of Gallia had begun.

Yet the strength of Gallia could not prevail against the full forces of the Empire, and during the long days of marching, glimmers of another cause returned to him — the bodies of Seymus's Servants burnt to ash in the Black Pass, the boy called Reev Nax transformed into something more than human. As Gallia fell into darkness, hope still remained, although now that hope was vanishingly faint.

It was late in the day, and the sun was shining brightly, the thickness of the summer heat laying thickly over the land, when Fortunato spotted something he hadn't expected on the westward-leading road. There were people walking down that road, civilians in civilian dress, dozens of them, yet in their hands were weapons of war. They were burdened with packs, and their horses and donkeys were laden with saddlebags. They were clearly not from Gallia, but they did not have the look of Imperials.

Fortunato signaled, and the three thousand men under him began to approach.

The passersby regarded them with looks of alarm. Some began to back away, but they did not flee.

And Fortunato took note of how healthy they looked, their faces fresh and lustrous in the way that warriors and athletes were. In complexion they varied from pallid to ebon, and as Fortunato and his men drew near, he began to count. There were thirty-seven of them, together with animals and a few wagons, heading down the westward-leading road in the direction of Galiope.

~

"Who are you?" Fortunato said. "Gallia is at war. We are under martial law."

And these foreigners, passing down the way, looked at him in surprise.

"We are competitors," said one of them, who was carrying something like a metal board in his hands. "We are competitors hoping to win the Victor's Crown."

Fortunato's soldiers began to surround the interlopers, and if they hoped to run away their pathways were being cut off.

"The Victor's Crown?" Fortunato said. "What are you talking about?"

The man with the board looked about, seeing he was now surrounded by soldiers. "The Victor's Crown... the Pan-Vardic Games are set to begin. Galiope is hosting them in this year, 1153... they were delayed to now, weren't they?"

Fortunato did not know what to make of these intruders. The Pan-Vardic Games... what was he talking about?

"Identify yourself," Fortunato said. "What is your name, and from where do you hail?"

The man with the board looked at him sidelong. "Am I to be treated like a criminal? I'm a competitor and that's all... and I *will* win the Victor's Crown."

Fortunato looked beyond them, to mixed tree cover and fields of wheat, scattered farmland which he'd soon order put to the flames. The Imperials were nipping at their heels.

"What is your name?" Fortunato said. "From where do you hail? Speak, or die."

"Spyke," said the man with the board, "and I am from Perremum. Are you satisfied?"

"No," Fortunato said, "I am not." He pointed to the crowd. "Have them bound. Seize their belongings."

Spyke glared, and his hands quivered. He looked like he was about to strike Fortunato with that board.

"Is this how the host of the Pan-Vardic Games treats it competitors?" he uttered as a soldier took the board from him, and bound his hands with rope.

But Fortunato had a feeling, inexplicable, that this was Imperial trickery. He had little doubt that this was some scheme of Nicollo.

Spyke, an improbable name… Perremum, where was that? And the Pan-Vardic Games — Fortunato had not heard of such a thing.

He turned, looked to Stenn, said, "Stenn, take your hundred. Remand these people to Galiope for questioning."

Stenn bobbed his head, and as other soldiers confiscated the party's goods, the men in Stenn's hundred began to lead them off-road. To Galiope, these interlopers would go, and the truth would be divined, one way or another.

The Pan-Vardic Games… who had heard of such a thing?

Chapter Thirteen: No Time to Waste

In the darkness of the House of Guard, Gastreel could see that night was falling. In their spare quarters, through the window, he could see the waning sunlight, and also the towers and barbicans of the Great Hoff. In the spare stone quarters, he and Wrinn were sitting at a table, Gastreel with pottage that was quickly growing cold, Wrinn with a hunk of stale bread that he refused to eat.

Despite the heat of the summer outside, the room was dry and drafty, and there was a dark air, one inexplicable, of shadow. The memories of his childhood had faded, and now the memory plaguing him was of a presence he forgot, a shadowy face, crimson eyes — what was he thinking of?

The door to the spare room opened, and a landswehr in full armor, his face disguised in a greathelm, entered. "Your Honor, the Green Wizard," he said, "I have an answer for you. The Grand Duke will meet with you on St. Kellen's Day, two weeks from now, and he looks forward to you having an audience with him — so he says."

"Two weeks?" Gastreel cried. "Galiope is under attack. Gallia is in the grip of war. And you expect me to wait and do nothing, waste time when many lives are at risk?"

"You must stay here, in the House of Guard," the landswehr continued, "until such time as you are summoned. You may once have been an Almanian, but you are no longer considered so, and no foreigners are allowed in the ducal city."

Gastreel snapped to his feet. "Enough of this… give me my staff. And give Wrinn his quarterstaff."

"You may have them back when you depart, and the Grand Duke sends you on your way," replied the landswehr.

Rage was pulsing through Gastreel's veins, all-consuming rage, turning to hot fury. The Grand Duke and his landswehr were treating him like a common criminal, when he was an emissary of the highest ranks of Gallia's government.

"Two weeks," he howled. "I do not have such time to waste. Give me my staff — I demand it."

He called up the weave, and though without his staff his craft was less focused, he could still summon magic — perhaps the ignorant landswehr did not know.

The landswehr staggered back as the room fell into darkness, as points of bright blue lightning appeared in Gastreel's palms. As those points grew to sizzling balls, he called up more magic, and in a voice made louder by the weave, shouted, "Where is my staff?"

The landswehr turned and ran… his faith in Heron was apparently not enough to quell his trembling heart.

"Come with me!" he called after Wrinn. "We will not ask the Grand Duke his help… we will demand it."

~

Out of the double doors of the House of Guard he walked, and the weave lingered on him. His staff, he sensed, had been stored far away in the Great Hoff, or in some other tower.

He walked and Wrinn followed, and he pushed past the crowds who seemed to part at the sight at him, and the rage coursing through his veins had not at all lessened.

He summoned lightning, and lightning sizzled; booming thunder echoed instantly, and the crowds in Alzdorf's Great Square began to flee. A path was cleared, and they began to hurry. The revelers fled, and they began to run.

At the Great Hoff more landswehr in greathelms stood guard, ten Gastreel counted in total. In their hands were spiked war clubs. In an instant, they began to charge. "Avast, traitors!" Gastreel said.

"Avast, cowards! Breakers of bonds…"

And he summoned lightning, a spear brighter than the one before it, larger though it was uncontrolled, and the landswehr fled, leaving the doors to the Great Hoff unguarded.

"Wrinn," he said, "tonight, we collect on what Gallia is due."

Chapter Fourteen:
Amulet

It was night in Galiope, and through the windows of Sunstone Manor Reev could see an eerie peace had come to the streets of Wodenscross Court. Soldiers were patrolling the alleys and thoroughfares, for the best of protection was provided to the rich and well-connected. In his guest room, all alone, Reev uttered a prayer that Gastreel would return, that even now he'd see him riding up the way on Ivy, and with him Wrinn… take him back where he wanted to be, among his friends, as war inevitably drew close to Galiope.

It was beginning to rain. A wind was blowing. Through a veil of clouds, the full moon was brightly shining. And there was a knock on the door.

He crossed the room and pulled it open. Standing there was one he had expected.

In the candlelight Aunt Ramona looked a ghost. She was pale, and shadows were flickering about her face. "Dinner, my nephew," she said. "Dinner is served."

~

In the dining hall, a meal was prepared, bowls of candied apples, roast pheasant and duck laden in a spicy sauce. In the brighter light of the chandelier, Aunt Ramona looked no less ghostly, and Reev could see bags under her eyes, as if she'd been crying.

Ash joined them, walking through the door. "Duranchese duck *again?*"

Aunt Ramona snapped at her son. "Sit down, you ungrateful — " She stopped herself and looked to Reev. "Sit down, Ash. You will have your duck, and you will like it."

Ash acquiesced, seeming to shrink at the harshness of his mother's words. He sat down, and as the rain outside began to patter ever harder on the roof, the young man Reev knew as Guy entered with a bottle of wine.

One by one the drinks were poured, Ash, Reev, Ramona.

"Ah, ah," she said, "a bit more."

And Guy poured until Aunt Ramona's wine was at the very edge of the cup.

There was the distant roll of thunder.

"Aunt Ramona," Reev said, and gulped. "Is everything all right?"

"Have your duck, Reev," she said. "Eat up. I think you'll like it."

He took his fork and his knife, and obeyed Aunt Ramona's instruction. The duck was tough, overcooked… and the spicy sauce tasted strongly of vinegar. He looked up and saw that Aunt Ramona wasn't eating, only staring at him, between sips of her wine.

"What is wrong?" he wanted to say. "What did I do?"

And there was a feeling deep in the pit of his stomach that she knew… she knew what Reev now knew.

Soon his plate of duck was all gone, and still Aunt Ramona hadn't eaten. Still, she was staring at him, still sipping her wine between dark looks.

At last, Aunt Ramona spoke. "Reev, nephew," she said, "why didn't you tell me you visited your grandfather's house?"

Thunder rolled; the rain picked up.

"I didn't," Reev said — a lie, and he didn't know why he said it.

"Don't lie to me," said Aunt Ramona. "Last night, I found your grandfather's amulet in your room. Why did you keep this from me? Why didn't you tell me you went to the High Country?"

"I didn't think it was relevant," Reev said. "I didn't think you'd care."

"And how is your pappy, Reev?" Aunt Ramona said. "How is he doing up there, in his house, all alone?"

Reev stared into his aunt's eyes, saw cunning, saw the faintest trace of malice now being revealed.

"He is dead," Reev said, "I buried him."

Aunt Ramona howled, and looked down. When she met Reev's gaze again, those eyes of hers were watering. "Dead," she said, "as I thought. That amulet of his hadn't kept him safe from *them*, as he'd thought."

"Them?" Reev said.

"Everyone was always out to get your pappy," Aunt Ramona said, "the neighbors… the hold-lord's warriors. Everyone was pursuing him, and we had to keep quiet, keep safe, in that house of his — yes. Ramona and Simeon weren't to leave his sight. But we did leave, Reev. I and your father *did* leave."

Ash seemed to be enjoying the tension, and as he observed them nearly have an argument, there was the faintest trace of a smile on his lips.

"Dead…" Aunt Ramona said. "Dead. Kal Nax. He disowned me when I said I'd leave the High Country.

"But that amulet… I hadn't seen him wear it since I was a little girl. Where did you find it, Reev?"

"In a chest," Reev said, "in his house. It was locked away, but the chain was rusty."

"So, you are a thief, too." Aunt Ramona seemed to instantly regret the words; she drew back in her seat, and appeared to shrink in size. "No, not a thief," she said, softly, "just a grandson, wanting to be part of a former world… A world that shall never again come to be."

She reached into her pocket, and from it produced that coin necklace, which she'd apparently taken from Reev's room.

"Have it," she said, "have it, Reev — it is yours. Wear it, and wear it proudly. It did not protect your grandfather like he thought it would, but I suppose he hadn't been wearing it at the end."

She tossed it across the table, and Reev took it in his hands. He was glad to place it once again over his neck. He felt that coin of inexplicable make belonged over his chest. And he did feel safer, somehow, wearing it.

"I was a terrible daughter," Aunt Ramona said, and her voice was almost a sob. "I was a terrible daughter indeed. I should never have left the High Country."

"Then Ash wouldn't have been born," Reev said.

And the darkness and grief in Aunt Ramona's eyes seemed to be growing, and her chest was heaving in and out ragged breaths. "Yes," she said, "for that, all this has been worth it. For Ash's sake, and the joy he has brought me, I would have gone through it all again."

Gone through what, Reev wanted to say, but he kept silent. He had so many questions yet about his aunt.

"Perhaps, I should have taken that amulet with me," Aunt Ramona said, "with me, to the west..."

She still had not touched her food, though through the cloudy glass it appeared the wine was all gone.

"That amulet," Aunt Ramona said, "your grandfather said it was special, so special. It could protect from fire; it could protect from rain. It brought good luck and good fortune. It has been an heirloom for generation unto generation."

The water in her eyes was building; her lips were beginning to tremble.

"I should have brought it with me," Aunt Ramona said. "It can protect from fire, he said. Even the fires of our hearts..."

Chapter Fifteen:
At the Bridge

Fortunato raced through the night darkness, under the moon which was being veiled and unveiled in gray wisps. Behind him were the three thousand men under him, and that number was growing by the day. They were an hour out from Galiope, and the Imperials were not far behind. They would cut the Imperials off at Balem's Bridge, he had thought… he had thought…

There was a howl, piercing the night silence, a wolf's howl, sharp in its timbre.

Fortunato, riding on Tyra Jade, looked back for any sign of the beast, but he could make out nothing. He signaled for his men as they approached a few stands of trees, as the wind whipped through the willows and pines, and the heat of the summer day lingered long into the night.

At Balem's Bridge, they would cut the Imperials off, surround them, harry them from afar — weaken them, cull their numbers, and when they reached Galiope's walls they would be weakened. That was what Fortunato intended.

But racing down the road, he could see no sign of that bridge, though they had been journeying long, and each second and minute seemed to blend into the next, and in the darkness and the dim moonlight he was disoriented.

There was a trumpet sound — no Gallian horn.

Call off your dogs, he wanted to say to Nicollo. Leave Galiope alone. Must every state be subject to the Empire?

The ground was ascending, and the road was winding upward. Far in the distance, on cliffs, were the lights of a yeoman's cottage. Beside silver pines and quiet lakes, somewhere, somewhere — was Balem's Bridge. Or so he had thought.

Pursued at the heels by the Imperial Army, Fortunato had had no time to rest. He had been reacting, not acting, and Nicollo was driving him wherever he wished, wherever he wanted him to go — or so he thought.

"Make haste!" Fortunato shouted, and the trumpet blew again, from behind, and then another, to the right — an Imperial trumpet, not a Gallian horn of low and soft timbre.

"Make haste!" he said again, as the ground took him up a steep embankment, and a river and stream appeared below.

The bridge was in ashes, burnt to a shell — dark shapes were in the distance, Imperial soldiers in helmets and metal armor. Fortunato cried out in despair… they had been outwitted.

But something else he noticed in the light of the full moon, a dark shape moving across the moon's breadth. There was a shrill cry, and up in the night sky, Fortunato took note of two gleaming red eyes.

Wylocks were here, putrid beasts from the Dragonteeth Mountains. *Wylocks*… what did that mean?

The Imperials at the bridge were approaching; the Imperials from behind were making up lost time. But something Fortunato noticed, in the dark of night — beside the river, beyond the soldiers, a robe black in color wafting in the wind, and five others behind him. Whenever the clouds unveiled the moon, there were glints of light reflected on iron masks, six in total.

The Imperials were ravaging through Gallia, but something darker was here.

Chapter Sixteen:
Mordblood

The rain was pattering on the roof of Sunstone Manor, and as Reev cowered in his guest room, that pattering of rain was turning to a downpour. The shutters of the window were banging against the wall, and as the wind howled in shrill ghostly tones, there was a spear of lightning, striking the street just ahead — sizzling sparks, and a deafening boom.

The light of that heavenly spear reflected on a face — now standing inches from him.

His Aunt Ramona was standing there, and in her hands, she was gripping something — a painting, underneath it the words "Madame Ballens."

"What were you doing snooping around in the cellar, Reev?" Aunt Ramona said.

He had left everything as he had found it — or had his secret not been safe with Ash, after all?

About an hour had passed after dinner, and Aunt Ramona appeared dazed and gaunt, having not touched her food. In her eyes was inchoate rage, lips trembling no longer with sadness and reflection but wrath.

"I didn't — " His lie was swallowed up by his own trembling heart, and the feeling that lies would do him no good, anymore.

"I'm sorry," he said instead.

"Sorry!" she said. "So sorry!

"I've housed you, I've fed you, I've treated you better than you deserve. Sorry! Why were you snooping through my things? Who do you think I am? What did you think you'd find?"

There was another spear of lightning, another gusting wind. "Aunt Ramona," Reev said, and he felt his resolve harden, and the coin amulet around his neck was like a testament to who he truly was.

"Why did you have a Black Book? Why were there black candles scattered among your things?"

Aunt Ramona howled; she grabbed the portrait by either end, and she tore it in two. In two pieces it fell to the floor, and as lightning speared and deafening thunder crackled again, she seemed to lurch forward, as if she were ready to strike him. "Ah, Reev, it is so like you to bring up such things, at my most vulnerable. You are your father's son!

"When Elfraine sent me and our son away, I wanted to remember not just the good times, but also the bad. I wanted to remember the company he kept, his unfaithfulness, his cruelty, so that I would not despair at a time such as now...

"Jauchevin Ballens, his lover... curse her name! On her naked body the worshippers of Seymus in the capital would set black candles, and utter prayers to him — the Dark One. They signed his book, and they participated in the Black Rite. My husband was among them. I will not just remember the good times — I will also remember the bad!

"That was my shrine to dark memory... and you intruded upon it."

"I'm sorry," Reev said.

"Sorry, sorry," Ramona said, and the wrath in her eyes had not lessened. "Sorry, you are... oh, you have not only your father's eyes and hair — you have his heart. He always thought so little of me, his baby sister... *he* was revered, but I was the social climber. Everyone called him selfless, but I knew him better than that. He wanted glory! Fame! And what did I want — a happy family, enough money to go around."

"And you got it," Reev said.

Lightning flashed; thunder crackled, and the light in her eyes was like chthonian darkness.

"A happy family!" Ramona said. "Yes! So happy. When my husband of thirteen years sent me away for… for…"

"For what?" Reev dared to say.

She picked up one of the pieces of the portrait and cast it at him. "Still at it, hmm? Still snooping?"

Her watery eyes were building to tears — grief and anger competed against one another, and some infernal combination of the two was bursting outwards.

Reev cowered back, against the bed, but he resolved he would not let Aunt Ramona control him, anymore… he would not let her make him a coward.

"You accused your own aunt of being a demoniac — a worshipper of the Dark One!" she sneered. Lightning crackled, thunder roared, and the storm was raging throughout the city.

"I only noted that you had a Black Book," Reev said. "Who else would but a demoniac?"

"I did not sign it," Aunt Ramona said.

"But why did you bring it with you?" Reev said.

Aunt Ramona leapt up, and her menacing moves were like a dark dance. "Oh, you ungrateful wretch, raised by rats, a creature of Gastreel — "

And wrath was now being born in Reev, indignation, righteous anger.

"A shrine to the bad times, so I would not only think of the good!" Aunt Ramona shrieked. "I will not be judged by you. I did not sign the book."

"And neither did Elfraine," Reev said.

Aunt Ramona struck him; Reev felt blood against his cheeks. He hurried away, scrambling toward the door, to cries of "Don't you defend him!" and then "Get out! *Get out!*"

He ran through the halls, past Ash's bedroom and that of Guy's, past the upstairs parlor and the ballroom, the upstairs conservatory and the family archives. He sped down the grand staircase, to the door, and in the shadows of the corner of the room saw Ash's dark eyes, and a quiet grin.

Without his belongings, wearing only his clothing and his grandfather's amulet, he fled from Sunstone Manor, into the wind, and the lightning, and the rain.

Where, now, would he go? He had left behind Gastreel's keys in that house of horrors, to which he would never return.

Chapter Seventeen: Green Wizard

Gastreel marched through the halls of the Great Hoff, and Wrinn followed.

They were unarmed, the both of them, but at Gastreel's presence the landswehr within the Great Hoff seemed to give no resistance. Gastreel's reputation had followed him; none would try the Green Wizard, even without his staff.

The landswehr watched and waited, statues of living flesh, as Gastreel and Wrinn passed through the high stone halls, past forgotten rooms and iron doors, through the spartan living quarters of the Grand Duke — his castle.

Yet as they made their approach up a set of stone stairs, in the light of torches and hanging lanterns, a faint noise began to reach Wrinn's ears, and soon after, Gastreel — music, growing louder, the rolling sound of a waltz.

And Wrinn recalled the festival which he had seen in Alzdorf's central square, and he guessed that there was a feast day under way. The Grand Duke was in the midst of a celebration, at which now the Green Wizard would appear.

Crowds, billowing crowds — noise. A perfect place to run away… a perfect place to escape, and seize that sunlight and cloudless day Gastreel had so naively spoken of.

There was nothing for him left in this world. He had lost his freedom, once again. He would not return to servitude — and that was what this was.

~

The landswehr at the great doors did not so much as draw their clubs. They stood statuesque like their predecessors as Gastreel laid a hold of the knobs and heaved the great door open.

Beyond, the spartan décor of the Great Hoff gave way to splendor. The scent of cooking meat and dough hit Wrinn head on. And beyond, in a golden hall, were marble floors and wood-paneled walls and amid that great space, hundreds of men and women dancing.

Gastreel pushed on, and Wrinn followed.

As the music of the waltz swirled, women in green and gold houppelandes twirled and stepped to the beat. Men in hose and kirtles, some of whom wore crowns, were joining them by the hand, and dancing with them.

An orchestra was playing in the far corner of the room, men and women furiously strumming viols and playing pipes and pounding drums. And at the carefree attitude and opulence of these, Almania's nobility, Wrinn felt his own resentment build — yes, about their broken promises to Gallia, but also old hurts and wounds… among them, standing in the far corners, tending to the food, doting on them, were elves — elves, in servitude.

On a throne, watching the dancers and their gaiety, on the opposite side of the room, was a man plump and fat, dressed all in green, with a purple cap over his graying blond hair. On his right hand was a gold ring, and in his left hand was a scepter.

"Martin Durkheim!" Gastreel shouted, and his voice carried louder by magic. The waltz stopped; the dancing ceased, and everyone stared at him in silence. "Grand Duke! You have betrayed your bonds…"

As the dancers froze in place, the lights in the room seemed to dim, and the air grew colder, though there was no wind. On Wrinn's tongue was a taste like sugar crystals. All in the room was darker, save Gastreel's form, and on the grand duke Martin's face was a look of abject terror.

But from the darkness near the throne stepped another, a man in a red robe and a red pointed hat, with a long gray beard — in his right hand a shapely black staff. A Red Wizard he was, an order that did not prohibit one's sale as a mercenary and magician for hire. The darkness lessened, and the Red Wizard's form became as bright as Gastreel's. In his left hand grew glittering motes of green light, being formed into a ball.

"Radobod, cease this!" Gastreel cried. "You know who it is you intend to strike — your leader. And you answer to the All-Seeing Eye. Under the laws of wizardry you are foresworn."

The Red Wizard, "Radobod," slunk backward, and the glittering light motes in his hand winked out one by one. Darkness returned, and Gastreel's body again stood out, bright green against a dark canvas.

Martin, grand duke, laughed nervously on his throne. "What is this about, Green Wizard?"

"You made a promise to Gallia," Gastreel said. "You have not upheld it."

Martin rose. "I said I would meet with you two weeks from now, St. Kellen's D—" he began.

But as eldritch light appeared in Gastreel's eyes, he said, "I will not be held captive to you. I do not have the time, nor does Gallia, nor does the Northern World as a whole…"

Martin smiled sheepishly. "Of course! Of course! Tomorrow I will hear you — such a matter requires thought and discussion, and not after I have had so much wine. Is tomorrow good enough for you, Green Wizard?

"I was only trying you — only testing you, to see if your reputation is true."

"Do not lie," said Gastreel, and the darkness faded, and the terrible light in his eyes was gone. "Tomorrow at dawn you will hear me — and not a moment later."

"So be it!" said Martin, grand duke. "Say, Gastreel — do you know how to waltz?" He lifted his finger and the orchestra began to play again its swirling tune, and the dancers began anew.

A woman in a white dress, with her gray hair tied up in many tresses, lurched forward and grabbed Gastreel by both hands. Around the room there was laughter, as the Green Wizard, the leader of the wizards of the north, joined the dance.

Crowds, blaring noise… distractions — and Wrinn remembered anew what he had vowed himself, what he had promised to do. At an opportune moment, he would run away and find a future.

There was nothing, nothing at all for him here. He was a servant — no, worse, a bondservant. And as the dancers danced and the musicians played, he turned, speaking the words aloud, "There is nothing for me here."

He turned, toward the door — and standing there, directly before him, was an elven maiden slight and slender, with brilliant blue eyes, a face pretty as could be. In her hands was a broom, and on her lips words seemed to hover, ready to escape.

Wrinn had never seen a girl so pretty before.

"What's your name?" he said to her.

She answered, "Rosalie."

Chapter Eighteen: Something Stronger

Reev ran into the night darkness, and as he passed by the mansions and estates of Wodenscross Court, the rain was lessening and the clouds were parting to reveal the stars. The storm was subsiding but not his worries and anxieties — *Where will I stay?*

The Dragonpaw was the easy answer, though he worried that Glenda had been insulted at his long absence. Nevertheless, *the Dragonpaw* — that was where he'd go.

Through the misting rain, his run slowed to a jog, his jog to a hurried walk, until he passed through the gates of Wodenscross Court into Middletown. Far in the distance was the sound of music rising… all about him was filth and squalor, and even late into the night people wandered about, some of whom were carrying mugs of ale in their hands.

He hurried through the streets, the sting of Aunt Ramona's words only now beginning to hurt. *Raised by rats*, she had called him. *A creature of Gastreel.* He was glad to be gone, but sad his aunt's love for him had grown so cold, if it was ever there.

He slid past a young man who was vomiting in the street, and two young women, his friends, beside.

He pushed through a crowd of men wearing floral wreaths on their heads, as the music grew louder and louder — the strain of the viol and the pounding of timpanis, joined now with the audible strain of the voice… and he was in City Square.

The Dragonpaw was in view.

~

Yet as soon as he took a step a young woman had jumped in

front of him, on her head a feather headdress, in her hand a wooden stick shaped into a serpent's caw — the Staff of Summer.

She was joining in with the revelous song.

"Summer is a-coming in. Loudly sing, yes you."

She wouldn't let him past her. Her eyes gleamed with mischief.

He turned to find another route, and a man was there in a flower bonnet, a giant mug of ale in his hands.

"Summer is a-coming in. And the pipers too!"

"Here! Drink!" the man said.

A festival was raging in City Square, even late into the night.

Reev gestured… "I don't want— I don't want—" he started, but the man crossed the distance between them and shoved the mug to his lips. He took the slightest of sips.

"Summer is a-coming in! Loudly sing, yes you!"

The song was rising up into the night. Just ahead, a young man was chugging a bottle of wine.

"Summer is a-coming in! And the pipers too!"

The noise was overwhelming Reev, and to the noise was added brilliant flashes of light. The revelers were burning something in the middle of the square.

"Drink!" the young man ahead of Reev snapped at him. "Drink! Again!"

He shoved past the woman in the feather headdress, and as he walked, he was beginning to stagger. Dizziness — and that glass of ale hadn't been ale at all, but something stronger.

There was a roar of something — a jet of flame bursting into the sky, and the revelers cried out. A cart was racing through the square, and the revelers were chasing after it.

"Summer is a-coming in! Loudly sing, yes you!"

Whatever Reev had drunk had been strong indeed. And he could hear the young man behind him, running toward him — "Drink! Drink!"

And Reev half-fell, half-ran, away from the riotous noise, from a place of light and color to one of darkness — the damp wetness of an alley.

~

Reev was stumbling in the darkness, and his mind was swimming. He'd just had one sip — what had been in that drink?

He felt nauseous and cold, but away from the revelers he felt safe, secure… he was alone.

He looked up. *No, not alone.*

Standing before him, in his hazy, shifting sight was one he knew, one he thought he would never see again.

"Ivan Xandrast," Reev cried out.

He was there, the man who had once cut him with the Dark One's own sword, but whose evil had been purged from his soul, and who had pledged himself to Reev in a bond of loyalty.

But that had been oh so long ago.

He lurked there in the distance, his black hair as shaggy as Reev remembered, over his body loose white linen clothes, strapped to his back that double-sided sword Reev recalled, the butterfly blade.

"Ivan Xandrast!" Reev cried out again. "Help me — " And he fell to the ground.

Ivan Xandrast helped him to his feet.

"Help me — " Reev said. Something had been in that drink — it wasn't ale or wine or anything like that at all. "Help me… to the Dragonpaw…"

Ivan Xandrast's black eyes gleamed. "I know a better place to go."

Chapter Nineteen: Fate

Cries of alarm were rising from Fortunato's men, as they brandished swords and raised shields. Rain was moving in from the south, drizzling mist. And the Imperials were charging from one side, and another.

"Retreat?" Thingel's voice called out amid the darkness.

"No!" Fortunato said. "No!"

"We fight!" he continued, with inexplicable resolve, a feeling and not a strategy, perhaps rage born of Niccolo's constant victories, of him driving them wherever he wished to go. "Draw swords! We fight! To the death! For Gallia."

And as the winds changed, and the misting rain moved in, fog was rising from the marshlands and the fells around. Imperial trumpets pealed and Fortunato signaled — and Gallian horns blew.

Astride Tyra, Fortunato charged the approaching Imperials. He brandished Danenhir as his heart grew faint. All rested on this — he knew it. On this battle rested the fate of the war.

Chapter Twenty:
A Midnight Idyll

The poison in Reev's mind was only just beginning to clear, and he was staggering down the way in the shadows of the night, with Ivan Xandrast's muscular form as his guide. Past shapes he pushed — no, they were crowds. Past mazes and twinkling stars he walked — no, those were street lamps and buildings.

"Where are we?" Reev said.

A group of men shoved past him roughly, and he almost lost his balance. He splashed forward through a puddle.

"Where are we?" Reev cried, louder, a shout at the highest pitch of his lungs. "Where are we?"

"The Bowery!" said Ivan Xandrast, a shape far ahead of him, now much farther ahead than Reev would have liked.

The Bowery… Riverside. A place that was warned against. A hive of criminality.

"The Bowery! The Bowery!" Reev said, and as the poison swirled in his mind he raced ahead, cutting the distance between him and Ivan Xandrast until he was almost on top of him.

The lights reflecting in the River Galios gleamed, and the moon now bare of clouds was a pale mistress. The stars shone on the city below, as Reev stumbled through the dark streets, as the paved road became descending steps, slick with water, and a building of stone appeared, and a black iron door.

"What is this?" Reev said, still poisoned.

And Ivan Xandrast said, and Reev read the words on the sign above the building's lintel — "The Salty Dog."

There was a line at the black door, and at the black door a brutish hulk of a man in a torn woolen shirt. He was examining the would-be entrants as they passed by him, and when they pleased him, he would open the door, and when they didn't, he would shove them toward the river below.

"I don't like this!" Reev said, and he thought his voice was swallowed up in the noise of the crowd, but Ivan Xandrast replied, "Don't be such a baby!"

At last, it was their turn, and the hulkish brute of a man was more intimidating close-up than he had been from a distance. His face was pocked with scars and bruises, and his jaw appeared crooked — perhaps from a fight.

"How tough are you?" the hulkish brute said to Ivan Xandrast.

"I'm wanted for death in three foreign nations!" Ivan Xandrast said. "I am a criminal of war! I would set the heads of the defeated on pikes, for all to see!"

"Not good enough!" the brute said with a scowl on his face.

"Want to see?" Ivan Xandrast said, and from his back quickly drew the butterfly blade.

The black door opened, and he passed through.

Reev, dazed, mind still swimming with poison, lurched forward, hoping to pass the brute by.

But his giant hand pushed Reev back.

"How tough are you?" the brute said.

"I'm not t—" Reev started, but he looked down to the river below, where the brute with a strong push could easily send him.

"How tough are you?" the brute shouted, irate.

"I'm the Prince of the Dawn!"

~

Through the doors of The Salty Dog, Reev walked, and there beheld a sight unlike anything prior.

Amid the pulsing light of the flashing lanterns, on a floor scattered with bones and breadcrumbs, sailors and painted prostitutes had gathered in a circle to watch a cockfight. One rooster with his eye hanging free was darting at the other, to the delighted sighs of some and the grumblings of others.

"Hey! Reev!" A voice stirred Reev from his voyeurism. Ah, yes — he was not alone.

He stumbled toward Ivan Xandrast, and through the haze of his poison followed him, past tables where more sailors were sitting, and others — ruffians, hoodlums in grease-stained cloaks with pipes in their mouths. The smell of pipe smoke was everywhere, but worst was the noise, a snare drum constantly beating to the flashes of the pulsing light — a singer on a lonely stage crooning some ineffable tune.

At last, Reev was at the bar, exhausted, wondering at his lapse of judgment, how he had gone from the staid discomfort of Wodenscross Court to here — the most dangerous part of town, the most dangerous tavern in the city… or so it would appear.

"A round of grog!" Ivan Xandrast said, and signaled with his fist.

The barkeep, a vixen in a tight red dress, her hair dyed some shade of blue, nodded and signaled back. "Coming right up, Xan!" she said.

And before Reev knew it, he was being dragged through the crowds, past two sailors who were drunkenly fighting, stepping on dry bread crumbs and discarded bones, amid the gleam of shattered bottles.

And Reev was sitting at a booth, still dizzy, mind still swimming. How much time had passed? — he did not know. Through the tavern that vixen from the bar was coming, and a platter was set before them — two glasses of horn, and a large pitcher.

"Grog!" Ivan Xandrast said before Reev could ask what it was, and he was pouring Reev's glass of grog before he could refuse.

"Drink up!" Ivan Xandrast said, and partly by the force of his stare, and partly by the thought a bit of drink would lessen the effect of the pulsing strobe lanterns and the constant percussion of the drums, he did just that.

He spat it out — it tasted like bleach.

"Come on!" Ivan Xandrast said. "You're not a baby… you're the Prince of the Dawn."

And again for that respite, he took a sip, and determined he would swallow. The harsh, fiery venom slid down his throat, into his stomach. And despite the taste, he found he did feel a little better, after all.

"Where have you been, Reev?" Ivan Xandrast said. "I haven't seen you at the Dragonpaw in weeks."

Nausea filled him; he keeled over, to the side of the booth, but his stomach remained firm — he did not vomit.

"Another drink!" Ivan Xandrast said.

And Reev took another swig of the foul grog.

"Where have you been, I said?" Ivan Xandrast wouldn't leave him alone until he'd answered that question.

"My aunt Ramona's house," Reev replied. "Where have *you* been?"

"At my house on Canary Street," Ivan Xandrast replied, "between trips to the Dragonpaw, and trips here, and my work on the docks…"

Another sip — the grog was foul, but the more of it he drunk, the less offensive were the pulsing light of the strobe lanterns, and the cheering of the cockfight spectators behind him.

"You look rough," Ivan Xandrast said.

"You, the same."

"What's bothering you?"

"Not your business.

"*What's bothering you?*"

"My aunt… my aunt…"

~

Another round of grog, and how long had Reev been in The Salty Dog?

The platter had been set before them, and Reev wanted no more, but Ivan Xandrast apparently had not yet had his fill.

"A Black Book," Ivan Xandrast said. "A Heth figurine.

"And your cousin, so strange…"

Had he told Ivan Xandrast all in this past hour, thanks to the grog? The poison was leaving him, but the grog was coursing through his blood.

He had told Ivan Xandrast all this, at some point in the night — Ivan Xandrast, and was he worthy of trust?

"Have you considered the fact that your cousin might be the one prophesied?" Ivan Xandrast said, and maybe it was the drink talking.

"Have you considered the fact he might be the one warned against? Wouldn't it make sense that if you, Reev Nax, are the Prince of the Dawn, that your cousin Ash might be the Dark One's Hand? Blood against blood — a good tree, against a twisted one."

It made terrible sense, and Reev's heart began to pound. Blood against blood — good, versus evil. Could it be so? Could it be so?

Could his cousin, Ash, be the Dark One's Hand?

Chapter Twenty-One:
Back Home

Reev's head was throbbing, and when he opened his eyes the light from the windows outside burned them. Where was he? Where had he been?

As he came to, he saw it was late, in the morning, and he was at his room at Gastreel's house, Rosetree Manor.

He was back at Rosetree Manor, but how? He hadn't had a key.

His head ached, he felt nauseous. What a night he had.

More of it came into focus… The Salty Dog, round after round of grog. A midnight walk, staggering, through the streets.

And at some point in the early morning hours, after Reev had purged his innards, he had said to Ivan Xandrast, "I'm locked out of Gastreel's house," and he had said, "I have a key."

Reev's head was throbbing. His body ached. It was late in the morning, and he had survived that most dangerous of nights.

And he remembered Ivan Xandrast's words in the early morning. "I have a key," he had said. "I have the Skeleton Key."

There was a thunderous knocking downstairs, and Reev in a panic leapt to his feet. He scrambled into his clothes, as the knocking began, and he thought in the haze of his exhaustion — he had come to Gastreel's house. *Where is Ivan Xandrast?*

In his trousers and tunic, and with the coin amulet he now even wore to bed, he scrambled through the hallways, down the stairs, to another thunderous knock — and the front door shaking.

He opened it, as was polite, to bare the tranquil scene of Wodenscross Court… manors, buildings, a cobblestone street clean and pristine — and a sight which he hadn't wanted to see: Aunt Ramona, behind her a bevy of servants. His belongings were piled at her side.

"Reev," she said, "nephew… your things. You left them at Sunstone Manor last night."

Reev stared at her in silence. In the daylight, she was not so terrifying. In the daylight, those dark eyes did not intimidate him.

Far off, lurking in the bushes, he could see Ash. It was a collection of people he hadn't wanted to see, of people he never wanted to see again.

"I wanted to say I'm sorry," Aunt Ramona said. "Sorry to you… and sorry to me. When I saw I had kin I hoped to make something of the Nax family, to have those cordial relations that your pappy Kal and your nanna Trita never could seem to create. I hoped we'd get along, Reev, but I'm a bit high-strung and you're… you're…"

What would she say? Would she insult him now, again, in the daylight?

"A happy family," Aunt Ramona said. "A dream, dashed. But I brought a peace offering." She looked back. "Guy?"

And Guy appeared, and handed her something.

"A Witchenwald gateau," Aunt Ramona said, "like your nanna Trita used to make — or tried to."

The cake was on a platter, formed of three ascending layers, a dark brown, with cherries poking through. It seemed to jiggle as Aunt Ramona took it, and Reev could see the edges of the cake were lined in white frosting, and at the top was a white figure made from fondant.

"A Witchenwald gateau," Aunt Ramona said. "Perhaps, it can't make things right. But it's something."

Reev took the unwieldy cake in his hands, and balked.

"And something else," Aunt Ramona said. "Something more valuable.

"You are young, Reev, but I put in a good word, and the Lord Eventide was delighted at the suggestion. You are now a part of the Council of Galiope, a member of the city government. We meet today at the Townhall, when the *tridium* bell rings."

Reev didn't know what to say.

"Farewell," Aunt Ramona said, "with love."

Love — but what love did Aunt Ramona have for him, in all?

~

He carried the cake as it jiggled left and right, up and down, through the narrow corridor, to the kitchen. He set it on the counter, and out of the corner of his eye noted he was not alone, as he'd hoped. Ivan Xandrast was there in his loose white clothes.

"Your aunt brought you something," he said in a voice that was almost a grumble. "I saw her coming. I should have warned you."

"There is no need," Reev replied.

"Here," Ivan Xandrast said, "I'll try it, make sure it isn't poisoned."

Reev scoffed as Ivan Xandrast grabbed a butcher's knife and cut himself a piece. He picked up the sticky morsel and dropped it into his mouth. "Delightful," he said, "cherry and cream. It's safe to eat, Reev… your aunt hasn't poisoned you."

"My aunt wouldn't poison me," Reev said.

But as he spoke those words, he was amazed at how uncertain his voice sounded.

"But your cousin… your cousin…" Ivan Xandrast grumbled.

And another thing Reev recalled from that long night — an accusation that had been formed. Ivan Xandrast said his cousin Ash might be the Dark One's Hand. That had been the grog talking, hadn't it?

No, no — at the accusation Reev's stomach twisted, and he felt ill, and he felt faint. *No, no,* he thought.

He would need more than a Witchenwald gateau to get through this day.

Chapter Twenty-Two: The Heer Meister

The sun was rising over the White Mountains, and not all was right with Gastreel. The warmth of summer had moved in, full and true, but after the pomp and celebration of the grand duke's banquet, an unsettled feeling had overcome him — a sense of danger, and when he walked from the High Porch through the corridors of the Great Hoff to their planned meeting, he found himself uttering prayers and supplications to the gods. The landswehr watched him as he passed them by… he was sure of it, despite the greathelms that covered their faces. Plotting, planning, like everyone in the Great Hoff — and there was no one to trust, and no one more in danger than Gastreel the Green Wizard, though he was strong in the powers of the weave and the arcane.

He realized he was missing something — no, someone. Wrinn, bondservant of the Council of War, had gone off somewhere. He was more than a bondservant, he was Gastreel's bodyguard, and the only one in this den of vipers that he could trust.

Wrinn, where was he? As always, his curious mind and emotions had gotten the better of him. But Gastreel would have to attend to this meeting alone.

Where was he? It no longer mattered. As Gastreel passed from the grand corridor to the throne room, toward the Hall of Counsel, he uttered prayers for help in this task — this task, on which the fate of Gallia rested.

~

Where was Rosalie?

As Wrinn walked through the halls, he kept an eye out for her, for her with whom he'd danced, with whom he'd talked last night on the palace balcony. They had had the best of times, and then she'd slipped off, nymph-like, away.

He knew he had duties to attend to; he knew Gastreel was counting on him. But that night — that night... for the first time, he had felt alive. For the first time, he had felt there was something worth living for.

He knew Rosalie had duties; he knew she was overburdened with work.

"I cook," she had said. "I clean. I do whatever Martin tells me."

"So, you're a slave," Wrinn had said, "like I used to be..."

Her luscious lips had perked up; a bit of anxiety had appeared in her eyes, for the first time in the night, as they shared a bottle of pilfered wine on the High Porch. "Not a slave," she said. "And don't let the master... I mean, Lord Martin — hear you say it."

The baffling comment had gone unexplained, as the conversation ventured to other topics. The wine had been gone, the bottle emptied, as the sounds of the banquet faded. And a look of panic had entered Rosalie's eyes, and she had said, "I must go."

With the suddenness of someone who had been caught doing mischief, she had disappeared, into the night, leaving Wrinn scrambling but eager to see her again.

And now he was here, searching for her — but as he passed through the west corridor to the chapel, it dawned on him he wouldn't be finding her anytime soon. The grand duke's palace, called the Great Hoff, was a city unto itself, with so many rooms that many remained unfurnished. There were hundreds who lived in it, and many hundreds of elves who tended to the ducal family's every whim.

"Rosalie," he said under his breath, "I hope I see you again."

"You — *quilit*," a voice stirred him from his concentration.

He whipped about and saw a man standing there at the chapel's doors.

Quilit… elf, in the Almanians' tongue.

"What are you doing?" the man said. He was tall and strongly built, and had eyes blue like the cloudless sky. From his spangenhelm a bit of blond hair escaped, and at his side was a sword, and a bulky coinpurse. Though he wore a cloth kirtle and hose, it was clear he was a man of war.

"Have you gotten lost?" he said. "What task were you assigned today, elf?"

Wrinn bristled at the implication of his words, that as an elf he was by nature a servant. Somehow, he gained control of his rising anger, and through gritted teeth said, "I am Gastreel's bodyguard."

"Gastreel is nowhere in sight," the man replied. "Perhaps, you ought to come with me."

~

In the Hall of Counsel, the grand duke had set up court. In the burning light of lanterns, he seemed reduced and small, and without the help of his throne Gastreel could see that he was short — shorter than most.

"You offered help," Gastreel repeated himself.

At the grand duke's side was his wife Freya, with whom he'd danced at the banquet last night. Her gray hair was no longer tied up in tresses, but in an elaborate bun. Where Martin was short and mealy-mouthed, the opposite of impressive, Freya had the poise and canny speech expected of royalty, and the presence to match. She was taller than her husband, and Gastreel was glad to be negotiating with Martin, rather than her.

The gloomy light of the Hall of Counsel reflected in both their eyes, and on the helms of the landswehr behind them.

"I said so," the grand duke replied, "that I would give Gallia the full force of our arms. But the king in the west is gone. The throne of Zarubain is no more; the Empire has brought him to ruin."

"You promised," Gastreel said. "The words on the Durkheim seal are 'I say; I do.'"

Yet the mealy-mouthed shrinking creature before him seemed to have little of the character and martial valor of those Durkheim grand dukes before him. To Gastreel's eyes he was pitiful, small.

Pitiful — but cunning.

Martin turned and made a signal, and the landswehr turned and departed, as if they were cogs in a machine. Through a curtained door they walked, and Gastreel and Martin, and the duchess Freya, were alone.

"You know, Mr. Wizard, that the grand dukes of Almania live in fear of the landswehr," Martin said softly, "and in truth are cowed by them. They obey my commands, but only to a certain limit. They call themselves the Poor Brothers of the Temple in Danarion, but they are bold, and they will not listen to my call — they will not answer to aid Gallia. I have no choice, you see."

"So this is a question I must bring to the high priest at the Greatminster—"

"No! No!" Martin answered Gastreel, and a frenzied look appeared in his eyes, as a door opened and shut, and all of them turned.

In the dim light were two figures — Wrinn, and another.

"Heer Meister Friedrich!" Martin Durkheim said. "And you have brought help."

"My help," Gastreel replied, "and I hope he doesn't wander off again."

"He won't," said Friedrich, the "Heer Meister." "He's had a good talking to."

At those words, Wrinn's confident sexpression turned to a bitter scowl.

The Heer Meister approached, tall and strongly built, in a spangenhelm, and where Martin Durkheim was a timid mouse, the towering figure before Gastreel carried himself like a lion with every bold step. "Green Wizard," said the Heer Meister, and made an ostentatious bow. "Greetings to you. I hope this day finds you well."

"It does not," said Gastreel, "for now it seems the Durkheim family will break the central promise of its words — 'I say; I do.'"

The Heer Meister's blue eyes glinted in the soft candlelight. "You come here, asking what?" he said.

"Aid," Gastreel replied, "aid, for Gallia."

The Heer Meister's eyes were piercing, and Gastreel found himself shrinking slightly backward. Where Freya's presence was strong, this Heer Meister's was overpowering. Yet Gastreel vowed to himself he would not be intimidated.

"You know we do not control the actions of the Poor Brothers," the Heer Meister replied. "They are vowed to protect the grand duke and his fief. Anciently they were called to do so — to protect Almania and no other."

"And yet," said Gastreel, "in times of peril and war, a mustering is called… peasant soldiers and knights, called up from the masses — squires and engines of war. You know this."

The Heer Meister's bright blue eyes glistened, and he smiled, bearing white teeth. "You ask much," he replied. "Almania is not at war."

Not at war, apparently, and how strange — when the king in the west had been brought to ruin by the Empire.

"And yet," the Heer Meister said, "our word is our bond. Right, Martin?"

"Right!" Martin piped up sheepishly.

"Something we must have in return," said the Heer Meister, and his smile anew was dark. His blue eyes became like a serpent's. "Something dear, something precious. A favor for a favor."

Chapter Twenty-Three:
It Is Decided

The *tridium* bell was ringing, and Reev remembered in that moment that he had been named a member of the Council of Galiope, and that that council was meeting, now, at the Townhall. He scrambled through the halls of Rosetree Manor, bidding Ivan Xandrast farewell, rushing past the door, remembering he hadn't had a key.

"*I have a key,*" Ivan Xandrast had said. "*I have the Skeleton Key.*"

So much of that night was forgotten; so much of it remained unremembered. And yet Reev had a duty now — a duty, apparently, to give advice for the war. Was that appropriate, in all, for a boy of sixteen?

It did not matter — they had asked, and they would receive.

~

"Victory! Victory!" he heard a man shouting on Kalend Street. "Victory — at Balem's Bridge."

And the city crowds passing through the thoroughfares and alleys were talking and remarking at the news.

Victory — another victory. When, ever, did the Empire lose?

It was good news, on good winds — and summer was about to begin in earnest. When ever did the Empire lose? Reev would surely learn more at council.

~

At the doors of the Townhall, two guards in full plate and red capes stood watch.

"I am a member of the council — " Reev said, one face amid the crowd in Lion's Square. He wondered if they wouldn't let him pass, if this had been some fanciful tale told by Aunt Ramona, but they stepped aside, and the doors opened.

Beyond those doors were lanterns, a great stone hall — splendor, vaulted arches, statues of monks and the city's great heroes in alcoves… and an open door. Beyond it, his Aunt Ramona was beckoning him.

~

Reev took his place behind the lectern that was given him, and saw the faces of the council for the first time, names he had heard spoken but whose faces he had not seen. The Lady Llewyn of Leyshaw — cold and gray featured, whom he'd heard a ruffian complain about at the Dragonpaw. He had owed money to her estate. The Lord Rivien, Galiope's lord of horse. Eventide and Fiona — whom he'd met before. And there was the Lord Alden, dressed all in black, red-haired and freckled, with eyes that appeared silver in the high windows' light.

Reev had entered to a storm.

In the center of the room, around which the lecterns circled, there was company. There among the council were a group of seven men, their hands all bound, and in charge of them a soldier dressed in quilted jack armor, carrying a spear.

"Say it again, Stenn from Sauer's Brook, so that our esteemed new member can hear it," Eventide intoned.

And "Stenn from Sauer's Brook" turned, and faced Reev, and looked about. "These men were found at the roadside, claiming to be participants in the 'Pan-Vardic Games.' Fortunato had a thought it was Imperial trickery."

Reev was only sixteen, only a boy, but he had a thought — though the supposed criminals were clearly foreign, garbed in a motley assortment of clothing, from tunics and trousers to kirtles to long skirts, they had the look of athletes full and true. And why would the Empire resort to trickery, when they were the stronger force?

There was silence in the council for a while. At last, the Lady Llewyn spoke. "Why has Fortunato bothered us, the council with this? They are no threat to us. The Pan-Vardic Games — "

"The Pan-Vardic Games," said Eventide, "a memory, faint. I remember something about them.

"A tournament of strength and skill, I believe, that the wizards in the north host every thirty-three years. Is it possible that Gastreel, in his distracted state, forgot to cancel them?

"They are not criminals, but misguided…"

"I know indeed what the Pan-Vardic Games are," Aunt Ramona spoke. "I remember them, so well. They are where my brother, Simeon, met Gastreel… and they had been held that year in the town of Naines, not far from Zarubad."

Silence ensued, a few brief moments of thought.

"There was war at that time," Aunt Ramona said, "even then… but Naines remained untouched. The city that hosts the Pan-Vardic Games is not allowed to be attacked, and the Empire respected that truce then."

Reev wanted to hear all about the victory at Balem's Bridge, but this was the topic apparently chosen.

"Gastreel did not cancel the games," Aunt Ramona said. "He forgot to, too distracted, too absent minded… and thank the gods for that, for once."

"The Empire was beaten back again," said the Lord Eventide darkly. "Another victory, thanks to Fortunato. They are currently pushed back to Estenmere. Why would we halt this war now, when we are winning?"

"We will not be winning for long," said Aunt Ramona. "I promise you that. This Fortunato you speak of is apparently a great tactician — but he is no demigod. He cannot halt the forces arrayed against us."

"He halted them again," said the Lord Eventide, "just yesterday — and we thank him."

Reev stared at the stoic faces behind the lecterns, one after the other, wondering why he had been chosen, he, a boy of sixteen. He did not know the art of politics, nor was he wise to the movements of armies and wars between nations.

He was not a politician, or a man of war — but this course of action to him seemed like utter folly. The Empire had been beaten back, yet again, a stinging blow it wouldn't forget… why let off the pressure?

"If we announce these games," Aunt Ramona went on, "and the Empire abides by the truce, as honor demands, we'd buy Gastreel time to gain Almania's help. We can lay traps. We can call on forgotten allies — make ambushes."

"I think," said the Lord Alden, red-haired, with eyes like silver, "that the Lady Nax speaks sooth. Gastreel needs time… but more importantly, the Grand Duke Martin needs time, to muster his troops, and summon together his knights."

The Lord Eventide had seemed at first unconvinced; but now his lips were pursed, and he seemed to be considering the matter in earnest.

What would Reev say? How would they take the words of a sixteen-year-old boy? Perhaps silence was best, but this bothered him. He wished to speak.

The would-be participants in the Pan-Vardic Games, clad in a variety of garbs, and of different complexions, were prisoners, but to Reev it seemed they liked what they were hearing. Their grim, distressed expressions were giving way to interested gazes.

They would have the Pan-Vardic Games — and Galiope would make a mistake.

"It is true," said the Lady Llewyn of Leyshaw, cold and gray-featured, her hands folded neatly on the lectern. "The Grand Duke will need time to muster his army, even more so to do it in secret, without raising alarms from the Imperials.

"And what of asking other allies? Leyshaw, my town, and Cardunnon have long had ties with the war chiefs of the Wilderlands. Will they not too fight for freedom? Surely, they know that they would be next in the Empire's sights…"

The Lord Alden was smiling; Aunt Ramona seemed proud that she had made such a suggestion.

"To me it seems wrong," said the Lord Eventide, "but Gallia is not a tyranny, and the Lord Chancellor's vote is only one. Almania —"

"And what if Almania refuses?" said Reev, and silence followed his words, total silence, and eyes staring at him all at once. "What if the Grand Duke is not in good faith? What if help never comes?"

"Don't be so pessimistic, Master Reev," said the Lord Alden, and his gray eyes sparkled, and his smile revealed brilliant white teeth. He spoke to Reev in a patronizing tone, like that of an old man with his grandchild. "You can't be so untrusting. You can't see malice where there is none. What is it that is said… those who do not trust others are unworthy of trust?"

But why would they trust a foreign potentate, the leader of another country who had yet to honor his vow? Reev did not trust him, Martin, the Grand Duke — and he did not trust so many of the people in this room.

"Fortunato will be disappointed," said Lord Eventide.

"Fortunato is our servant!" snapped Aunt Ramona. "He answers to us… he is the General of the Army — not the Chancellor, or even a member of the Council of War.

"Born a poor boy, I hear, in some insignificant Imperial town."

Reev began to snap back at her, "He delivered victory better than any noble could — " but members of the council all began to shout at once, until at last the Lord Eventide struck his lectern, and an uneasy silence followed.

"Gallia is not a tyranny," said the Lord Eventide. "We take a vote. As for me, I throw my lot in with Master Reev. The matter is before the council… shall we bide time, and host these Pan-Vardic games? May our ancestors and their gods guide us…"

Reev had forgotten he was among heathens… or, at least, a delusional heathen, and those too cowed by him to resist.

Hands were raised, and the clerk stepped forward, and counted them.

"The yeas for this course of action are fifteen — the nays, fourteen. One remains undecided…"

Reev looked about the room, and saw that the Lady Llewyn of Leyshaw had crossed her arms — a position, perhaps, indicating she was noncommittal.

A council, hopelessly divided, had decided on what seemed folly. And as Reev observed the faces of the council, he thought he sensed a new air, one of fear, a sense they had made a mistake.

But law was law, and the chips would fall where they would. Reev hoped to the gods, not the useless gods of Eventide's ancestors, that Gastreel's efforts would bear fruit.

Chapter Twenty-Four: Anything

Ramona exited council quietly, a silent rage threatening to build within her. As she stepped outside into the filth of Middletown, seeing the proles and the gathered masses just inches away from the council's dignity, she nursed that hurt — she had thought of a great idea, and Reev her nephew had led the rebellion against it. She'd driven him away last night, said some things which she regretted… told lies, and nearly chased him out of the house. But she had more than made up for her slights, with that cake baked by the best pastry chef anyone would ever find in this backwater city, and with that council seat which Reev had so quickly used against her.

It didn't matter. Time would provide new opportunities to get back at him, and perhaps he'd think of a brilliant idea at council which she'd eagerly demolish and leave him stunned and hurt.

As her guards swarmed around her for protection, she glared in the direction of the city crowds. They stood so close to the Townhall in Lion's Square, selling, buying, and loitering. She recalled the glory of the west, now fallen — and the king's council which had not seen her fit to be a member. There would not be such a sight there, peasants, in the view of the noble.

With her guards ,she began to make her way back home, nursing hurts old and new, at her nephew Reev — the freshest. But there was also one hurt that wasn't so old either, that had stung her, a slight she hadn't forgotten.

When she had dismissed Amée, Amée had called her a *mordblood,* and she had called Ash what the parish priestess, and the peasants, and Elfraine at the end called him — *Abollondon.*

She would not forget… she could not forget. Amée had breathed in the free air of Galiope, and gotten a view of herself that wasn't accurate. She was of peasant stock. She was not fit to hurl such accusations at Ramona. She'd run off, into the night… but Ramona would find her, and exact her revenge.

~

Back at Sunstone Manor, she changed into more comfortable clothes. Ash was sitting near the unlit hearth in the downstairs parlor, reading. The manor was sweltering, and she began to order her servants about. Eventually, she was outdoors, sitting at the table in the fresh air, a glass of wine in hand, and Chalmet and Guy were fanning her.

"Chalmet," she told her servant, a tall and strongly built, swarthy specimen, "you used to keep Elfraine's record books. You are smart. I'll pay you a bonus for a special task — a bonus, and a few nights off."

"Anything for you, my sweet," Chalmet said.

He had always been such a charmer. "Find out where Amée has gone off to. Find out if she's found employment. I badly want to know."

Chapter Twenty-Five: The Man in Orange

Bala, sitting in the booth at the Dragonpaw Inn with a cup of milk and a hunk of bread, was struck by something amid the music and celebration, the singing and the dancing: he wanted more.

He wanted more than this, Glenda's partial attention, his Mountain Folk friends he'd made, the tasty food and the comfortable bed and the agreement to look the other way when he went off to search for blood.

Something he remembered as he watched Miss Dolley singing on the stage and strumming her harp. Something he remembered as the Mountain Folk girls and boys hooked arms and danced in circles around the Dragonpaw Inn's main hall.

It was something he had been afraid of, but now something he realized he badly wanted. It was something that he had abandoned, or, rather, something someone had abandoned on his behalf.

He wanted to be a wizard, he really did. And he hadn't seen his teacher, Mr. Aleksander, ever since he'd extended his magical powers on those iron masks, and told him what he sensed, and knew — there had been no magic on them.

He wanted to be a wizard, yes, he did, a powerful wizard like Mr. Gastreel. But Mr. Gastreel had been gone, too, and Bala hadn't seen him in weeks.

He felt his eyes water and he began to cry. He pounded the table and shook his feet and let out a wail, so that Ms. Dolley stopped and Glenda came walking over to his booth from the corners of the room.

"What is it, Bala?" Glenda said.

"I want to be a wizard," Bala sobbed softly.

Then he spoke in a more serious tone. "I want to be a wizard, after all…"

"Well," Ms. Glenda said, "that's not something I can do for you. That's something your teacher Aleksander has to show you to."

"I don't know where he is," Bala said.

"The wizards' tower," Glenda replied. "That's where all the wizards live, isn't it?"

~

Outside the Dragonpaw Inn, City Square was crowded, packed with people, and in the heat of the growing summer, it stank — it stank, with the scent of people, with the scent of trash, with the scent of the tanneries and also the scent of smoke. Bala hadn't left the Dragonpaw for a few days, but now he had formed a new goal, an adventure… and he *would* be a wizard, he promised himself, he *would*. In the summer air, he extended his finger — a pinky promise — as good as done!

Through Middletown he walked, and as always, as ever, the wizards' tower was in view, stretching above the tallest of the houses and shops. He waddled through the crowds, past a sword-swallower, past men and women drinking, through the slowly building heat of the day. The sun was beating hot down on him, on his top hat that was perhaps a bit too thick for summer, but he made his way nonetheless.

Up some stairs he walked, down a street, and the immense tower was his compass, his guidestar. At last, the walls of the Tower of Pythor loomed above him, and the great gate which blocked all passage.

He was an ant before the walls and the looming tower, but as he waddled ahead, into the open space before the gate, he heard a voice — "Bala Rabaam!" and up above was the gatekeeper, a woman wizard in light white robes, and she made a signal. "You are welcome into the tower…"

He had been recognized — he had been welcome. And he would soon see Mr. Aleksander, or so he hoped, and he'd have his training like before — he'd become a wizard sooner than anyone knew. He knew it… he had made a promise to himself, and by the most certain means possible, his pinky.

~

Wizards were in the courtyard before the great tower, wizards — grown-ups — in many different colors of robe, red, green, white, gold. There were dozens ahead, and dozens before, and they seemed to be congregating around a man who was standing on a podium, wearing a bright orange robe, with a long gray beard and two piercing green eyes. He was speaking.

"Wise men and women from across the North," he said, "I ask to you this — who is your enemy? Consider it… in the coming weeks, a decision must be made.

"The city is our ally, it is true, and we are sworn to protect it. But our highest goal, and our only care, is the storing up of knowledge for posterity…"

As he spoke, his orange robe seemed to fluoresce. It was cinched with a gold-colored rope, and to it were tied several wands of white crystal. Aleksander had taught Bala what those wands could do — they were repositories of magic charges, so that necromancers could cast a ball of flame, or pyromancers could send a withering ray. This man, it seemed, was an expert, and those gathered near him were listening intently.

"Knowledge," said the man in the orange robe, "and the pursuit of it… that is what we hold dear. The recovery of the remaining two All-Seeing Orbs — past, present, future. To seek knowledge, to grow stronger — the defense of the city, yes, as was agreed to in law. But what are our true goals?"

Bala stopped in the afternoon light, looking at the gathered crowds, wondering if he should join them. But he was not a wizard, and now he hadn't a teacher — that, he vowed, would soon change.

~

He waddled into the doors of the great tower, and as he did his heart was welling in excitement, excitement, yes, and sadness — excitement at the sight of the teleportation pad, which could take him to any floor of the tower, excitement at the sight of the bowed black ceiling and the thought of the tower's many secret chambers, but sadness that he had lost it all.

He'd failed to remove the magic from the iron masks, because that magic wasn't there, and now it seemed that not just Aleksander but also Gastreel had abandoned him.

Where was Aleksander? He didn't know where to look.

And so he did what he knew best to do when something wasn't going his way. He stamped his feet, and puffed out his cheeks until he was sure they were red. He squinted his eyes and balled his fists, and he produced tears on command — he bawled, and he bawled, and he bawled.

A door seemed to open from nothing, the black metallic walls folding into an open doorway. And across the white marble floors, a person walked — a person, but not quite.

She — Bala knew it was a she — was a figure of light, white yes but shifting prismatic colors, glints of red and blue and yellow occasionally flashing, like a rainbow. Bala looked up at her, and thought he saw two eyes, brightness distinguishing itself against a bright canvas.

He knew this woman, if she could be called a woman. He had heard Aleksander talk to her. She was called Betha, and Aleksander had called her an "assistant."

"Bala," her changing voice was like music, like a windchime

blowing in the soft summer wind. "You have summoned me. What is your request?"

"I want Mr. Aleksander," Bala said. "I want to be a wizard, and now."

"Floor 48, Room 18 are his quarters," Betha said. "You know this, Bala. Don't bother me with such trivialities again."

And the being, of pure magical energy, shifted in the light, and glided back away, and the doorway folded in again, into the wall.

Floor 48, Room 18… he hadn't known it, and Aleksander hadn't told him. Aleksander had told him to "wait." But Bala couldn't wait any longer. He would be a wizard, and now.

~

In a dark room was a burning brazier, and at that brazier a chair, on which Bala's former teacher sat. The coals of the brazier were lighting his eyes in a way that frightened Bala, and the way he sat, with his knees halfway up his chest, showed how tall and gangly and misshapen his former teacher was. He looked how Bala thought a creature of the undead might appear. He was pale, and though Bala had disobeyed him, he didn't shout or grow angry. He didn't move — he was staring out the window, toward the ground, where the wizard in the orange robe was speaking.

Without looking at Bala, Aleksander spoke. "My student," he said, "you have come at a challenging time… for me, and for the wizards as a whole.

"Why have you graced me with your presence, Bala? Don't tell me; I know. You are eager to grow, and learn the art of magic. It is easy to see why… you are bright, precocious. And I am sorry I have not resumed our training… I have every intent to.

"But things behind these tower walls have grown troubled, and I and others are at the center of a storm."

"What storm?" Bala said. The sky was clear.

Aleksander turned and fixed his beady black eyes on Bala. "Gastreel; he shall be back soon, won't he?"

Why was Aleksander talking about Mr. Gastreel?

"He must hurry back; I must send him a letter, by hawk, by pigeon. I could send a courier by horse to Almania, but the Imperials have seized the North Country…"

He was talking to himself and himself alone, not hearing Bala's concerns, not caring for Bala's worries. Bala wanted to be a wizard, and he wanted to be one right now.

"Gastreel… have you heard from him?" Aleksander said. "What a silly question! But it was he who introduced you to me. It was an act of his council that legalized necromancy again. His council, his council! Ah… at times I do believe I might faint."

Something was wrong with Aleksander, and Bala didn't know what.

"Bala," he said, "I don't think the Tower is safe for you, nor really for me. Go back to the Dragonpaw! I give you my word I will train you, even if I have to flee back to Palaskov with you in tow."

Palaskov… where was that?

"I want to be a wizard," Bala said. "I want to have my training…"

"And you will," Aleksander said.

"I want to use magic," Bala said. "I want to practice."

"You can practice, Bala, without me," Aleksander said. "You are allowed to use the weave outside city bounds. You may wield your power, as long as it harms no living being, as long as it helps and does not hurt."

Bala had thought it wasn't allowed.

"Go, Bala, outside city walls, in the wild… practice summoning and calling, as I taught you," Aleksander said. "Go, practice, and wait for me, while I monitor all this." His gaze returned to the window, where far below the man in the orange robe had been speaking. "Flee the tower, Bala, and wait for me. Practice outside.

But run from this place.

"Run, before Sestriel takes notice of you."

Chapter Twenty-Six: The Skeleton Key

As Reev walked home in the building warmth of afternoon, stunned by the Council of War's folly and stung by it, it dawned on him that his concerns should be elsewhere.

When he saw a man in a black cloak, he thought of Ash's black hair and eyes. When he saw a washer woman in a white gown, he thought of Ash's pale skin. And when he saw a group of monks in frocks exiting the slums, he thought of the eschatological figure that priests had warned about for millennia, the one who would appear at the time of Varda's end — Seymus's deputy in the mortal world, the Dark One's Hand.

Could it be Ash? Could he have shared quarters with Seymus's deputy? Was he connected to that deputy by blood?

The Prince of the Dawn, and Seymus's champion, from the same family — as Ivan Xandrast had said, a good tree against a twisted one.

Reev fell back; a cart full of asparagus was racing down the way. A woman scowled at him. "Watch where you're going," she snapped.

And as Reev resumed his walk toward Gastreel's house, he realized he still didn't have a key.

~

At the door of Rosetree Manor, Ivan Xandrast was waiting to lead him inside.

Ivan Xandrast was a changed man, yes… the dark evil within him had been purged, but it was he who had inflicted Reev with the wound on his left forearm. It was he who had taken the shard of the Dark One's own sword, and injured him with it. Could Reev fully trust him, now that Ivan Xandrast had assumed by his own will the position of Reev's bodyguard?

"Ivan Xandrast," Reev said softly, "hail."

"Call me Xan, as my friends do."

"Yes," Reev said, "yes, I think I will."

~

In the kitchen, the Witchenwald gateau remained, partially eaten — it seemed Ivan Xandrast had helped himself generously to it… Ivan Xandrast, or rather "Xan."

And Xan had followed him into the kitchen. Reev spun around. "Perhaps, you ought to tell me something," Reev said to him.

"Like what?" Xan said, lurking in the corners of the room, fingers on the edge of the kitchen island.

"Like how we got in here, last night," Reev said, "how you had Gastreel's key."

"I didn't have Gastreel's key," Xan said. "I told you, I have the Skeleton Key. That's how we got in…"

"The Skeleton Key," Reev repeated, and examined Xan's eyes for untruth. He saw none.

"Want to see?" Xan said, and beckoned him.

Near the hearth, beside the divan on which Xan had piled pillows and blankets and was apparently using as a bed, something had been placed on the table. Xan picked up the small object, and cupped it in his hands.

"Here," Xan said, "a relic of my past life. An artifact I was given during those lost years, which I cannot much remember. A tool, perhaps of evil, but that work of evil is faint, for I can use it though I am now changed."

Changed… no longer a warlock.

"See? Hold it. It only burns slightly."

When Reev took the so-called "Skeleton Key" in his hands, there was slight discomfort, and in the dim light of the room it appeared to emit heatless smoke. It was like a bulky key with many segments and grooves, and its edge was in the shape of a skull.

"Faint, the power of darkness is in it," Xan went on, "but it has only lost a little of its effectiveness. When fitted to any lock in Varda, that lock will be opened. No door or secret chamber can hold me back."

A warlock's tool remained from Xan's former life. He had not gotten rid of all of those artifacts he had used, but Reev hoped he had gotten rid of the shard of *Serpentax,* the Dark One's own sword.

The skeleton key, in Reev's hands, was beginning to burn his skin. He looked into Ivan Xandrast's dark yet bright eyes. "Xan, you haven't used this for criminality, have you?"

The way Xan said "No" did not convince him in the least.

Chapter Twenty-Seven: A Voice He Knew

For days, Fortunato had pursued the Imperials, and for days, the hunters had become the hunted.

On Tyra Jade Fortunato was riding through Estenmere, keeping a slow pace to accommodate his footsoldiers. His army had swelled to four thousand, and patriotic Gallians — once cowed — were joining by the day, hoping to be a part of the Empire's coming defeat.

The battle at Balem's Bridge had not been one Fortunato designed. When the fog rose up on the fells, obscuring sight, the motley Gallian army had taken advantage of the confusion. One thing had led to another; dominoes had fallen, in a manner of speaking, and now proud Nicollo Maiodore was on the run.

Amid the chaos of the battle, in the fog, in the night, the Empire's forces had disintegrated — and they were reduced to this. Estenmere, southeast of Gallia, was a place of rich farmland and forest and those farms and forests were before Fortunato — rolling hills and towns, and Nicollo's forces were on the run.

It was not lost on Fortunato that such a victory would not last long. It was not lost on Fortunato that the Empire had infinite resources, and when they decided to end this war, they would. It was not lost on him — but he had dealt them a serious blow. He had wounded his archrival Nicollo's pride... a casualty of a sort, even if that casualty was small.

No... not small. A devastating victory. A terrible defeat for the Empire. And it is due to me... due to me, and the gods' favor.

Fortunato made a signal. The sun was beginning to set at this late hour. They would set up camp for the night. And tomorrow they would clean up the remnants of Nicollo's legion, and hope that the powers that be in the Empire would consider the war in Gallia no longer worth it. But what were the chances of that? In Fortunato's experience, a defeat drove the Empire's elites to all-consuming rage.

They will not stop…

They would not stop, and where did that leave Fortunato?

He turned, and as his soldiers fanned out and began to erect their tents, he remembered something, a faint memory. He remembered Stenn, consumed by some dark power. And he wondered if that dark power remained.

~

It was twilight. The frogs were trilling in the ponds, and the birds were singing their last songs. The heat lay all about, and summer in truth had begun, even if it had not begun by the calendar's reckoning.

This summer — would it be Fortunato's last summer alive? Would he not live to see the end of Gallia's war? He supposed he did not want to see the inevitable defeat.

Thingel was calling him over to the bonfire. This day, they would eat richly — to their daily slop now was added salt pork, and a bit of wine.

Four thousand were under Fortunato… but as the day darkened, and the heat of the day lingered, he was overcome with something — a feeling of doom. Stenn's sightless white eyes flashed in his mind's eye, his lips chattering, his tongue uttering some incomprehensible language that everyone in their own way could understand.

The army's chaplain had not explained it, and when Fortunato had inquired in the ensuing days, that chaplain insisted he had not seen such a thing before.

At the bonfire, soldiers were gathered, and other bonfires were there too in the distance, as the twilight darkened and turned to night. The moon was a sliver, the stars twinkling, and Fortunato had had his fill of the slop and bacon bits, though the wine he refused to touch. He needed to be alert, capable, in case Thingel suddenly fell to the ground and began uttering perverse things, or the moon turn to blood red and the stars fall from the heavens, or if the moon glint on the metal of six iron masks.

Something was not right; something evil was at work in Gallia. And for some reason, Fortunato's victory did not feel like one.

The fog had appeared so suddenly; the Empire's panic had overcome them in the span of an instant. And Fortunato was left with a hollow feeling, though a victory had been had, and that victory was in his own name.

Fortunato of Rîva… would his mother Alessa be proud, even though he had dealt a blow to his erstwhile homeland?

Thingel had taken out a fiddle. Bart was singing. Gaillon was patting a cymbal and Nigel was tapping on a drum.

Their song was rising into the summer night.

Gallia, Gallia, land that I love
Land where the tyrants of old found their end
Gallia, Gallia, under stars in the sky,
To death we shall fight for you, for exile, for friend

The thousands camped in this place were joining in the song, and the jars of wine — provided by the farmers of Dark Harrow — were being emptied much faster than Fortunato had instructed. But in the dark, he vowed not to correct them. Under the starry sky — as the song had said, Fortunato would let them have their respite, unwise as it may have been. They had won a victory which to Fortunato had inexplicably felt hollow, but that victory had been hard fought. They had seen many of their brothers-in-arms die.

And when the winds inevitably changed, and news of the defeat reached the emperor on his white throne, the full resources of the enemy would be fixed on this place. What then? Defeat… the death, the destruction of an entire people. Gallia would be no more.

Yes… let them have their wine.

~

The revelous song was behind Fortunato as he walked away from camp, away from the light of the bonfires. Fortunato was walking into the woods beyond, through a copse of oaks and maples. His combat boots were treading the carpet of fallen leaves. The heat of the summer day had not at all left, and sweat and grime lay thick over his skin. They had marched, and they had not bathed. Filth accumulated over days and weeks, and the pains of the long days and the lack of rest was wearing on Fortunato's muscles.

He felt tired… drained. But up ahead, amid darkness, was light — light, so faint, shining down from above. What was it? It was not the Imperials — in sight of that light, Fortunato's heart felt at peace.

He walked in the direction of that light, and fell to his knees.

~

"Fortunato of Ríva!" He knew that voice, a woman's voice, though in the midst of the vision he could not remember who it was.

Light was all about him, brilliant light — but a light was ahead of him, a figure, from which brighter light than the rest was flowing.

"Why do you bother yourself with this?" she said — that inscrutable figure. "You know the hour is late. You know the Enemy is on the move… not the one you fight, but the foe of the gods and of all our souls."

The light was distinguishing itself, and the figure ahead of him was clearly humanoid, dressed it seemed in a white veil and gown.

"What is Alonar compared to the final battle? What is the fate of Alonar compared to the life of the Sage? Hurry, before it is too late… take him, and flee with him to my father's kingdom!"

"Nenré!" Fortunato screamed. "Nenré! It's you!"

And his heart soared, at the thought of those lush red lips, those brilliant eyes of blue, that fair face — and the fact she wished to see him again.

"It cannot be." — She had lied.

~

"Nenré! Nenré!" Fortunato was shouting, but the light was gone — he was back in the woods, back in the darkness of the night, in Gallia, a nation threatened with extinction. He was back… and a voice was speaking, one which he hadn't wanted to hear, like the other before.

"Fortunato," said Thingel's voice. "What is wrong?"

He turned to face the army's cook.

"Fortunato… there is someone here to see you…"

The outrider was dressed in a blue robe, and he had ridden in on a brown stallion. The emblem of the city, a hawk, was emblazoned on his robe and he had surely ridden at a swift pace.

"Fortunato," he said, "you are being recalled to Galiope. You, and all your men."

"What? Why?" Fortunato said. "Victory is at hand — "

"The honorable Council of War has also requested I ask you something," said Eventide's messenger. "Fortunato of Ríva… how quickly can you build bleachers?"

Chapter Twenty-Eight: Archival

The sun was over the White Mountains, reflecting through Gastreel's window. In the streets below, the common folk of Alzdorf were beginning to stir to life. And Gastreel, lying in bed, with a tray that had been brought by the castle servants on which was toasted bread and fresh fruit and cream and, best of all, a cup of tea — was busy eating.

He was eating, until there was a tapping on the window.

The slight figure was so small Gastreel could not easily notice it. It was the size of his fist — a bird.

It was a hawk, and in its talons was clutched a letter.

Gastreel hurried out of bed, setting the tray aside, and ran to the window, unlatched it and let it free. The bird darted in and dropped the letter onto the room's marble floors, then flew away.

On the letter was a seal, holding it together, imprinted with an insignia — a mortar and pestle inlaid with a skull. This had been sent from Aleksander, Bala's teacher.

Gastreel wondered what trouble the poor tyke had gotten into.

He grabbed the letter and shattered the wax seal with his finger. It quickly fell open.

Gastreel Osiris:

Greetings. I, as always, give you my best.

Your mission to Almania is considered of utmost importance here in the city we both love and which we have sworn to defend. You should know that you forgot to cancel the Pan-Vardic Games, and that these games will soon be underway. You have been given time, plentiful time, months... the Empire and every nation has always respected the Pan-Vardic truce. You have precious time, so do not leave Almania without success. Do not leave Almania without securing Martin Durkheim's help.

That, however, is not why I have written. You should know that your archnemesis Ariya the White Wizard has been seen within the tower walls. She has been seen often in the company of a member of the Ruling Council, Sestriel of the Orange Robes. I was appalled, but no one else among the full wizards seems to have raised an alarm, even after what was done with the missing iron mask.

I wished to keep you apprised of this. I at first thought you should swiftly return, but on further thought the mission to Almania is of gravest importance, and I and the other god-fearers among wizards are capable of handling the situation. I will keep a watchful eye and, to you, make all matters known.

Yours...

For the All-Seeing Eye, Aleksander Ivic

The room was sweltering and warm, but Gastreel felt his heart grow cold.

Ariya the White Wizard, by wizarding law a renegade, treated as not so by they who dwelt in the Tower — what did this mean? Sestriel of the Orange Robes was a man Gastreel had hand-picked for the wizards' council, one of the Twelve, but that selection had been made on the advice of others and Gastreel did not well know him.

Ariya had committed an act so vile it would echo in eternity —

she had placed an iron mask of the six Servants of Seymus over her face in an effort to gain its power. And now, if Aleksander's letter was true, she had been welcomed back.

Gastreel's enemies among the wizards were taking advantage of his absence. What would he return to? What vipers would have to be dealt with?

And what had the other members of the wizards' council known, all along? Had Ariya acted with their consent?

No, it was impossible.

No, no, Gastreel thought. *No…*

She had survived the battle in the Vale of Ahorne. She had survived the wounds she'd been dealt at Council Rock. She had survived despite her act of evil, and now, it seemed, she would thrive.

What would Gastreel return to, when his mission here was done?

The door to his room opened, and the eyes of the Heer Meister Friedrich gleamed. "Mr. Wizard," he said, "His Worship Martin wishes to speak with you."

What would Gastreel return to? If this mission was not a success, he would return to a city, and a nation, in extinction.

~

Gastreel was trying to focus on the mission at hand as he followed Heer Meister Friedrich through the Great Hoff's halls and corridors. He was trying to think about nothing else but this, the mission to Almania, and securing the Grand Duke's help… but memories were flashing before him, memories of this past year — a battle of might and magic in the snow, Fortunato and Gastreel against Ariya and her apprentice Durgo. Memories were swirling in his mind, dark memories… and he and Fortunato had defeated their two enemies. Ariya had been left to die among rokahn — but somehow, she had survived. Gastreel had underestimated his foe, and now she was back, back in Gallia, and the wizards had accepted her, if Aleksander was to be believed.

What, then, was there to be done? What, then, could he do now?

Nothing now — nothing, and he would try not to worry, try not imagine what was going on now behind the tower walls. He would focus on Gallia, on Almania. He would.

But Ariya. *Ariya… alive, and ready to strike.*

"Here, Mr. Wizard," said the Heer Meister, Friedrich, and showed Gastreel to an open door. They were in a wing of the Great Hoff that Gastreel had not been before, and though it was crowded with people the rooms beside had mostly been empty. Yet from the door to which he had been beckoned was coming a steady bright light.

He passed through.

The chamber before him was vast, with ceilings of teak, and a great chandelier. Every wall was lined from top to bottom with shelves, and in those shelves were books and codices and tomes, their spines facing outward. Each shelf was marked, and some books were in Almanian, others Gallian, others Elvish. It was like a paradise, for Gastreel's taste, on earth… heaven, in literary form — the Grand Duke's library.

The Grand Duke's slight form was standing there under the light of the chandelier. He was dressed in a green tunic, with white hose and a felt purple cap. In his hand was a cane, but he had not been disabled — it seemed in Almania a man of respect was not to be seen without a walking stick.

"Green Wizard," said the Grand Duke, "I know that in addition to the study of magic, you are the world's premier bibliophile. These are the archives of I and my fathers, throughout the centuries, from the time the priests' book was copied in the North for the first time, until now. These archives are all at your disposal."

"I am glad at your generosity," said Gastreel, "but in truth it is not why I have come. We must speak… we must strike a deal."

"In time!" said Martin. "In time enough… have you not heard? The Pan-Vardic Games have begun. The war will be postponed."

The news had reached Martin's ears already. Gastreel peered into his eyes, and again, wondered, again, thought.

Delay, delay, delay… but I will not leave without this help from him.

Martin wished Gastreel to be distracted, wished him to busy himself with books and reading… to what end?

"We must speak," Gastreel said, "and now."

"You have time," said Martin. "We have time."

Martin was looking past Gastreel, and Gastreel looked back, and saw Friedrich's blue eyes staring into the room. So quickly, Friedrich vanished out of the doorway.

"'I say; I do.' Those are the words on your seal," Gastreel said, and as he stood in the archives' light he noted one of Almania's standards on the wall.

Almania's insignia was on the green-and-gold standard, its token animal a manticore — a lion's body and a scorpion's tail. But the standard was so large, taking up much of the wall, that Gastreel noted writing just below the manticore in black, in elaborate letters: "T.T.I."

It was not the standard of the landswehr, but that of the national army. It was not the standard of the Durkheim house, but that of the nation, and one little used, and little seen. It was one Gastreel had seen in his childhood at festivals and certain public occasions, but not at such a great size.

Gastreel's eyes were fixed on that standard, and on those letters, "T.T.I." Martin looked back with him.

"Pardon, Martin," Gastreel said, "my curiosity. I noticed something I hadn't before. 'T.T.I.'… on Almania's flag. What does it stand for?"

"*Teli Telantari Indion*," Martin Durkheim said to him. "Don't ask me what that means. Sounds Imperial to me…"

"It's Elvish," Gastreel said. Martin had not pronounced it properly. "Elvish…"

"It is an old flag," Martin said, "not much used anymore… our most ancient one, before the kings gave up their kingdom and became 'grand dukes.'"

"*Teli Telantari Indion*," Gastreel repeated, murmuring softly. "Mighty 'Telantari' Kingdom."

Martin seemed puzzled. But Gastreel had learned something.

"He shall be *telantari*," Gastreel said, repeating the ancient prophecy. "The Sage shall be *telantari*."

As Martin walked off, away, joining Friedrich, Gastreel vowed he would not rest until he uncovered the meaning of this. *Teli Telantari Indion* — that was what the Almanians had anciently called their realm.

Chapter Twenty-Nine: Signs

Reev in Rosetree Manor was sharpening Doomblade while he sat on the bed, making sure it was sharp, ready for the time of battle, ready for the time that they'd flee Galiope and its imminent doom — and they would, wouldn't they? They had to.

Iron could not sharpen *estirion*. Nor could common stone. For the purposes of sharpening *estirion* swords, only *estirion* could be used. And sometime in the past year, Gastreel had given Reev a second present from his long-lost father, an orb of *estirion* Gastreel thought he had misplaced, but which had been found and recovered.

Outside, he could see the wizards' tower, a black basalt-colored pillar amid the city skyline, and as he sat there, he thought he could see smoke rising from nearby it.

As he sharpened Doomblade, he kept his eye also out on the street below. It had not been long ago that he'd caught Ash snooping, peering through his window, and after what Ivan Xandrast had said, the very thought of his cousin caused his heart to race and his lungs to strain to breathe.

"Reev! Reev!" he could hear Ivan Xandrast — or Xan as he liked to be called — downstairs.

And downstairs Reev walked, sheathing Doomblade as he made his way there.

~

Xan was standing beside the front door, his butterfly blade strapped to his back. The front door was slightly ajar, and a warm wind was lightly blowing it against Xan's boot.

"Reev," he said, "I must show you something."

And Reev followed Xan outside, into the thick warmth of the afternoon.

He followed Xan around the side of the house, past the bushes that had grown misshapen and tangled, through the narrow space between the fence and the wall. He stopped at a window that overlooked the kitchen and pointed down, at the ground.

Two footprints had been made in the last night's rain.

"I was doing my rounds," Xan said, "securing the perimeter… making sure you were safe. I noticed this — "

He pointed to the footprints.

"And this…"

And Reev saw that there was damage to the window ledge, paint that was peeled off and wood that was torn away.

"A crowbar," Xan said. "Someone was here last night, while we slept. They tried the window, saw if it would come undone. You should thank the gods I was with you."

I can take care of myself, Reev thought. But could he, really?

"They must have seen me, or seen that I was here," Xan said. "They ran off like the cowards they were…"

"My cousin," Reev said aloud, and his heart grew faint, and his breath was cold. "My cousin…"

"What?" Xan said.

"I saw him peeking through my windows before… looking into them. My cousin, Ash… it had to be him."

But as Reev looked to the ground he saw more than just those two footprints — there were more, scattered, faint. Could it have been Aunt Ramona too, or Guy, or some other servant?

"Your cousin," Xan said, "the one — "

"Don't say it," Reev said to him. "Don't say it…"

To accuse him of being the Dark One's Hand was a terrible

thing, for the sake of that at all, but also because Reev and Ash were connected by blood. They shared a grandmother, a grandfather… and Simeon, Reev's father, was Ash's uncle.

Xan had drawn back. His dark yet bright eyes were fixed on Reev.

"I must find what is said about him," Reev told Ivan Xandrast — he wouldn't call him Xan. "I must find the prophecies… I must prove you wrong.

"I must go to St. Sigmund's… I must ask a priest."

"I think you had better stay here — " Xan started.

"No, no," Reev said, "you aren't my master… nor are you my bodyguard. The gods rescued you from darkness, Xan… don't presume more about yourself than there is."

And Reev, with Doomblade at his side, heart and fingers trembling, did what he had resolved to do, exiting Rosetree Manor, walking toward the gate of Wodenscross Court, in the direction of Cathedral District.

Chapter Thirty:
He Shall Be

For hours, Gastreel had pored through the archives of the Great Hoff, paging through book after book of Almanian history, as early as he could find it. He paged through tomes in forgotten dialects which he could barely comprehend, and also books unrelated but which he hoped would miraculously tell him what he wanted, and needed, to know — *Teli Telantari Indion.* The Great *Telantari* Kingdom. What was *telantari?*

He was reading, out of desperation, a biography of Grauens Durkheim, the first of the Durkheim Dynasty, when the door to the archives opened to bare a familiar figure.

It was Friedrich, the Heer Meister, dressed all in black, a longsword at his side and over his neck a manticore necklace.

"Mr. Wizard," said Friedrich, "tea is served in the solarium, and with it oat cakes. Shall you celebrate the arrival of summer with our household?"

Gastreel looked up at him, peered into his piercing blue eyes, his cold lips. "I... I..."

"What are you looking for?" said Friedrich. "I am a man of war but also a man of letters. I believe I have read every book in these shelves."

"*Teli Telantari Indion,*" said Gastreel, "the letters on Almania's most ancient battle flag. Great Telantari Kingdom — what does it mean?"

Friedrich smiled, and his blue eyes twinkled. "A good question, Mr. Wizard. I know our library is vast. It is easy to miss the forest for the trees."

He walked over to a book Gastreel had sworn he had read, though one that was unmarked and unlabeled.

"In olden times, many kingdoms shared similar names," Friedrich said. "For then the glory of the Old Dominion was fresh, the memory of the True Empire that had ruled the world in peace and justice was one still thought of.

"Everyone wished to be thought of as a Telantine Kingdom. Everyone proclaimed they were Telantis Reborn. But they were not, for the True Empire was long gone… their city was by the slope of a great mountain, and in the span of an hour the Telantines were brought low — by fire, by smoke, and their city and their kingdom fell into the sea. Disaster was on them in the turning of a moment, and now they are all gone."

"No," Gastreel said, "there is a remnant."

"What?" Friedrich snapped.

"There is a remnant of them left," Gastreel said. "'He shall be *telantari*.'"

Chapter Thirty-One: The Priest

The spires of St. Sigmund's Cathedral were before Reev, the gargoyles and votive statues and the great rose window. The double doors were twice his height, but one was open. Under that door he strode, into the dim light of the cathedral proper.

There were no worshippers inside; the pews were empty. It was not a feast day or a holy day for Gallia, but some nations, he knew, had a calendar different from their own.

The nave was before Reev, and the stained glass windows portrayed the ancient stories. Most prominent of all was a window in the apse, which Reev could see, showing St. Sigmund slaying a dragon.

The cathedral was cool, chilly even, despite the summer heat outside. And Reev, for a reason he did not know, began to question his actions, began to rethink all this.

Xan has placed a thought about Ash in my head, and it isn't true. I should turn back.

But he could hear footsteps now, coming from the south transept. In the light of the stained glass, a figure distinguished itself from among the wooden pews and the altarpiece far beyond.

It was a man, slight, slender. It was not the rector Bartholem, but someone else.

He was dressed in a black cassock, which itself was fastened with a length of gold rope. His eyes glinted in the light. Though he was young, his brown hair was speckled with gray.

"Hello, good sir," he said. "Have you come to make an offering to the gods, on behalf of St. Sigmund?"

"No, I… I…"

And the young man, the priest, was standing just feet from Reev in no time. "I am Tyrol, rector of the Cathedral," he said.

"Bartholem — " Reev began.

"Bartholem is gone," was the reply and this Tyrol instantly seemed to grow cold. But then his eyes brightened. "The Lord Alden, as minister of religious affairs, dismissed him."

"A pity," Reev said, and he meant it — Bartholem had been a good man, and worthy of trust.

"So why have you come?" Tyrol said. "Tell me."

"I… I… it's nothing, really," Reev said.

And he peered into this Tyrol's eyes. He wanted to say nothing, to say nothing at all, but as he stood in the cathedral's dim light Xan's words echoed in his mind, the accusation that haunted Reev day and night, the fears he had that his cousin was his own mortal enemy.

"It's my cousin, Ash," Reev said, "and the prophecies… the prophecies…"

~

In Tyrol's office were statuaries of the four Gods of the Winds, and on the red-and-gold walls paintings of St. Sigmund in his dragon-slaying glory.

Tyrol had taken a seat behind a desk, and Reev took a seat in the corners of the room.

"What is this that troubles you?" Tyrol began.

"The Dark One's Hand… who will he be?" Reev said. "What do the prophecies say?"

Tyrol smiled and his eyes twinkled amid the light of the candles on the desk. "That seems to be a worry on every worshipper's mind," Tyrol said. "Their friends, their neighbors… everyone is the Dark One's Hand. The world is coming undone, that is what they think.

"But in my experience — "

"Reev."

"In my experience, Reev, it is best not to take the words of the gods literally. What are they, truly? The gods are what we make them... the Book and its prophecies speak differently to each reader. The gods are all of us.

"There is no Dark One's Hand," said Tyrol. "Nor is there a Prince of the Dawn coming to save us."

The Prince of the Dawn, and that's what Gastreel thought Reev was... it had never seemed so unlikely. "You're a priest," Reev said, "and you believe this..."

Tyrol's smug smile had not waned. "The city is consumed with this talk, and in the world there seems to be a dark fever. You are not alone in your fears, Reev, for I've spoken to many worshippers at this cathedral of the same. Your cousin is not the Dark One's Hand, Reev... no one is."

But that to Reev was patently false — wasn't it?

"Reev... a name very rare. Reev Nax, you must be — a name I've heard often. You were a hero in the war against the wizards. But some in this city accuse you of being the serpent's son, the Dark One's Hand. Doesn't that seem ridiculous to you, in all?"

It did — but now his heart was racing, and he realized this false priest Tyrol would be of no help. Nothing proved or disproved, no prophecies unveiled.

"Lord Alden appointed you," Reev said, and the memories of that member of the Council of War, red-haired and silvery-eyed, flashed in his mind. "Lord Alden..."

Chapter Thirty-Two: St. Kellen's Day

The solarium of the Great Hoff was twice the size of Rosetree Manor back in Galiope, but to Gastreel every table appeared to be occupied. Amid the bright light of the sun and the potted fan palms that had no business growing so far north, the sound of clattering silverware and tableware was deafening.

Friedrich, the "Heer Meister" beckoned Gastreel. "Mr. Wizard," he said, "the best seat in the house, for you."

And he led Gastreel past rows of tables, nobles and servants alike feasting, up to a raised dais on which was a table with a red cloth. There, the Grand Duke Martin was sitting with his wife Freya, with a pot of tea and cups, together with small cakes.

"Wizard," he said, "you have joined us. Welcome."

Gastreel took his seat on the edge of the table, though his mind was focused on other things. *Telantari*, the name of an ancient people, and not an attribute of personality like Gastreel had thought. They were a people he had found no record of amid ancient texts, but in some parts of the world, apparently, that memory lingered.

From the dais he looked down, and he could see that the solarium was divided by a curtain into two sides, and that on one side Martin's distant relatives and his human servants were sitting, and on the other side the elves. The elves' partition of the room was much bigger, and they outnumbered the humans.

"The celebration is cloven in two," Gastreel noted.

The grand duchess Freya laughed softly. "Ah, it is the eve of St. Kellen's Day — St. Kellen, who proclaimed us all equal. And we in Almania are enlightened, but elves and humans eating in the same room… that is a bridge too far, even for the House Durkheim."

Her words were like a bitter lash. And Gastreel looked down again, this time sadly, to the elves, whose tables were not so brightly decorated and whose teapots were rudimentary objects of metal.

He made out Wrinn sitting among the masses of elves, at a table, with others of his own kind. He was laughing and talking boisterously — it seemed even amid the poorer treatment, he was happier among his kindred.

~

"We have a whole day off on St. Kellen's Day," said Rosalie. Her blue eyes glinted in the light of the solarium's windows, and her red lips teased Wrinn into the slightest of smiles. "One day off work… and we will do what we may."

"What will you do?" said Wrinn.

The others at the table were smiling along with her.

"We're hiking," she said, "up to Rathulf Falls."

"Hiking?" Wrinn said. "On your day off? Why?"

"For fun," Rosalie said.

Hiking, for fun… Wrinn had never heard of something so ridiculous. But if that was what it took to be in Rosalie's presence, a grueling hike was a small price to pay. "I think I'll join you," Wrinn said.

"We'd love it if you would," Rosalie replied.

The day wore on; the party ended. And Wrinn counted down the hours until that most ridiculous of things — a grueling hike for no reason at all.

~

Already at dawn, outside the city walls of Alzdorf, the thick blanket of heat had arrived. And before Wrinn and Rosalie and the others had reached the trail, their clothing was drenched and wet.

It was a terrible proposition, and Wrinn would have liked nothing better than to stay back, but for Rosalie he'd do this — yes, for Rosalie.

The maples and elms loomed above them, but the heat was too thick for the shade to do any good. With his quarterstaff as a walking stick — his quarterstaff, which Friedrich had given back to him, at his insistence, a few days ago — Wrinn made his ascent, struggling up the winding dirt path. To his amazement, the other elves seemed more spritely than he, hopping up the trail, though he was a warrior and the better athlete.

"Say!" Wrinn said, "they call these the White Mountains… but all I see is green."

"You should be here in the winter, and you'll see," said Rosalie, racing up ahead of him.

But would he? He wouldn't be here in the winter, he'd be gone. He was on a mission and he would have to say goodbye to Rosalie, unless, by some chance, she could come with them.

No, no… I won't think about that now.

The path wound up the mountainside, staggeringly steep, past creeks and over bridges, beside the knotted roots of trees and in view of squirrels and hedgehogs and minks. Wrinn's tunic was dripping and his sides burned, but Rosalie and the dozen others in their party were racing along, keeping up a breakneck pace. At times the trees would peel away to bare stunning vistas of the Green Mountains, which though tiny compared to the Dragonteeth in the north, were as challenging to scale as anything Wrinn had done.

The elements seemed to be withering — the trees, crying out amid the blazing sun. All the water in the world could not help them and then… then there was a sound like gushing rain, and the brush fell away to reveal a towering waterfall.

The gushing crystalline water was flowing down the sides of a rock cliff, so quickly the stream below had formed rapids. In the light of the sun, flowers and bushes were growing, vines and what looked like unripe strawberries.

"See it? See it?" Rosalie said. "Aren't you happy you came?"

And Wrinn was happy he came, though not for the reasons of the waterfall, beautiful though it was.

One of the elves had with them a basket, and from it produced what Wrinn had been told were traditional St. Kellen's Day food, oily fried cakes drizzled in honey. And another of the elves had brought a large bottle of wine.

It was about noon.

~

With the fried cakes in hand, Wrinn found himself wandering in the company of Rosalie. They dipped their feet into the ice-cold waters which flowed from the waterfall, and then wandered off, following the stream, to the edge of a cliff, at the bottom of which was a deep green valley.

"Wrinn," Rosalie said, "will you tell me something?"

"Anything," Wrinn replied.

"That quarterstaff of yours… it's a weapon, right?" she said. Wrinn bobbed his head.

"Have you ever struck anyone with it?" Rosalie asked.

"Plenty," Wrinn said, "and I've killed many rokahn, and given many humans a good beating. I was a pit fighter, back when I was a slave. Humans surely like their blood sports… they're such cruel creatures, don't you think?"

Rosalie turned silent; she wasn't even nibbling her food. Wrinn realized he had said something that would cause a severe reprimand at best in the Great Hoff, a beating or something worse most likely.

"Sorry," Wrinn said, "I shouldn't speak so loosely. I wouldn't want to get you in trouble. You aren't free, like I am."

But was he free? A "bondservant" of the Council of War… he supposed it was a status that was only temporary.

"Slavery," Wrinn said, "I don't know what I'd do if I was forced back into it. Maybe jump off this cliff… I can't imagine your strength, Rosalie."

"We aren't slaves," said Rosalie. "We are free, technically. Servants, that's what we're called. Servants… indentured. We are paying a debt. The Grand Duke has outlawed slavery."

"You really believe that?" Wrinn said. "You really think you're free?"

Rosalie fell silent a while. The chirping of the birds was like a chancel choir. And the heat of the summer lay thick about them both.

"An indentured servant," she said. "It isn't slavery, that's what we're meant to say."

"Well," Wrinn said, "Martin doesn't seem like the worst of masters. At least you can't be bought."

"No," Rosalie said, softly, "debt can be leveraged. We are all paying off a debt for our freedom. Other masters, or, rather, supervisors, can buy our indentured servitude."

"Sounds silly, doesn't it?" Wrinn said. "There is no difference, except Martin feels a bit more proud."

"I suppose," Rosalie said, and at last took a bite of the fried oily-cake she was holding in her hand. "I suppose I am not much better off. I wanted to think I was. But I am not."

Wrinn would do anything to free her, anything to take her with him when he returned to Galiope. He imagined purchasing a townhome in Market District, little children running about, he and Rosalie growing old — but wouldn't Galiope soon be no more?

"You know, Wrinn, I hear," Rosalie said, and her tone had grown deathly serious and somber, "the Empire, when it moves into a territory in the North, it grants the elves their freedom. I've heard of elves in the countryside, in other duchies and counties rising up against their masters, and fighting alongside the Imperial legion."

"It's only a strategy," Wrinn rebuffed her. "The Empire doesn't have our good in mind, or anyone besides themselves."

"Perhaps," Rosalie said more softly, more softly than ever. "Perhaps… but I wonder if they'd free indentured servants, too…"

Chapter Thirty-Three: Godfrey's Wood

It was the fifth day of the heat wave, as Bala had counted, and it was the fifth day he intended to brave it. It was the fifth day of the blazing sun and the sweltering warmth and at dawn now, the air was no cooler.

In the Dragonpaw's main hall, Glenda had opened all the windows, but her tunic and trousers were spotted with sweat at this early hour, and those kitchen staff who were preparing the day's meal were drenched as they hurried about.

As for Bala, he had put on the same clothing he had always worn, and he wore the same top hat he had always loved. He planned on doing what he had done every day since the heat wave began, ever since Aleksander gave him permission: he would practice, and today, he thought he'd venture out a little deeper, into the woods.

"Bala!" Glenda called after him. "Will you have some breakfast? Buttered toast, and some cool water from the well."

"No thanks, Miss Glenda," Bala said. He supposed that after he spent the day practicing, he'd fill up his stomach on cow's blood. The farmers never seemed to notice.

And he waddled off, away, through the Dragonpaw Inn's doors, into City Square outside.

~

The heat had brought the city to a standstill. The air wavered even now in the early morning, and some had taken to sitting on their porches and fanning themselves. Others Bala saw were spraying themselves with water as they walked about the way.

In the middle of City Square, some Mountain Folk youths had stripped down to their undergarments and were splashing in the fountain, against the law and all proper protocol.

Bala wasn't enjoying the blazing sun either, but he had a purpose now, and a challenge. He wanted to be ready when Aleksander finally restarted his training. He wanted to be ready to ascend to the rank of full wizard, and become a mighty wielder of the weave.

He waddled down High Street, past a few Mountain Folk men he suspected of being pickpockets, lurking by a street corner, past a sword swallower and a juggler whom the heat had defeated — they were sitting down and sweating in the blazing sun, with the tools of their trade beside.

Bala himself was beginning to struggle, his youthful gait beginning to falter just a bit, when at last he passed outside of Cathedral District, past Godsgate, to the farm fields beyond.

There was a wood not far away where Bala could focus, where he could close out his mind and hear nothing but the breeze and the chirping of the birds. There was a wood and he began to walk toward it, through the thick heat and the burning sun, past roads and farms and thoroughfares, a pigpen, chickencoops, a cattle ranch…

Greenery greeted him but also something else, loud noise — a vigorous saw. There were shouts, and amid the wood about a mile from the city, people walking about… dozens, and a hundred.

Some were wearing metal helmets despite the heat, others thick padded clothing. Against some trees leaned spears and shields.

And for a moment, Bala forgot all about his training, all about his intent to practice, following this incredible curiosity. There were people, hundreds he could see, wandering about this once-untouched wood.

~

There were not hundreds… there were thousands.

They were soldiers, some in armor and some who had disrobed to tunics and trousers, all working vigorously. They were chopping down trees and sawing them into workable logs and boards under the sunny sky.

The forest where Bala had been just once before was quickly disappearing. He would be sad, or aggravated, but instead he just stood in the heat, overcome with confusion — confusion, and wonder.

"Bala!" said a familiar voice, a voice filled with youthfulness and life. "Bala!"

And Bala turned around, and there saw a grown-up he knew approaching, Fortunato.

He was dressed in shorts and a thin white tunic, and his face was marred by grime and dirt. He was smiling that brash smile Bala remembered. His sword was gleaming in the sun's light.

"Have you come to watch us work?" he said.

"What are you doing?" Bala inquired.

"Staging the Pan-Vardic Games," Fortunato replied, "and these bleachers will soon seat ten-thousand. Games of might and magic, and best of all an end to the war…"

Bala had known there was a war underway, but his life had remained unchanged — his nights spent at the Dragonpaw, his days wandering about.

"What are you doing here at Godfrey's Wood?" Fortunato said. "Or what's left of Godfrey's Wood…"

"Practicing," Bala replied. He hadn't known these woods had a name.

"Practicing what?" Fortunato seemed amused.

"Summoning," Bala said. "Calling."

"Magic, in other words," Fortunato said, and then he added, "You should participate in these games, Bala. Magic is part of them.

You could win a prize, or something more."

Something more… something more…

Like what?

Chapter Thirty-Four: At the House of Sunset

Ramona watched crossly as her nephew Reev stumbled into the Townhall five minutes late.

The council had convened unlike at other times at Lauds, early in the morning, but Ramona had expected better of him. Each member of the Council of War had received their summons last evening, and absolute punctuality was expected of all of them.

She hid her glare as Reev looked her way. She glanced to Eventide as he began the meeting a bit later than he surely hoped, and vowed to get back at Reev soon — for this, and for so many other reasons.

"Members of the council, welcome," Eventide said, and there would be no invocation. Tyrol the new rector had offered to say a prayer, but Eventide was still wrapped up in this heathenry play-acting that Ramona found so childish. No prayers would be said to the gods Eventide claimed "had abandoned them all."

"Members of the council," Eventide said again, "you are summoned here today because I have in my possession a letter from His Honor Niccolo Maiodore of the 1st Kheroan Legion."

"Do not call him 'Your Honor,'" the Lady Llewyn of Leyshaw hissed.

"Honor, in war," Eventide replied, "it is here stated: 'The Pan-Vardic Games are inviolable, the truce of which the White Throne has respected since time immemorial. Thrice has the Empire been glad to host them, in 1053 in Latera, and back-to-back, 1086 in Ovisaris and in 1119 Sycaria. The wizards have borne witness to me that these, the games of 1153, were long planned.

"Pardon if we participate, as is our custom… all nations and tribes and races may vie for the Victor's Crown. The truce is respected, but may it be known that it is also custom that no machinations of war be undertaken in the truce city. I request you do not meet until the games are finished. — Nicollo."

"He hasn't the right to tell us not to meet," Reev said. "We should continue to meet — it is imperative."

Ramona wanted to lay into him, but she couldn't think of anything clever.

Instead, the Lord Alden spoke, Lord Alden with his red hair and his eyes that looked silver in the high windows' light. "We may meet in secret in my estate on Ammon Lake…"

"No, no," said the Lord Rivien, Gallia's second in command, the Lord of Horse and the most senior of this council, "your estate is far too public. We must meet in the secret groves you have constructed, Eventide — in the secret groves. You have, after all, instructed that no one of the common people enter them."

The sacred groves, the repositories of heathenry that Eventide had introduced — and Ramona took in Reev's offended expression in delight. "Yes," she added to the chorus, "let us meet in the secret groves, and continue to plan the war quietly."

The vote was eighteen to one, and Ramona's nephew was the odd one out. If he wished to continue to participate in this Council of War, he'd have to do it among those trees spattered with the blood of ewes, from whose branches hung entrails and straw-made fetishes. He would have to endure it… or resign to public shame.

A mighty blow, dealt by Ramona. But she hoped it wouldn't be the last lash.

~

Ramona had found a way to avoid the gathered crowds outside the Townhall, the peasants so close in view to the nobles. Unlike the others, she had begun making use of a secret passageway, one that would take her and her guards under the city through a dark corridor. If she took it to its furthermost extent, it would lead her outside the city, to a cave no one knew of. But one doorway led her to the Arcades, a part of the city which, though not nearly of the character of what she was used to in the west, at least was less populous and had a bit less of the squalor. Besides, when boredom struck her, she could avail herself of its quaint shops. Many of those shops and markets were fit for a commoner, but there was a gypsy woman she knew of who sold interesting trinkets and a dressmaker of tolerable quality.

Her guards bore torches as they traversed the dark, damp tunnel. The stone ceiling dripped water every few moments, and Ramona shuddered at the thought of the unruly rabble walking just above.

But in time, the stair opened up — a doorway, and the dank humid air of summer greeted her… stench mixed with the scent of produce and cooking food, arches all around… and a gypsy woman sashaying about in a dress.

Her dress was billowing, and her hair was crowned with red and blue flowers. She had the look of a young maiden, and as she strutted about she was calling out in her own tongue. Others had gathered to watch her.

"Lady Ariel," a woman said to her, also a gypsy, "tell us — will Gallia lose this war?"

Lady Ariel, if that was her name, took a red flower from her hair and cast it on the ground. She stomped onto it with her feet and crushed it under her sandal.

"No, they shall not," Lady Ariel said, beholding the smothered petals.

A man strode forward, a non-gypsy in a tunic and long trousers. "Will the Dark One's Hand soon appear?" he said.

Lady Ariel took another flower from her hair, this time blue, and cast it on the ground. She pulverized it again with her sandal, and examined it — seemingly carefully.

"Yes," she said, "he will."

Ramona had stopped her walk to observe the spectacle, half amused, half interested. She did not know if she believed in gypsy fortune telling, but her neighbor in Wodenscross Court Beatriz swore by it.

"Who is he?" said a young woman in a light floral gown, one of the gathered faces of the crowd.

Again, Ariel took a flower; again, she smothered it with her sandal, and again, she examined it.

"He is here, the Dark One's Hand, is — in this crowd," said the gypsy woman Ariel. There were horrified gasps among the crowd. "Yes, he is here — he, or the one who bore him."

Ramona peered into this Ariel's eyes, wondering, waiting. Of all her servants Chalmet was the smartest, and it was he whom she had assigned to track down her archenemy Amée, her former servant who had called Ash *Abollondon*. Beatriz swore by this seeming nonsense. And Ramona supposed there was no harm in trying.

"Ariel!" Ramona was approaching, pushing past the safety of her guards. The faces in the crowd turned to her and looked all at once, some, seemingly in fear. Ariel gazed into Ramona's eyes.

Ramona said, "I have a question for you."

Silence followed, total silence.

Ramona pushed on: "Where is Amée?"

Ariel turned rigid; she took a step back. Her breathing seemed to grow shallow; there was paleness in her face. At last she plucked a flower from her head, red — and another, blue. She cast them onto the cobblestone and ground them to a pulp with her feet.

"At the House of Sunset," the "Lady" Ariel said. "Now leave us! Leave!"

Chapter Thirty-Five: At Dusk

Back at Rosetree Manor, the heat had not at all lessened; no, it was turning afternoon, and when Reev stepped within he found he could scarcely breathe, and to his trouble was now added a headache. He believed that he might faint.

The sweltering air had all settled into this heat trap — and then he realized something, that the windows all were closed… Ivan Xandrast had shut them.

One by one, he walked up to them, the windows on the first floor, and a bit of the air and the wind was felt, but not enough. He marched upstairs, to his own room, and opened those windows too, and the windows of Gastreel's bedroom, and the guest quarters.

He felt a presence behind him. "Where have you been?" said the voice of Xan.

Reev turned. "I told you," he replied, "the Council of War."

"I shut those windows for a reason," said Xan.

"Did you?" said Reev. "You aren't my master, and your position as my bodyguard was one you forced on me."

At the words, Xan was unbowed. "How can I not give my all," he said, "to protect the Prince of the Dawn?"

Reev looked at Xan with suspicion. He was dripping sweat, and his tunic was drenched. He couldn't imagine how he'd be able to sleep tonight, in this humid air. "Xan," he said, "where is the Skeleton Key? Show it to me…"

"Don't you trust me?" said Xan.

"Where is it?" Reev said again, insistent.

And Xan reached within his pockets, and from it produced that artifact of evil, or what he had called faint evil.

"I don't feel comfortable with a warlock's tool in this house,"

Reev said.

But Reev would let him have it, on second thought, just the same.

Chapter Thirty-Six: Sending

The bleachers were taking shape, and Fortunato was watching as the flags of the wizards were installed on posts throughout the game grounds. They were as they had been sent — the All-Seeing Eye, white on a blue field. And as his soldiers worked furiously, hour by hour, minute by minute, as afternoon passed toward evening, they were being joined by spectators — among them wizards in robes of green and orange and fluorescent blue.

Fortunato had a thought he would participate in these games, and display his skill at the sword for all to see. Maybe, Ambrass would see it, or hear about it. Maybe…

Ambrass — the thought of her stung him, sent him reeling. He had best not think of a story that was no more.

"Pardon!" there was a voice, and Fortunato looked away, to his right.

A man was standing there, white bearded, with a robe colored flame orange. In his wrinkled hand was an ash-colored staff with spirals of crystal winding up its top. On his head, balding, was what looked like a crown, inset with gems of bright red and luminous blue.

"You are Fortunato of Ríva," said this man, clearly a wizard of some power. "Fortunato of Ríva, into whose hands the gods delivered the Imperials. And now you are reduced to this — building seats for a game, on behalf of the All-Seeing Eye."

Fortunato did not much like the words this man was using. "This for the city, too," Fortunato said, "following orders. I won't question Eventide or the city's leaders."

"Won't you?" said the wizard in the orange robes. "Sestriel is my name. Shall you bow?"

"I don't think I will," said Fortunato, and looked back to surveil his men's work. The bleachers towered toward the sky, each board artfully placed, each perfectly sawed and sanded — masterful craftsmanship. In a week, they'd be filled with people.

Fortunato turned back to look at Sestriel, whom he sensed had not left.

The wizard's eyes were dark, but there was a luminous glint within them. "Will you contend with the contenders?" said Sestriel. "Will you hope to win the Victor's Crown?"

"Wreaths and medals mean nothing to me," said Fortunato.

"There is more than accolades to the Victor's Crown," Sestriel said, "as you will see, if you will win it."

Fortunato wished to be left alone — how could that be made clear? Sestriel couldn't seem to take his eyes off him.

He saw there were more wizards coming up the way. "Sestriel," said Fortunato, "if you don't mind… we are rather busy."

"We have come for a reason," Sestriel said, "and that reason involves a friend of yours."

"Really?" Fortunato said. He had come to believe these wizards would not leave him alone. And so, he made a motion for his men to stop their work.

A break — a precious break. They would drink some water, and have a bit of rest, away from their labor in the blazing sun.

~

Fortunato led Sestriel into a grove of trees. "What is it you want?"

The wizards behind him, male and female, were in robes of all colors, green, white, blue, all clutching staffs in their hands. Despite the sweltering heat they did not seem bothered, though their robes were of thick cloth, and most of them looked old.

"Gastreel the Green Wizard," said Sestriel, "you know him."

Fortunato peered into this Sestriel's eyes suspiciously.

"You accompanied him, on a journey, into the mountains last winter."

It had been the month of Brightleaf — fall. The winter he had spent under the mountain.

"Did you bear witness to him doing battle with a wizard, up there, in the snow — a wizard in robes of white?"

"Yes," Fortunato said to Sestriel, "yes, I did. And it was I who slew her apprentice… I'd do it again. She was wearing the mask of a Servant of Seymus, trying to channel its power…"

"And where did that mask go?" said Sestriel. "Where did Gastreel take it? Do you know?"

Fortunato peered into Sestriel's eyes. He noted, in the sun's light, that small white motes of light were orbiting around that strange crown he was wearing. He noted, in the sun's light, that those eyes of his could not hide his guile.

What had happened to the iron masks? He did not know, and he would not tell them.

"Further, tell me, Fortunato," said Sestriel, "were you there when Gastreel did battle with the Baron Tuck in the castle called Grimmburg?"

"I think you had better go," Fortunato said. "I'll tell you no more. I have nothing more to say."

Sestriel pursed his lips, continued examining him, continued looking at him in that strange way, in the sun's light. His fingers were wrapped tightly around that staff of his, and though his eyes and face were emotionless, Fortunato thought those fingers were trembling — perhaps, with rage.

"You slew her apprentice," said Sestriel, "so it was you, that killed Durgo…"

Fortunato drew his sword, and Danenhir glinted in the light of the sun. The gold letters on its side seemed to flash. "Away, wizard. This conversation is over."

"Yes, it is," said Sestriel. "Yes… it is."

~

It was night. The moon was glowing brightly above-head and the stars were twinkling amid the vast expanse. A wind was whipping through the air, and the clouds up above were scattered silver wisps. Fortunato and his men were sitting on the bleachers, which they had finished, and as reward, the city had provided them with ale — much ale, several pints each, but which Fortunato was not drinking.

Thingel was sitting next to Fortunato, and Stenn was nearby — Stenn, who had not taken part in the victory at Balem's Bridge.

The strange conversation lingered, the peculiar line of questioning that wizard had taken. He wondered why Sestriel had been so insistent, why an entire crowd of wizards had been with him…

That, however, was the past. The future was ahead of him.

And though the war had not ceased in truth, but only been delayed — though Gallia's destruction seemed no further off, he thought he might truly pursue that Victor's Crown. He might truly compete.

The moon up above was brightening, and light seemed to be pouring down. There was a flash, and another flash, but Fortunato seemed to be the only one to notice. Blinding light, all about — and all that was before him, and all, up above, was brilliant white.

He was in another world — but there was a figure, distinguishing itself from among the luminescence.

~

That figure was little more than an outline, sitting on a chair, and amid the brilliant white light Fortunato could just barely distinguish fingers on the arms of the chair, and on those fingers many rings.

A voice called out, clear, powerful, deafening, "Fortunato — why do you bother yourself with such useless things?"

That voice was one he knew, a voice it seemed from another life, another world now forgotten. It was the voice of an elf, and a powerful elf — a lord among them.

"Perhaps, if you will not listen to the king's daughter, you will listen to me, *quilenthi*, you, who have earned our trust and whose deeds even the king has heard of.

"If you shall not listen to Yanenré, listen to a voice you have heeded before. Run; depart tonight. Take the Sage with you, and flee Alonar before it is too late."

The vision was all about him — all he could see was the brightness and luminescence, the faintest outline of a chair and fingers, the slightest hint of eyes, a face, and long white hair.

"I don't know where he is," Fortunato said.

"Find him, then," said the elf-lord, sitting on a chair. Calion — Calion, that was his name. "Find the Sage, and depart at this very hour to the land of the elves, for the forces of darkness are moving, and the Shadow has at long last begun to fall…"

"I can't," Fortunato started, "my friends…"

"On you rests this now, the hope of elves and mankind… do not fail us. Take with you the Sage — flee, this very night."

"I can't," Fortunato said. "Gallia…"

"Do it, now, this very moment," said Calion, "or the world shall fall…"

Chapter Thirty-Seven: Pig!

Reev woke to the sound of shattering glass. He leapt out of bed and dove across the room, grabbing his sheath and drawing Doomblade.

More noise echoed —footsteps, a scream. And Reev jerked to the door, and, throwing himself to the ground, braced his body against it.

There was the thunderous sound of ascending footsteps — a muffled cry, a wild howling in the night. Then, someone began to slam against the door with all of his might.

Reev heard a shriek come from the first floor, then more footsteps, and the person throwing himself against Reev's bedroom door ran off. Reev stood to his feet, locked the door — then rushed to his window. Scattered shadows were fleeing the manor, in the night.

~

When Reev finally mustered the bravery to descend to the first floor, Xan was lying unconscious in the hallway. A bull's-eye lantern was flashing at Reev, just ahead, and the man holding that lantern was a member of the town guard, with a hawk tabard over his armor.

Other guards were wandering about, in the vestibule, in the kitchen. Reev looked to Xan.

"Is he okay? What happened?" He looked down and saw what looked like a burnt-out metal ball by Xan's side.

Xan was immobile — but he was breathing.

"So you *are* all right, Mr. Nax," said the guard with the lantern, "though a crime has been committed. This man — you know him?"

"Yes," Reev said, "yes, Xan."

"So he was not among those trying to kill you," the guard said.

"Kill me?" Reev wondered what hour it was — it was surely the middle of the night.

"The General of the Army, Fortunato of Ríva, told us to check on you," said the guard. "He was right…"

"Henrik! Look!" someone called out from the library. And as the guard with the lantern walked past Reev in the voice's direction, Reev's focus again turned to that burnt out metal ball beside the unconscious Xan. He stooped down and took it in his hands.

~

In the library, books and shelves were overturned — the divan had been thrown on its side. And on the wall a picture had been painted in bright red blood.

Reev took a step back; he grew dizzy, faint, nauseous, as his own blood drained from his face.

The bright red blood, smeared on the walls, depicted what looked like two serpents, one devouring the other.

"What is this?" said the guard with the lantern.

And the guard who had called him said, "Pigs' blood… a message of some kind."

In the distance, Reev made out the sound of Xan groaning and moaning — he was waking up.

Henrik, the guard with the lantern, turned to Reev. "You are a member of the Council of War — and you have no protection? This must be remedied, at once."

But as Reev looked at this Henrik in the light of the lantern, he noted a folknut necklace about his neck, and that on the other guard's arm was a dragon's eye tattoo.

Heathens.

"I think you shall leave us," Reev said, "leave us… at once."
And the guards looked at him warily.

"Leave us… leave me, now."

~

Xan was just coming to as the guards filtered out of Rosetree Manor. He was still staggered, still dizzy — clearly out of sorts.

"Reev — " he at last said, and then he opened his mouth in a silent scream. "Did they get you? Did they hurt you? It all happened so fast…"

Reev was still reeling, and still his heart was pounding. Still, his forearms were lined in icy cold sweat.

"I was nodding off in the vestibule… almost asleep when I saw them. They broke through the window. There were dozens — they threw something at me. There was a flash, and noxious fumes — and here I am."

Reev held up the burnt-out metal ball to the light of the candles.

"Yes, that must be what they threw. That must be what knocked me out," Xan said.

But what was it?

One thing was clear, Reev was no longer safe in this city, no longer safe, even in the presence of a skilled warrior like Ivan Xandrast. He'd come within inches of death, and if the guards were to be believed, a fortuitous warning by Fortunato and a summoning of the town watch had saved his life.

"We had better not stay here," Xan said, "or in one place, for long. It seems there are people in the city intent on killing you. But why? Why?"

Reev was still trembling, still breathless, still faint.

"Let's go to my old flat," Xan said, "on Canary Street."

"Canary Street? Isn't that in Greenwater?"

"Anonymity is what will keep you safe… blending in and not

being noticed. No one knows me from Solarias; they won't look for you in that house of mine."

Who? Who had tried to kill Reev? Who was after him? Who had tried to deal him death?

They had clearly planned the attack in advance, incapacitating Xan and then rushing into the manor by the force of numbers. Then, inexplicably, they had painted a picture on the wall in blood.

"Come on," Xan said, "let's get you out of here. I'll keep you safe."

But he hadn't kept Reev safe, not at all, and he dreaded living with him in closer quarters. Reev was not safe and he could not be in this city, where so much darkness lay just beneath the surface.

"Come on! Come on! Grab all you need, and hurry!"

~

When Reev walked through the doors of Xan's rented room, mice scurried away, in view. On the floor were remnants of food and a tin of spoiled milk. The entire flat was little bigger than Reev's bedroom in Rosetree Manor. But it was tucked away, anonymous, hard to find. It overlooked a narrow alley.

Beside the filth and grime and discarded bones was a mattress, spotted with dirt.

"Oh, dear," Reev said, aloud. "Oh, dear."

~

By morning, the word had spread all over the city of Galiope that an attempt had been made on Reev's life, but that Reev had miraculously survived. Those would-be murderers, people stated on street corners, had been captured to a man.

"No one lies to a thumbscrew," one said, in earshot of Reev the next day.

"The truth will out!" But at night new news arrived, the would-be assassins had been carrying with them vials of poison. They had tried to kill Reev, "six young men from good families" — but to keep their mouths shut they had taken their own lives.

Reev vowed to remain inside, to stay within Ivan Xandrast's rented room, to survive until Gastreel's return.

"Gastreel," he said softly under his breath that night, before bed, "come home…"

Chapter Thirty-Eight: Gray and Crimson

It was dawn, and the city of Alzdorf below Gastreel's window was being painted in dawn's colors. Gastreel had arisen, and if he remembered correctly, it was the 10th of Aurelios. The Pan-Vardic Games soon would begin.

He was rising, stretching, preparing for what would be said today. Martin Durkheim had made vague promises of help, but a concrete commitment and the beginning of the mustering had not yet emerged.

There was a tap on the window, and Gastreel's old heart raced within his chest. He fell a bit back and then realized what this meant. A hawk had been sent, a message… *Aleksander. He will keep me apprised.*

The letter in the hawk's talons he took, and read it, softly, aloud, "To Gastreel Osiris — I am your stalwart friend and ally. It brings me no pleasure to tell you what I have learned. Ariya, the White Wizard, who attempted to use the iron mask to her advantage, was seeking to harness and tame the power of a creature called 'Orm Huluk.' Does that name bring anything to mind?"

It did not.

"She wished to tame it and bring it into the power of herself and the wizards — but the iron mask seized control over her mind and spirit. She could not direct the iron mask; she could only be directed."

Wizards always played with fire, always tried to manipulate nature. Their error had so often brought them to ruin.

"She became enveloped in the crisis in the mountains. You freed her from the mask's spell. I do not know if she did what she did with the sanction of others. I will keep learning, and I will keep you informed. Yours, for the gods, for goodness — Aleksander."

Gastreel let the letter fall from his hands.

There was a flash of light, and then a flash of darkness. He saw a shadowy face, two red eyes. "Thou fool!" a voice seemed to say, and to echo. "He is mine…"

He felt his knees give out.

~

And his eyes were blinking, faces, hovering above him. He was in the infirmary of the Great Hoff, and doctors were beside him.

"Gastreel!" a voice called out, one he knew, Freya.

"He is alive!" she howled.

Gastreel sat up on the bed, seeing the doctors — priests and nuns — before him and about him.

"We found you collapsed in your bedroom!" said Freya. "You were breathing only slightly."

The grand duchess was standing a ways off, her silver hair tied up in elaborate tresses.

Gastreel was still in a haze. He felt his heart had gone still. And something came to him — "My staff! My staff!"

They had taken his staff when he arrived in Almania. It was, supposedly, in the grand duke's keeping. He would not be parted with it anymore.

"You must give me my staff!" said Gastreel. He stood up on his two feet, amid the beds and the gathered doctors, the sick and infirm laying still. "You must!"

Freya furrowed her brow. "Green Wizard — it would not be appropriate. A weapon — "

"My staff!" Gastreel said.

Why had they taken it from him? He did not know.

A door opened in the distance. He saw Wrinn and the grand duke Martin walking through.

My staff… my staff…

It was in their safekeeping… safe — and he would have it back.

He could suffer such an indignity, if it were for Gallia.

My staff… my staff…

Chapter Thirty-Nine: Might and Magic

Trumpets blew, first six, then seven. Drums pounded and cymbals clanged. A whole host of Gallians were in the bleachers that Fortunato had built, and Fortunato was watching from a distance in the thick summer air.

With his sword clipped to his side he kept watch, as riders on white horses galloped through the game grounds, announcing the beginning of these, the Pan-Vardic Games. Beside the bleachers merchants had set up shop, some selling "chewets" — handheld pies in which was spiced and minced meat. Others he had heard, shouting of "Wine of Orr!" and "Highrock Mead."

That, however, was not Fortunato's concern. From the shadows he was watching as the games began, observing all, plotting, planning, wondering where all this would lead.

A woman walked out into the game grounds wearing a blue gown. It was the mistress of ceremonies.

In the private box Fortunato had built, Eventide and his wife were sitting, together with other nobles. One among them was there with them, with bright red hair and freckles, dressed all in black.

Alden.

"Today we announce the beginning of the Pan-Vardic Games," the mistress of ceremonies was droning on, but Fortunato wasn't listening. He was focused on the crowd, focused on the faces he saw, common and noble alike, sitting in the stands.

"Games of might and magic!" said the mistress of ceremonies. "Games of all kinds of strength!"

Why had the council done this? Why had they agreed? Why had they postponed the war, when victory had been at hand?

Nenré... Lord Calion. Had those visions been delusions of

overwork? Had he truly heard from two people he thought he'd never see again?

And then he saw it — Ambrass's face in the crowd. She was there, and beside her was a gypsy man.

At the sight of him, he felt his heart seize up. What was his name? Gaius… Gaius… to whom Ambrass had been betrothed, long ago. And now she was back with him, back in his love.

Fortunato had known this; he had heard, and it had been told him. But the sight — the sight — he felt nauseous, then angered, then determined.

I will participate in the games… I will compete. I will remind her of who I am, and what we once were…

"The games are divided into three parts," the Mistress of Ceremonies went on, "the Sword, the Staff, and the Wand. Whoever wields one of these the best will win the Victor's Crown, and all that entails. Welcome, our judges."

Fortunato's gaze was fixed on Ambrass's face, and the face of her erstwhile, and current, suitor Gaius. *Have they been married already? Have they already said the vows?*

He felt sick, and he staggered a bit back, as the "judges" walked by him.

I will win her back. I will…

~

The "judges" walking by were wizards, ones Fortunato had seen. There were eleven of them by his count, one among them he had seen before, Sestriel in his orange robes, his white beard almost touching the ground, in his wrinkled hands a staff of cinnamon color, at the top of that staff an orb.

"The Archwizard is not present," said the Mistress of Ceremonies, "so these, the games, will be judged by eleven and not twelve."

There were scattered mumblings in the crowd; some it seemed had forgotten that Gastreel was gone, gone on a diplomatic mission — and so these games, which had occurred because of his absent-mindedness, would go on without him.

Fortunato gazed at the wizards only briefly. His heart, and his eyes, turned to Ambrass, who now was resting her hand in Gaius's.

I will compete in the games. I will remind her of who I am.

He sensed a presence behind, and turned in the afternoon's light. Some men were approaching, all young and muscular, one he felt he had seen before, carrying a sharp-edged board in his hands.

His face was dark and swarthy, and his eyes equally so. Muscles were visible through his light dun tunic. He carried himself with confidence. He met Fortunato's gaze. "Hello again."

"Again?" Fortunato said softly, in the afternoon's light.

"You were the one who captured me," the man said, "the one who remanded me to Galiope, remember? You are Fortunato, the general, aren't you?"

Fortunato peered into those eyes of his, which though familiar he couldn't place. Something about him he remembered, but the travails of the war had been so long, so many decisions had been made, so many tasks undertaken.

"Spyke," the man with the board said.

"Yes, yes," Fortunato said. He remembered that unusual name. "Spyke, from Perremum. We caught you crossing through Gallia Shire not long ago…"

Spyke, from Perremum — he had come from wherever that was for these, the "Pan-Vardic Games" and Fortunato had almost spoiled his plans. Now those plans had come to fruition — at the cost of the cessation of the war, which Gallia had been winning.

What fools are in the Council of War…

"Perhaps," Fortunato said, "I will meet you in the arena."

"Spyke" from Perremum's eyes twinkled. His lips perked into the slightest of grins.

~

Night had fallen over the city, and in The Green Girdle —
despite the war that had been raging for months — Fortunato saw
that not much had changed.

Its booths and stalls were packed with people, and the dim-lit
chamber echoed with the sound of idle chatter and of pouring
drink. This was the place he had taken Spyke, the place he had
recommended… his favorite tavern in the city of Galiope, one he
had missed during the long months on the march, whose beers were
of the highest quality, and whose wine was the best he could find
in Gallia.

"This?" Spyke said. "This watering hole? This is the best tavern
in Galiope?"

"I've always thought so," Fortunato replied. "Not much,
maybe, but it's always suited me…"

~

At tables the serving girl came by. Spyke had beer, Fortunato
wine. And as drinks were poured, and drunk, more Fortunato began
to learn about this Spyke from Perremum, though he was most glad
to be off duty, away from the travails of war.

"I will beat you," Spyke said, softly. "Just you wait."

"We'll see," Fortunato said, softly, "we'll see…"

Chapter Forty: Memory

The *compline* bells were ringing when the doors to Sunstone Manor at last opened, and Ash walked through the door. Ramona had been up late, waiting, and her mind, swimming with wine, was in a daze. "Ash! Ash!" she said. "I've been worried sick — "

He'd been gone all day, for hours, and memories were returning of a former life, one she had thought she left behind.

Her son's dark eyes gleamed in the light of the hearth, which, in the other room, was turning to embers.

"Ash," she said, "where have you been?"

In her hand was a glass of wine, her fourth of the night. In her struggles with her son, wine had so often been her comfort, her medicine. Now, she had half a wit, but she was glad to see him at long last.

"Where have you been?" she said, insistent, as from another room the lithe form of her servant Chalmet emerged.

"Looking after my cousin, as you asked me," Ash said.

"Your cousin? Reev?" Ramona said. "Why, why," and her voice grew hushed.

She recalled what she had asked him to do long ago, with motives that had varied, reasoning that had waxed or waned, and changed. Reev, Reev — his cousin, her nephew, a part of their family... but no longer.

"You are a doting cousin," Ramona said, "but you know what has happened... you know what has been done. You know what I told you. You know his heart."

Chalmet's form was like a dark silhouette.

"Rosetree Manor is ransacked   it's empty, and the door is open," Ash said.

"You know this," Ramona said. "You know what happened… you know what has been done."

And the attempt on Reev's life had brought her great consternation, but Reev… now, what was Reev to her? Not her nephew but her opponent in the Council of War. He would want nothing to do with her, after the words she had said. She wanted nothing to do with him, after he had turned against her.

"He is in the company of a common criminal," Ash said. "A known robber and bandit. A murderer, some say — his name is Ivan."

"And how did you come across this knowledge?" Ramona snapped. "Where did you find this information? Where have you been, my son? Where have you *been*?"

Ramona, beside herself, wished to strike her son, but also meet him in an embrace from which he could not leave. She imagined her son wandering wild through the streets of Galiope, wandering among the gathered proles and common hoodlums. Ash had prince's blood… it was no place for him or anyone like him, nor really was this backwater city — but that was a topic for another day.

"Where have you been?" Ramona said, again, beside herself. "How did you learn this?"

She saw his face was edged with grime and his fingers were caked with dirt.

"Others told me," said Ash.

"Who? Who?" Ramona said.

Ash didn't want to seem to say.

"Chalmet! Draw him a bath!" Ramona said. "Clean that *filth* from his hands, and wash those clothes of his.

"Ah, Ash, this is like olden times… like before."

And the darkness in Ramona's soul was complete.

~

Ash had bathed, his clothing had been changed, and he had been sent to bed. Ramona, in her own bed, watched the door open, and Chalmet's muscular form appear. He was a servant, the child of servants, but had nonetheless kept her company in this room the past few nights. Elfraine had been blue-blooded, a noble of the finest pedigree, but he had not had such fine arms, such dark complexion, such eyes the color of midnight. What would Elfraine think at the sight of this? Perhaps, she'd send him a letter.

"Chalmet, Chalmet," Ramona said, "why don't you shut the door?"

If Ash found out, his wrath would be incalculable. And at that wrath, as Ramona learned, lives could be destroyed, worlds undone, existences ruined. She could not risk such a wrath again.

"It's not about that," Chalmet said, "not about tonight… I just remembered something. Ivan — it's a name I'd heard before. One spoken from the lips of someone you know… someone you hate."

Hate… her mind for some reason flashed to Reev's face, though hatred — in her estimation — required respect.

"Amée," Chalmet said. "Amée had an admirer she used to talk about, someone who wouldn't leave her alone when she went to bars and taverns. He was obsessed with her. His name was Ivan Xandrast. Could that be the Ivan Ash was talking about?"

Who else in Galiope was named Ivan?

"Perhaps," Chalmet said, "if we follow this Ivan, he'll lead us straight to Amée."

"Too much talk," Ramona said, as she viewed Chalmet's virile form. "Shut the door."

But as Chalmet obeyed, she thought it over… yes, yes. Perhaps Reev and his poor choices in companionship could be of use to Ramona after all.

Chapter Forty-One: Neither Sword Nor Staff

In the heat of the summer morning, Bala was dressed as well as he ever had been. The prior night, he'd asked Glenda to wash his clothes and top hat, and now, despite the thick fabric, he was beaming and proud as he waddled down the road. He was following the crowds, and soon enough they led him where he had wanted to go.

He saw bleachers, and he saw people in them. He saw a dirt arena, rectangular in shape, and colorful tents set up all around.

They were the Pan-Vardic Games, where Mr. Fortunato had said he could participate. And with all his practicing over the past few days and weeks, it was his turn to try, he guessed, his turn to win the Victor's Crown.

He waddled down the road in the sunlight, past a family, past two young men, past a street artist painting a picture of a man in the grass. He waddled past a man selling meat pies from a stand, and a woman selling "Highrock Mead!" by the cup. He waddled past all the vendors and tents, toward the arena — and almost bumped into a man in a bright orange robe.

He looked up, and those two dark eyes caused him to shrink back. He felt he was being examined, felt that when this man was looking into Bala's eyes he was peering deep into his soul.

"Hello," Bala said, weakly, and his voice was almost a squeak.

The man in the orange robe didn't answer for a while, only stared at him.

The staff he held was the color of cinnamon, and the orb atop it was of crystal blue, overlaid with a gold dragon.

"I'm Bala," he replied.

"Bala," the man in the orange robe said, and his eyes seemed to glisten. In those eyes was something like the waters of the ocean, a sea of storms — an endless abyss. Bala felt his knees weaken, and his heart grow cold. "You are Aleksander's apprentice. Why are you here?"

"To compete," Bala said, and he remembered something Aleksander had told him, *avoid Sestriel of the Orange Robes.*

"I do not think that is fitting for someone your age," said the man — "Sestriel" perhaps. "Besides, your training has only just begun, according to the records provided by Gastreel."

He spoke the name "Gastreel" like it was a curse.

"You have no chance," he said.

No chance — Bala felt his shoulders stiffen. He felt his gaze harden. "No chance," Bala said. "We'll see."

He wondered why Mr. Aleksander had told him to avoid Sestriel, and as he waddled away, he felt Sestriel's eyes on him. He had a thought that Sestriel was up to no good.

~

In the square dirt arena before the stands, there were people practicing, young men some shirtless and some in midriffs, muscles glistening in the sun. They were striking at each other with swords or with axes, with bats or with spears. Bala watched their work in the midday light.

The heat was building; the spell of hot weather had not ended, and the elements themselves seemed to be withering away in the face of the sun. The young men grunted and shouted as they struck at each other, careful not to shed blood.

Bala looked to the stands, saw Ambrass's face — Ambrass's and another.

At a stall was a wizard Bala thought he had seen before, a woman in a gown of gray. Her yellow staff was strapped to her back. Bala began waddling over to her.

The wizard regarded him with surprise, and alarm, as she took note of the apprentice's robe that Bala wore. Bala guessed this was where the would-be participants announced their intention to compete in the games.

He gave a cursive glance back, and noted that Sestriel of the Orange Robes was still standing where he had been, staring at him. At the sight of Sestriel's eyes, a shiver passed up Bala's spine.

Dare I?

Yes, I do.

"I want to compete!" Bala told the woman in the gray robe, standing behind the stall.

"I want to compete!" he said, again, and the woman seemed to stiffen, to look, briefly, beyond him.

"How old are you?" the wizard said, staring down at him in bafflement.

Bala held up the five fingers of his left hand, and added two from his right.

"Seven," she said, softly, "seven years old. I don't think there's a rule against it… but… but…"

She seemed to be looking to Sestriel for permission, but as soon as she did, he walked off. In the thick warmth, Bala looked up at her, his heart eager with anticipation and hope, but also with fear.

"I shall not stop you," she said, "but the games are dangerous. The battles of the Sword are controlled, but of the Staff and the Wand many die."

"I want the Victor's Crown," Bala said. Perhaps, if he won the Victor's Crown, Aleksander would hear about it, and be so impressed that he would start his training at once.

All this to commence his training… all this, he vowed, and under the folds of his robe, extended his pinky.

Another promise.

"So be it," the wizard said. "I will not stop you, though at the age of seven I'd hope you'd have a father or a mother to stop you instead. You are an apprentice, and so in the battles of the Staff you will not contend, but of the Wand, with the aid of magic tools."

That was just as well, so long as Bala won the Victor's Crown, and Aleksander was impressed, and his training commenced. It was just as well, and Bala was eager.

"You will be competing against men and women much older than yourself," said the wizard in the gray robe.

Chapter Forty-Two: Ink of Atälos

In the days since the games began, Fortunato had busied himself quietly with the war. As the General of the Army, the Council of War — meeting in secret — kept him apprised of their every action. Help was being requested from the Wilderlands, from Kav, from even the elves of the plain. Negotiators were sent in all directions, favors being called in, hoping to add to the troops for the inevitable battle when the Victor's Crown was handed over, and the Pan-Vardic truce expired into the summer sun.

He was in his quarters, a tent a few miles outside the city one morning, when a messenger arrived, one of Eventide's men he had seen before. Over his neck was one of those heathen necklaces, and on his finger a ring on which was the heathen symbol of the Four Corners. The heathenry, Eventide believed, would aid the war, invoking the gods of his ancestors, but Fortunato had a thought that the gods of his ancestors — those of the Empire — were much stronger to prevail. Only wit and wisdom, the gods' own luck, would see them through this.

"Lord General," the messenger said, and his face was ashen, "Niccolo's legion is approaching."

"They are breaking the truce?" Fortunato said, and his heart seized up — he felt faint.

The Empire took pains to appear honorable, but he supposed in achieving victory they would endeavor to do anything, even betray their word and commit dishonor if necessary. Did they consider it necessary after the blows Fortunato had dealt them? Had their dual humiliations caused them to stoop so low?

"We will meet them," Fortunato said, "come what may. Put the city on alert."

~

In the span of an hour, Fortunato's men had gathered, just two thousand in number now, having donned quickly their quilted jack armor and armed themselves with spears and shields. From camp they marched, and over the day they walked, until, about a mile outside the city, there were red standards gleaming.

The sight of an Imperial army was like nothing else, and though Fortunato had witnessed the legions marching many times now, it still stole his breath. Their armor was polished to shine in the sun, the red crests of their helmets were crimson — the color of blood. Their eagle standards rose high above those marching, red and gold… and they marched as one, as a machine. At the head of them, riding on a white horse, was Niccolo.

Fortunato on Tyra Jade rode out to meet him.

"Niccolo!" Fortunato said. "The Empire has dealt much violence to the North, but I have not yet seen them betray their words. Will you attack us now, now that you have agreed to the Pan-Vardic truce?"

Niccolo's cold blue eyes had no emotion in them. Coldly and emotionlessly, he spoke: "The traitor general speaks of honor," he replied, "riding on a wolf — the steed of a rokahn.

"Do not worry, Fortunato of Ríva. I am not a traitor like yourself. I am not a worm or a weasel. We come merely to participate in the games, as is our right. And I am here to observe. Young men in their prime, full of life, doing battle. Will I see you among them, traitor?"

You will. Fortunato said nothing.

"Men of the Empire may participate in the games," Niccolo said, "as may people of all nations. You will not stop us, and if you do try, then the truce will be broken, and Gallia's destruction will come. You, however, will be taken back to your home, to die a traitor's death."

Fortunato stared into Niccolo's eyes for a while, and could not see a soul behind them. "We will not stop you," he said. "We just do not trust you. Nor should we. Participate in the games. Then the games will end, and we will settle the score."

Niccolo's dark grin indicated just who he thought would prevail. The Empire was the mightier force — but Fortunato felt that the gods were with him.

~

The games had begun in earnest when Niccolo and the others reached the tents. An observation deck had been hastily assembled the prior day, and the eleven wizard judges were observing from the opposite end of the stands. Chief among them was Sestriel in his flame orange robe, holding that cinnamon-colored staff, on which was an orb.

A banner on which was painted a wand flapped in the wind. In the dirt of the arena, a battle of magic was underway. As Fortunato rode near it, he was stirred into a panic. It was Bala participating in this deadly game.

He wanted to rush out into the arena and grab the little boy, but there were flashes of light, blue, purple. In the little boy's hand was a wand of white crystal, and facing him was a man perhaps four times his age, dressed in a larger version of that ash-gray robe of his.

The crowds in the stands were cheering with each arcane blow. The young man summoned up a gout of fire which exploded in smoke just above Bala's head. Bala sent back a scintillating sphere of purple energy, which hit the man straight on and burnt a hole in his robe.

Bala's opponent fell to the ground, barely breathing. A trumpet sounded. There was a voice from the observation deck. "Bala, victor!"

What a terrible idea it seemed to Fortunato, but Fortunato was not Bala's father. Bala had a father, albeit not a good one.

"How old is that child?" Niccolo said as he dismounted from his white horse.

Fortunato said, "Seven years old."

As Niccolo walked into the dirt of the arena, there were gasps and a few screams. Others looked back at the soldiers and began to panic, standing up to run away or otherwise turning white-faced. But Niccolo kept up his walk, and raising his hands said, "Are we of the Empire not allowed to participate in these games?"

Eventide, in the official box, looked at Niccolo with bulging eyes. He glanced to Sestriel, hoping perhaps that Sestriel would give him a way out.

But it was not to be so. "Of course!" Sestriel thundered. "All nations may participate, all nations under Varda's sun."

Bala was walking away with a bit of a prance in his step. Fortunato was proud of him, despite what a terrible idea his participation had been.

Fortunato searched for Ambrass's face in the crowds, but he could not see her.

Will I participate, if she is not here? Perhaps, if he won the Victor's Crown, she'd hear of it from afar… remember him, and what they had been, and still could be.

~

The games of the Sword started in the late afternoon, after full wizards had dueled in sight of the crowds under the banner of the Staff, hurling balls of fire and jets of lightning, gouts of acid and beams of spectral light. In the light of Varda's sun Fortunato approached the wizard's stall and asked for the first time, "May I, as General of the Army, participate?"

~

"Here," the wizard in the gray robe told him, apparently in charge of all would-be entrants, "dip your sword in this."

Before them, in the sun's light, was a vat in which was something like liquid tar.

"What is it?" he asked her.

"Ink of Atälos," she replied, "so that your blows may not kill, but only injure. A touch of this and you will drop to the ground, wounded but still alive."

"Cowards," Fortunato said to her.

Her eyes turned to him with a look of dark anger.

"You Northerners are cowards," Fortunato said, "in the Empire, the swords and tridents in the arena kill, and gladiators face death."

"Cowards, you northerners are," he said, and he smiled.

"You are the North's general, no?" the wizard in the gray robe said.

But the North was not Fortunato's home.

Chapter Forty-Three:
The Old Haunt

In Xan's upper room, Reev had kept indoors, and when Xan went about his business, or his work in the docks, Reev would sit by the door, adding his body's weight to the force of the lock. The night in Rosetree Manor remained in his memory, a bewildering terror, and to this new danger was added thoughts day and night of his cousin Ash — could he be? Could Ash be the Dark One's Hand?

Doomblade was at his side, but a sword was only effective in the hands of a swordsman.

At night, he would lay awake thinking, and when he finally slept, his dreams were of the attack — the attack, and what would have happened if Fortunato had not given that inexplicable warning… the attack, and thoughts of his cousin Ash.

It was late morning, and still he was leaning against the door. He had slept hardly a wit and was beginning to wink, to nod, off and on. He supposed it was better to leave the security of the door than to fall asleep and lose all consciousness.

He stood up, and amid the filth of Xan's upper room remembered that once he had lived in better climes — a mansion well-kept with many halls and chambers, not this, this dirty stye. Still Xan hadn't cleaned up the food from the prior night, and his makeshift cot was unmade. Dirt specked the walls, and mouse droppings could be seen in plain view. Reev endured it all for the sake of anonymity.

He looked ahead, to the dirty window.

The window…

He cleaned some of the grime and fog with his hand and looked down into the streets below. People were passing down the way, not women in fine cote-hardies and gowns nor men in blue or purple tunics like in Wodenscross Court, but the least advantaged in the city, the urban poor. In tunics of drab gray or brown they passed by, on their way, hurrying to their laborious jobs or rushing to the markets to purchase food for their children, in their homes without ovens. Reev pitied them, but in the hearts of Gallia's nobility he had seen something infinitely worse than poverty, a disrespect for the things of heaven, a cruelty and pride for their subjects, and a total absence of the warrior virtue that was supposed to predominate the upper class.

As he sat on the windowsill watching, observing, he eventually exchanged glances with a young man standing at a street corner. As soon as their eyes met, the man turned and dashed away.

Reev could feel his heart begin to race. He wondered when Xan would return home.

~

When Xan at last barged through the door, oblivious, his butterfly blade strapped to his back, Reev rushed forward and at once began to shout. "They've found us!" he said.

But how did he know? He felt it… he sensed guile in that young man's eyes. He had been standing there, staring at the window through the upper room.

"How do you know?" Xan said.

And when he told him, Xan's eyes narrowed, and his thick pale lips perked up just a slight bit.

"Could just be someone looking into the house, searching about for something," Xan said. "People-watching, as it were."

"It could be," Reev said, "and maybe I'm too fearful, but I don't feel safe here, anymore. But where could we go? There's nowhere left to hide…"

The attack at Rosetree Manor had undone him that badly. But

he did not feel safe, and he felt he could not risk it, especially if what Gastreel and others said about him was true.

The Prince of the Dawn…

"Very well," Xan said, "I owe you my life, and now I will protect yours. That is my duty. I know of a place. If we keep moving about, perhaps, they'll lose track of you. None will know."

Xan crossed the room and took something in his hands.

"Here… take this."

A stained black coat Xan tossed into his hands, a coat with a hood to obscure his face. He would walk the streets of Galiope unmolested.

~

Reev followed Xan, who wore a cloak of his own, through the trash and ordure-strewn streets of Riverside, and as he walked, he was beginning to recognize the shape of certain buildings, the contours of a street as if it were from some half-remembered dream. Under the sunny sky he followed Xan, until the street fell away, and there was a sign he recognized: "The Salty Dog."

"Really?" Reev said. "You must be joking."

"They are an inn by daytime," Xan said, "and a den of ill repute by night. They have a few comfortable beds in the rafters for only a penny or two."

Reev heaved a sigh. "So be it."

Xan was his protector, at least for now… and where else could he go? Where else could he find refuge?

~

The beds in the rafters were little better than straw cots, whose sheet coverings were stained with dirt and grease and other odd things. It was a stye of its own, but Xan said he bought the whole room, so that they would not have company.

That night, the revel Reev remembered from before commenced, and though the noise overwhelmed his senses it made thinking and dwelling on dark things impossible. For the first time in many days, he slept and slept well.

Chapter Forty-Four: Midsummer's Day

It was Midsummer's Day, and the forests of Almania were alive.

Wrinn had been given the day off work, as had the other elven servants, and so — as always — he was spending his time with Rosalie. They were riding their horses through a forest outside city bounds, at times racing each other, at times gently trotting along.

Wrinn did not know how Rosalie felt about him, but he knew that he had fallen hopelessly in love, for the first time in his life. He wanted to be around her at all hours. Whenever he got a chance, he'd hover near her, and when his duties with Gastreel took him far away from her it was a savage blow. The thought of his imminent departure troubled him deeply, but some things were more important than love, he knew— duty, honor, the cause against Seymus and his servants in the mortal world.

"Here! Here it is!" Rosalie said. The trees began to fall away, and a pond appeared, its waters glistening and surrounded by bulrushes. The sun was shining gently down on it.

"This is where my friends and I used to swim," Rosalie said.

"A pond," Wrinn said. "What is it called?"

"I don't think it has a name." Rosalie dismounted and tied her horse, which she had borrowed from her lord's stables, to a tree. In her hands was a basket of food, and a bottle of wine. "We can watch the fireworks tonight from here…"

"Fireworks?" Wrinn said.

"Yes, every Midsummer's Eve there are fireworks," Rosalie said. "Our master Martin always buys them at high cost."

Her "master" — she had begun calling Martin that in Wrinn's presence. Wrinn seemed to have convinced her that an indentured servant was little better than what he had been.

As soon as Rosalie had set her basket on the ground, she had removed her supertunic to bare her brassiere and loin. Wrinn felt himself blush.

"Aren't you going swimming?" Rosalie said, and, rushing forward, dove into the water.

Wrinn hesitated only a moment before stripping his tunic and trousers, and joining her. The water enveloped him, cold and sharp, and the mud of the pond massaged his toes. As he swam in place, he looked into Rosalie's eyes, and he realized he needed her, now more than ever.

~

It was Midsummer's Day, and Gastreel was aware the Pan-Vardic Truce would one day expire. In his upper room, he could hear the bells of the Greatminster ringing, and he knew the ducal family was in the church conducting their solemn services. Each hour that passed, each day that went by, was a grave concern, as time slipped away toward the war's inevitable resumption. Martin had promised help, but no sign of the mustering had occurred, and firm commitment — *"I will fight!"* had not yet come.

When a shadow darkened his door, Gastreel was ready to lash out — and when he saw it was Friedrich, the Heer Meister, the dark thoughts and frustrations of all these months were threatening to spill outwards.

"Gastreel!" said Friedrich. "We missed you at the Midsummer's Day services…"

Gastreel rose from his chair, fuming, as the rage that had slowly boiled in the background was at last bubbling in full force. "Friedrich, Heer Meister," he said, "you have not begun the mustering… you have not made firm commitments. You have not said you would give Gallia aid, explicitly."

"But we said we would give it implicitly, no?" Friedrich's light blue eyes brightened, and he smiled, baring white teeth. "We said we would help… under a certain condition. Remember? I said there was one thing you could do, to guarantee our support. A favor for a favor…"

"And what favor is that?"

"Come," Friedrich said, "let us go for a walk."

Friedrich took him outside the double doors of the Great Hoff, into the city proper. The healthful and wheat-fed folk of Almania were walking about in their tunics and kirtles of bright colors. They had no fear, no cares in the world, for they had betrayed their vows and their oaths… they had not gone to war to aid Gallia, as had been promised.

Through the streets they passed by, until at last they were in a square near Alzdorf's wall, at the head of which was a statue. It depicted a soldier in a winged helmet, his foot on the back of a dying warrior.

"What is this?" Gastreel said, taking note that Friedrich had stopped his walk and his stride, and was staring at the statue in the sun's light.

"Not long ago, Almania was at war with a nation called Kav," Friedrich said, "a nation that lies near the edge of our borders. This statue depicts my father Hermann, who valiantly fought to free the land of Rodnerov from the Kavan yoke.

"We were trying to win Rodnerov's freedom. We were attempting also to civilize the Kavans and the warlike nations that lie to our east. Our war was just — but though we were victorious, justice was not done."

Friedrich turned to Gastreel, and Gastreel in that instant took a step back, winded, intimidated. Friedrich had a presence a hundred times the strength of Martin, and double that of Martin's wife Freya. He had a presence fit for a wizard, though he was a soldier and not much more.

"Galiope has in its possession a war criminal of Kav, a prince among them, who has escaped justice time and time again," Friedrich said. "He would set the heads of the defeated on pikes. Those who resisted him, he would impale while they still drew breath. He would sow productive farmlands with salt, and put cities and villages to the flame. He would pile the defeated's skulls in great mounds to intimidate those who would defy him. But the reason I hate him most is that he killed my father. An ambush, a night attack — he overcame a man much greater than himself, through a coward's tricks. His name is Ivan Xandrast."

Gastreel felt his blood go cold. He knew that name. He had seen Ivan, met him. He had watched Reev drive the evil out of him. He had witnessed him turn from evil to good. He had been a warlock, but now that poison had been purged from him.

"Give us Ivan Xandrast, and you will have your war," Friedrich said, "our troops, our soldiers… and that is my warrior's honor."

Something new dawned in Gastreel, something besides cold horror. When he looked into Friedrich's eyes anew, he saw a cunning mind. "You know that Galiope is a city that welcomes exiles, by law," said Gastreel. "You know this… you know that Galiope never gives up its citizens to foreign nations. You know this… you are stalling. Do you not intend to give us what I will?"

"Do you accuse me of dishonor?" said Friedrich. His cheeks flushed red — wrath. "I gave you my word. The Council of War can overrule its laws. Give us Ivan Xandrast, and you will have your war. Those are our terms. I am the Heer Meister, the ruler of the army. Not even Martin can defy me."

Friedrich's words were bold. Gastreel still did not trust him. But what choice did he have?

He would dispatch a letter to the Council of War. He would make this request to them. What was Gallia, an entire nation, compared to the life of Ivan Xandrast?

And yet — what was Gastreel's true struggle?

Reev Nax, the Prince of the Dawn...

~

Wrinn was swimming in the pond in the sultry heat, splashing, and eventually he and Rosalie were in close quarters, just inches from each other. He felt his lips drawing near hers without his voluntary movement — and then noise. Noise!

Curses!

Elves were walking through the trees, elves he knew, their friends... Joran and Kara, Lisette, Spatha.

"Hail!" Wrinn said, swimming, and he wondered what they would think, he and Rosalie barely clothed, swimming, alone.

Midsummer's Night would soon be here, and Wrinn would tell Rosalie how he felt, despite the presence of others. Midsummer's Night... he would make explicit what had been implicit.

Chapter Forty-Five:
Abollondon

In the rafters of The Salty Dog, where Reev had spent the past many days, the heat had welled toward the inn and erstwhile tavern's upmost stories, where he had been sleeping. Still, remembering his danger and what all had occurred, he remained hidden from view, cognizant that people were after him, trying to take his life.

Yet as he lay there — what day was it? He remembered, Midsummer… a voice stirred him from his solitary contemplation. It was a voice he knew, one he recognized — a laugh, a chortle.

Amée…

Ramona's servant, whom she had dismissed, that was the voice he heard, and despite his constant state of danger, he stood up and walked over, crept to the very edge of the rafters.

The Salty Dog, wherein he'd had that midnight idyll, was altogether different in the daytime. The bones and various scraps of debris had been cleared from the floor, and there was not the sound of pouring grog or shouting sailors… but there was Amée.

She looked worse for the wear, and her face was not so fresh. Her auburn hair was tied up with a ribbon, though, and the clothes she wore — a fine white chemise, and a small cap — ornamented her well.

Their eyes met.

Reev took a step back, almost shrieked — but the damage was done. Perhaps, he'd be able to convince Amée to keep quiet. Perhaps, if he told her he was being hunted…

But as he climbed down from the rafters, down a set of steps, other eyes saw him, eyes he did not recognize.

"Reev Nax! It's you!" one said.

I will have to move again… Xan will not be happy. But something inexorable was drawing Reev onward, and he approached Amée as she was sitting down in the booth.

"Reev," she said, and he took a seat across from her.

~

"Reev," Amée said, softly, again, "you are not here on behalf of your aunt, are you?"

"No," Reev said, "of course not…"

Amée's bright eyes seemed to darken. "Good!" she said. "That woman is a demon… pardon my saying so. And I thought the whole Nax family was that way until I met you."

Memories returned of the weeks spent in Ramona's house, the uncomfortable dinners, the secret investigations that Reev had undertaken. He remembered words from more than a year ago, and rumors that had spread across the city without answer. He remembered what Ramona herself, and what Gastreel had told him.

"I thought I needed that job," Amée said, "but now I'm making three times the money, and I'm much happier."

Much happier — when she said the words, she did not sound convinced. "Where are you working now?" Reev said, and as a serving girl came by with a cup of tea and a plate of bread, she gave her answer.

She said it as quietly as could be. "A stew on Porto Street."

Two things had bothered him over these days and weeks, the attack at Rosetree Manor and the surely false idea that Xan had planted in his head. "My aunt said that her marriage was annulled."

Amée looked up at him; her brown eyes sparkled, and her lips perked into a grin. She seemed delighted to tell Reev all she knew, now that she wasn't under Aunt Ramona's heel. "It was all because of *Abollondon*," she said.

"Abollondon?" Reev said.

"*Abollondon* — the thing of hell. That was what the parish priestess and the peasants of County Sareil called your cousin Ash, and by the time the High Priestess graciously granted the annulment, his father Elfraine called him that too."

Reev felt ill.

"When your cousin Ash was born in County Sareil, that very night, the moon turned like blood, and the summer after he was born there was an eclipse of the sun, the only one of this century. That year the crops failed, and when the peasants complained about Ash and what he had wrought, Elfraine was at first enraged, and punished the accusers to a man.

"But there was something wrong with Ash, gravely wrong. When he emerged from his mother's womb he had almost killed her; they had to open her up, and after they had done so she almost died. It was only lately, shortly before the annulment, that his true nature was shown.

"The count's dogs were going missing, one by one. From the kennels they were disappearing, and Ash's father found him one morning in the woods with a knife. He had sawed off the dog's head, and he had been dissecting it."

Reev's illness was growing, but an eclipse of the moon and sun — it could only be chance, an astrological phenomenon. The killing of a dog was cruel, but did that make him the enemy of the gods, the Dark One's Hand?

"That summer the crops failed again," Amée said. She seemed to be reveling in at last telling all. "Elfraine was already enraged at the killing of his dogs. The High Priestess does not grant divorces easily, but when he wrote to her, of all that had gone on over the years, the mishaps, the strange coincidences, she agreed — your Aunt Ramona was a *mordblood*, and she had given birth to someone not of this earth, but of an entirely different realm."

Reev felt himself shrink back in his seat. Ash, Ash, it could not be so — for if poison blood was in Ash's veins, then it was in his as well.

"The High Priestess arrived at County Sareil," Amée said. "She and her servants questioned Ramona for hours. She learned that Ramona had not disclosed her foreign origins, not of Zarubain or Gallia or the North, or even the Empire, but somewhere else, somewhere called *Telantis* — and the Inquisitors with all their expertise determined that Ramona did not even know of that place's location.

"*Abollondon* — a thing of hell. That's your cousin. And Ramona when the annulment was granted ran away, back home, with her tail between her legs. Ramona had not divulged her iniquitous origins… and so the marriage was considered to have taken place under false circumstances. Null… and void."

The blood had drained from Reev's face, and he was breathing only barely. The noise in The Salty Dog was rising, however, and some in the crowd were staring at him.

"Some," Reev said, "have accused my cousin of being the Dark One's Hand."

"Have they?" Amée said. "Have *you*?"

Amée's smug demeanor vanished — the glib light faded from her eyes. She was looking away from Reev. "Not you again!" she said. "The answer is no!"

Reev turned and saw Xan's form amid The Salty Dog. Xan's eyes were fixed on Reev and not Amée.

"Reev," Xan said, "what did I tell you?"

Amée stuck out her tongue. "You know Xan? You know this pest?"

"Hurry, Reev. Grab your things! What a fool you are…"

~

"Where will we go now?" Reev said amid the crowds of the street. His location again had been discovered, this time by his own hand.

He had learned things, though, some which he hadn't wanted to know, things he hoped weren't true, things he thought might best be left unknown.

They were both clothed in hooded cloaks, but they had been seen exiting the doors of the tavern and erstwhile inn. It was late afternoon, and the shadows of the day were long. Clouds were veiling the sun, and a dark fever seemed to plague the air. The firmament promised storm, but the greatest storm, to Reev, seemed to be raging in his own heart.

Chapter Forty-Six: Oath-Bound

The skies were painted in the colors of dusk, but clouds were moving in from the north. On the High Porch of the Great Hoff, Midsummer Night promised a summer squall. In Gastreel's hand was a glass flute of sparkling wine, and so too in the hands of Freya and Martin, and Friedrich, the "Heer Meister."

"See?" Martin said to Gastreel. "'I say; I do.' A favor for a favor. Give us our desire, and you may have the full force of our troops."

That was not how promises worked. As fireworks began to go off and erupt in the sky, as darkness prevailed over dusk, Gastreel wondered if this help would ever come.

When he shut his eyes, he saw a shadowy face and two blazing red orbs. A thought: *You are mine.*

~

The fireworks were echoing, bursting in red and gold and blue and yellow against the black canvas of the sky.

Wrinn and Rosalie were lying next to each other, and as they lay on the ground, beside the waters of the pond, he sidled up to her, even closer.

Others were in the distance, some standing, some sitting, under the starry sky.

There was a storm in Wrinn's heart, words buried in an abyssal sea. He could hide them no longer. "Rosalie," he said, loud enough for her and maybe others to hear, "I love you."

Rosalie sat up and looked down at him. Her eyes watered; her lips trembled. "I love you, too, I think," she said.

"You think…"

"But it cannot be. Martin has arranged all our marriages. He calls himself an enlightened monarch. Science, like horses bred for their best traits. That is how he thinks of us. Enlightened… that is how an enlightened man treats his indentured servants."

"Indentured servants," Wrinn said with a scowl. "Slaves — that is what you are." He sat up. "Rosalie, maybe, when I leave, you can run away with me."

"I will not live with a man I do not marry," Rosalie said.

"I'll marry you…"

Fireworks pulsed in the distance, red, green, then red and green.

"There is no ring," Rosalie said.

Wrinn looked to his left. He plucked a daisy from the ground and placed it in her hands. "I cannot afford a ring," Wrinn said, "but here… this is my promise to you."

Rosalie's eyes watered in turn. Her lips trembled. She held the daisy in her hand and peered into his eyes. "Joran is a good groom," she said, "I am a good cook. We are to be married according to Martin's will… it cannot be."

"It can," Wrinn said.

"No, no," Rosalie said, "a groom and a cook, and our child will be a husbandman…"

"No, no," she said, again, but before the night was over, she had placed the flower in the pocket of her gown.

Chapter Forty-Seven: Midsummer's Night

Rain was coming down in sheets, and there was lightning, and peals of thunder.

Reev's hooded cloak was sopping wet as he followed Xan through the dark streets, under the starry sky. From home to home, from inn to inn, he walked, but nature itself seemed to have turned against them, and with it the would-be hosts. "There is no room." "Sorry, Ivan." "Not again, after what you pulled."

They had at last come to Middletown, and the Bridge-O'er-Galios was in the distance. The rain was soaking through the cloak, into Reev's garments. "What shall we do?" he said.

As he spoke, a thought came to him.

"St. Sigmund's Cathedral," he said, "they offer space to the homeless — refuge."

But wouldn't his location there eventually be discovered? Wouldn't those who wished to harm him find him?

"Safe, in a cathedral," Xan said, "they will not harm you there — none would. And priests are sworn to secrecy of those who are under their care."

As Xan began walking south, in the direction of Cathedral District, Reev thought of Tyrol the false priest who was now St. Sigmund's rector. But, he supposed, it was too late to stop this idea from unfolding now.

~

In the night, in the rain and storm, the sharp angles of the churches and belfries and monasteries were a stunning canvas, and when the lightning struck and thunder pealed, the blue light illumined statues of monks and nuns and the city's heroes. From what Reev saw, he and Xan were the only ones on the road in this stormy summer night.

Following Xan, he walked south, and the illogic and impracticality of this venture endured, swallowed up by Xan's quick pace. Reev doubted this new venture would amount to anything. Perhaps, they'd spend the night under the bridge, or on the river-walk, where there was shelter.

At last, St. Sigmund's appeared, and the doors were open, and light could be seen from within. More remarkable, sound was echoing from within, the unearthly timbre of a boys' choir.

Reev wished to abort the mission at once — he'd surely be seen — but Xan ventured on regardless, into the light of the cathedral. Reev followed a step behind.

~

Lights were hanging from the ceiling on silver chains, causing the gold of the altarpiece in the apse to fluoresce. There were a few scattered people in the pews, and near the altar, the choirmaster was furiously conducting. It was Midsummer's Night, and the service was still raging, though few in the city seemed to be in attendance.

Xan was walking down the aisle. "What are you doing?" Reev would have said, in different circumstances.

The boys' choir was singing in their pure tone.

The Lord of Light, the Lord of Light, did teach us to obey
His words were taught by seer and sage in mountain valleys low

What was Xan doing? He appeared to be approaching the altar. Past the parishioners he was walking, and when he reached the altar, he knelt down. He bowed his head, and placed a coin in the offering plate.

From the shadows, Tyrol emerged, and he sprinkled Xan's head with palm oil.

It was the Midsummer blessing. Reev had not heard Xan speak much of religion, but perhaps, now that he had left the life of a warlock behind, he'd become as devoted to good as he had been enslaved by evil.

Yet he was lingering there, and when he arose, he began to speak to Tyrol. Tyrol glanced back at Reev.

Dear gods…

As Reev backed away, realizing anew what a terrible proposition this had been, what an impractical solution for a serious problem, there was a voice.

"Reev Nax!" that voice called out.

Dear gods again…

But as he fixed his eyes on the source of that voice, he was surprised at who it was. In the pews, near the middle of the church, was a woman with flame-red hair and brown eyes, dressed in a blue gown of dagged sleeves. Her hands, on the edge of the pews, sparkled with diamond rings.

It was the Lady Fiona, the first lady of Galiope, Eventide's wife. She was the wife of the Lord Mayor, and in St. Sigmund's church on this most high of holy days.

"Come here, Reev Nax!" said the Lady Fiona.

Could he resist her? Was there no limit to his distrust of others?

The Lord of Light, the Lord of Light, the master of us all
Of fen and field and dog and cat and meadow, mount and glen

Reev after a moment's hesitation drew near, as Tyrol and Xan continued to talk in the distance, between glances back at him.

At last, he sat in the pew behind her.

Alabaster king of gods, Amara mother too,

Fight for us in heav'n and earth and bring us soon the Dawn

"The council's been looking for you," the Lady Fiona said.

"Others are looking for me, too," Reev replied.

"Yes, I heard," the Lady Fiona said. "You refused Henrik's offer of official protection. I don't think we'll let you refuse again."

"Sometimes, anonymity is better than a sword," Reev said.

"I don't think so," she replied.

The boys' choir continued to sing. Xan and Tyrol continued to negotiate the arrangements.

"What are you doing in this church?" Reev said. "Shouldn't you be sky-clad, dancing around a fire?"

The Lady Fiona rolled her eyes. "Ah, my poor husband. He hasn't been the same since the death of Ethelbert. But deep down he still reveres the holy gods. This delusion will pass…"

Would it?

"Reev," the Lady Fiona said, "listen carefully. This city is not safe for you. The town guard is continuing to investigate the attack. What they've uncovered so far is nothing short of alarming. All members of the Council of War have protection, and you will too, whether you like it or not. There is a safe-house outside city bounds where no one will know to look for you. That is where you're going, tonight."

Fiona's tone was overpowering, yet Reev still bucked at the command. Who was she to tell him what to do?

"If you don't trust Henrik or the guards, trust me," the Lady Fiona said. "You aren't safe, and we will keep you safe."

Did he trust her? As he thought it over, he was more inclined to think "yes" than "no."

"You will be kept under constant protection," the Lady Fiona said, "until such time as this war is resolved."

Resolved — not won.

"No heathens," Reev said.

"What?" Fiona's eyes glistened.

"No heathens among the guards. No folknuts, no dragon's eyes, no hand-fasting," Reev said, "those are my terms…"

"So be it," Fiona replied. "Every guard will be vetted as you wish. All, pious reverers of the gods."

Xan and Tyrol were walking down the aisle. When they reached Fiona and Reev, Fiona was already speaking.

"Thank you, Ivan Xandrast, for taking care of Reev all this time," she said. "His security is in the hands of the city now. Now, leave us. Neither you nor Tyrol will be apprised of his location."

Chapter Forty-Eight: Under the Moon

Reev wandered out of Godsgate in the thick sultry air, underneath a moon partially concealed in darkness, under the starry sky. The sign of the Eagle was rising, and the sign of the Lovers would follow after it.

About a dozen guards were walking through the brambles and brush, as frogs trilled and night-birds chirped, as a wind blew that Reev thought he knew, a wind of change, of ill portent.

They were coming through some thick woods, under lamplight and starlight, and the guards were shoving through brush with boots and even their spears. In the dull illumination a wooden house appeared, overlooking a babbling brook. It was a cottage on a hill, and a deep valley could be seen below.

"Here," a guard said, "your quarters, Master Reev…"

The lamplight glistened on his armor.

Reev supposed his new climes were safer… safer, he guessed, from the city rabble, more guarded by steel. But it was a safety borne of trust, for he'd placed his life in the hands of the city, in the hands of Eventide and Fiona and others. He was at their mercy.

As he opened the door and entered, finding a dusty room, a bed, a chamber pot and little else, he was filled with regret — regret, and dawning fear.

~

It was late at night when he saw it, in the valley below, six figures so far away as to be inscrutable dots, moving about the broad expanse on beasts whose features Reev could not discern.

The ghostly light of the gibbous moon seemed to glint on

something, on six somethings. And as they maneuvered through the fields, horror filled him.

The Servants… the Six Servants of Seymus.

He hurried outside, to the guards standing at his door. "Go," he said, "summon Fortunato of Ríva at once."

Chapter Forty-Nine: A Breath in the Dark

Gastreel sat up from his bed in a cold sweat, his mind echoing some misremembered dream. There was a feeling of darkness in his heart. A face — Reev.

He felt Reev was in danger.

The night outside was deep and dark, Alzdorf and the Great Hoff utterly quiet.

No, no, he thought. *No, no…*

It was his imagination, surely.

He had pledged his loyalty to Gallia. He had a mission, hadn't he?

But there was a greater mission than this…

There was a flash of light swallowed up in darkness. There was a shadowy face, two red eyes, and another image — a hideous mask.

A thought: *Cut him down… bring me his heart…*

Chapter Fifty:
Two Against Seymus

When Fortunato stumbled into the safe-house, he appeared tired, but not bothered.

The valley below was empty, and the six dark figures could no longer be seen. "Fortunato," Reev said, "what are we doing?"

"Why have you summoned me, Reev?" Fortunato said.

"I thought I saw the six Servants of Seymus," Reev said.

"Maybe it was a trick of the light," Fortunato answered.

"Maybe," Reev said. "Maybe not."

His heart was still racing; his fear had not lessened… it had grown.

He turned to Fortunato. "Sorry for bothering you," he said. "I was scared. I trust you when I trust few. Gastreel is gone…"

He looked at Fortunato for a moment, still breathing raggedly, still in a daze.

"Fortunato, what are we doing?" he said.

"What do you mean?"

"Gallia, the war… why are we fighting?" Reev said. "What is our true purpose? It's not this, is it? It's to defeat Seymus."

"How will we defeat him?" Fortunato said.

"I… I don't know," Reev said, "but surely someone might know. Someone else."

Frogs were trilling; all else was silence.

"We should flee," Reev said, "but there is no safe place in Varda. Where would we go?"

At Reev's words, Fortunato pursed his lips. Did he know of a place to go?

"Do you want me to stay with you here, tonight?" Fortunato said.

"No" was Reev's response.

"Few are worthy of trust in this world," Fortunato said, "but the city will keep you safe. Eventide is delusional in this heathen nonsense, but he wishes you no ill. Here, the Nax name is revered. The ones who tried to hurt you won't be able to find you."

"How did you know I was in danger?" Reev said. "How did you know to send guards after me?"

There was a pause. Fortunato said, "I just knew."

Reev looked out the window.

"You are safe here," Fortunato said.

"The Servants…"

"A trick of the light."

"The murderers…"

"They are dead."

Reev turned to look into Fortunato's eyes. "Sorry to bother you. Just seeing your face has warmed my heart."

Fortunato smiled a half-smile. "Call for me if you need help," he said. "You are safe here, perfectly safe."

But Reev wasn't, and he knew it for a fact.

Chapter Fifty-One:
Mother and Son

Days passed, and weeks. Hot spells came and hot spells went. The city was in the throes of sultry summer, and Ramona felt she had turned a new leaf.

In the porch outside Sunstone Manor, she was thinking of Chalmet, of the secret rendezvous she had tried so mightily to hide from Ash. The affair had been kept quiet, for now, but she thought other servants might be suspicious, that others might have seen or heard things and what was done in the dark might soon be known.

As she sat, thinking, waiting, she thought on her time in Gallia, how difficult things had become. Ash had begun acting as he had before, of late, and it grieved his mother's heart. Peace there no longer was — for Zarubain's enemy, the Empire, had come at last to Gallia's doorstep, and there was little hope it wouldn't swallow the nation whole.

The hazy summer light reflected a figure at Sunstone Manor's gate, and at that figure's arrival the gatekeeper Titus began to open it in turn.

It was Chalmet, Chalmet in the summer's light, and as he walked down the way he regarded Ramona with a knowing smile, the smile of one who knew her intimately, the smile of one to whom she was intimately connected.

She stood up, wondering how she should act, wondering how people who weren't bedding each other behaved. She began flapping her hands. "Chalmet!" she said, "Hail!" The first thing on her mind — the first thing she thought to do.

Chalmet smiled even brighter, and she felt her heart race.

He is a servant, the son of servants.

"Hail, milady," Chalmet said. "I have a report for you…"

"A report…"

"I went to the Council Archives," Chalmet said, "I pored through every registry. There is no establishment called the House of Sunset, no inn, no eatery, no tavern, no shop… such a place does not exist in this city."

Not long ago, a gypsy woman had told her that Amée, her irksome servant, had found employment at a place called the "House of Sunset." She had ground flower petals onto the street and somehow by that divinatory method gleaned Amée's location. She had been wrong. She had led Ramona astray.

"Playing cards, flower petals, palm-reading," Ramona said. "Hocus-pocus. Drat! You tried hard, Chalmet."

Other servants in the yard were staring at her, including Titus the gatekeeper. Was she looking at Chalmet in a revealing way? She could feel her palms begin to acquire cold sweat.

"I will find her, milady," Chalmet said. "I give you my word."

She felt her heart begin to race. What a tangled net she had woven for herself. Still, under her breath, she said, "Perhaps, Chalmet, an afternoon treat…"

"Your wish is my command, milady," he said.

~

She and Chalmet were walking up the grand staircase, their appetites driving them forward, almost to Ramona's bedroom, when the double doors of Sunstone Manor slammed open and shut and a voice Ramona knew, the voice of the one she loved most in the world, wailed, "Mother!"

The hot passion within her vanished in a moment, and when Ramona beheld her son, that hot passion turned to cold fear.

Ash had a black eye, and his arms had many bruises.

"Mother!" he wailed again, and, taking a few staggering steps forward, dropped to his knees.

Ramona shrieked and ran down the grand staircase to the main hall, under the windows' light. She herself was weeping and wailing by the time she met her injured son in an embrace.

"Mother," he said, his voice now a sob, "mother…"

"What happened?" Ramona said, heart shuddering within her. "What happened, my son? Did someone at school strike you? Did the teacher do this to you? I'll have his head!"

"I haven't been going," Ash replied. "I haven't… I am sorry. I lied to you…"

"What?" Ramona snapped. "What do you mean, my son?"

"I was with a bad crowd," Ash said, "bad company… I met them at school, but I haven't been going."

"What?" Ramona was saying, "what are you talking about? What?"

"A cult, I now realize," Ash said. "A cult… they are trying to kill Reev. They are trying to make a poison especially for him. I went along with it until now."

"Why? Why?" Ramona said, howling, weeping. "Why did you do this to him? To us? To me?"

"They wanted my blood," Ash said. "I said no! I am lucky to have escaped with these bruises…"

Chapter Fifty-Two:
The Secret Grove

It was the fifteenth of Odens, and the grass in the valley below Reev's safe-house was beginning to turn gold. Not going in or out, he had done little except pray, and hope in vain that Gastreel would return. Food had been brought to him, day in and day out, week after week, from the city, and though it was finely cooked, and supplemented with whatever he wished to drink, more and more his focus returned to his true task. Gastreel said he was the Prince of the Dawn, the Hand of the Gods — that it was his mission to defeat the Dark One. But how?

Noon was turning to afternoon, the air in the safe-house was like a thick blanket, and Reev was struggling to breathe, when there was a knock at the door.

Normally, food was brought to him at Lauds and at Vespers, not now. He ventured to the door and opened it.

"Reev Nax, Your Honor," said the one at the door, a man dressed in the garb of a city official, a blue robe and a blue cap. "The council is meeting now…"

"I will not go to the secret grove," Reev said, "I've said it over and over… I will not participate."

"It concerns a message from Lord Gastreel," the official replied.

The conflict of conscience vanished; hope and fear drove him forward. Hope and fear propelled him to follow the official, north through the brush, around the city walls, north by northwest.

~

Conscience assailed him again when he reached the place of

evil.

The oaks of the grove were red with blood, dried and fresh, and though no wind stirred the crimson leaves seemed to shake and to twitch in Reev's sight, though it could have been a trick of the light. Fetishes of straw dangled by strings from the blood-soaked oaks' branches. No birds could be seen, nor animal, and silence greeted Reev — silence, and the faces of the council. The sense of violation and the degradation of nature seemed to permeate the outdoor shrine, not the heathens' gods, which were nothing, but a stain of evil, a testament to how low Gallia's aristocracy had stooped.

Reev was appalled.

"Men of the council," Eventide began the meeting, "welcome."

Standing in the secret grove, amid the blood-soaked ground, Reev counted thirty in attendance, including his Aunt Ramona. The council's size waxed or waned depending on who agreed to show up.

"A message from Gastreel, Archwizard and senior member of this council," Eventide said. From his tunic pocket he produced a packet of papers. "The message: 'An official notice from Gastreel, a servant of Gallia and her council, and from Wrinn, her bondservant: Almania, under Martin Durkheim and the Heer Meister Friedrich, the ruler of its army, has agreed to provide military aid to Gallia under the condition that you present Ivan Xandrast, your citizen, in chains to them. They wish to execute him for war crimes against their people."

There were a few scattered gasps. Rivien, the Lord of Horse and Galiope's second-in-command, said, "It is against Gallia's law, against our constitution as writ on the stone tables, to hand over a citizen to a foreign nation. We are of old a bulwark for the exile."

"The Tables of the Law can be altered," said the Lord Alden, whose eyes in the distorted light of the secret grove seemed red rather than gray. "By a unanimous vote, if all present consent, we may change our constitution. Let the clerk be my witness."

"It is true," the clerk said, sheepishly, from the shadows.

"What would our ancestors think?" the Lord Eventide said, the mayor and leader of the council. "Changing not just statutes but the Tables of the Law, prostituting ourselves, degrading ourselves for—"

"For survival," said Lord Alden.

The air in the secret grove grew hushed, and the blood and the fetishes, the growing sense of violation and transgression threatened to overwhelm Reev. But he remained amid these thirty despite the appalling spectacle, for he knew he held a man's life in his hands now, a man he loved like a brother.

~

Ramona was watching as the council bickered back and forth, amid the blood-stained oaks of the secret grove. Her attention turned to Reev at last, Reev her nephew. There seemed to be a glint in his eyes, and he had gone stiff.

Then he spoke, and when he spoke, all others were silent. A wind blew, and crimson leaves fell, and all there was was Reev's voice.

"Almania does not intend to help," he said. "They know well Gallia's laws. They know Gallia's established customs. They are delaying. They are preparing to lay Gallia low. They ask for what they know they cannot receive."

"Then let us prove them wrong," said Lord Alden.

"Quiet, snake," Reev said.

At his words, Alden was silent... so too were the others. Solitude fell over the secret grove. Eventide looked about the blood-stained branches, at the fetishes, at the crimson leaves.

~

"Here, our vote," said the Lord Eventide in the secret grove, "to change our laws, and allow the extradition of citizens to foreign nations… all saying yea, raise their hands."

They raised their hands, twenty-nine of them, Eventide, Fiona… the Lord Alden and the Lady Llewyn. The Lord Rivien, last of all.

All save Reev, twenty-nine against one.

"The motion is not agreed to," the clerk said. "The constitution is not altered."

"Gods help us all," said the Lord Eventide, and Reev did not think he meant the elemental spirits that the heathens worshipped.

"Gods save us," he continued. "We will fight the Empire without Almania's help."

Chapter Fifty-Three: The One Clothed in Light

It was Odens, and Fortunato was fighting under the summer sun.

As he did battle, striking blows against an elf carrying an axe, in view of the crowds in the bleachers, he glanced at his audience, hoping to see the one he had loved.

He did not see her, but he fought all the more. Perhaps, if he won the Victor's Crown, she would hear about it.

A lucky strike; a piercing blow. And Danenhir, lathed with Ink of Atälos, met its target. The elf collapsed to the dirt of the arena.

Niccolo was in the private box and a few other Imperials. Eventide was with him, and a few others of the council.

Fortunato thought he saw Ambrass in the crowd, but when he looked in the woman's direction, she glanced away.

"Fortunato, Victor!" cried Sestriel from the judges' box, Sestriel with his cinnamon-colored staff, topped with a crystal orb.

Fortunato would advance to the next bracket.

~

Spyke was victorious against his opponent, a tall and fearsome brute with a greatsword, a foe much larger than himself. To celebrate their victories, Fortunato offered him a drink.

It was late, and it was at late hours that The Green Girdle was the most alive. Drinks were poured, a beer for Fortunato and a beer for Spyke.

"What is on your mind?" Spyke said. "What have you been

dwelling on, lately?"

"Let me tell you a story," Fortunato said, "about a boy. A dark mountain pass, and a boy clothed in light. He is called *velati sonoren*, the Prince of the Dawn…"

Chapter Fifty-Four: The Weird Sisters

It was Sextil, the last month of summer, and in the Lord Alden's estate on Ammon Lake, the crickets were chirping. Ramona had a glass of wine in her hand, a fine Zarube vintage, and garbed in a small black dress she was wandering about the great hall. She felt she'd grown further and further apart from the Gallian aristocracy, further and further from this crowd, whom over the months and years she'd tried so mightily to impress. She was thinking of other things now, the world writ large… regrets she had, her hot temper.

Alden was on a couch before the fireless hearth, and two girls were at his side, redheaded, called by some the Weird Sisters, Dahlia and Desdemona.

"The Lord Alden has retired with his harem!" thundered the Lord Eventide to riotous laughter.

Ramona knew Alden was a libertine, that he had confounding views on conjugal relationships and thoughts on religion that befuddled, but she supposed she was not one to talk. She and Chalmet were not wed, nor would they ever. Ramona would not wed a servant, the son of servants.

Imagine Ash's fury…

"Life is too short for one woman," said Alden, and he looked to his wife Dora, a doe-eyed creature standing a bit away with a glass of wine in her hands, "or for women, one man."

Dora was speaking quietly to a man Ramona recognized as Alwin, the minister of the exchequer. Ramona repressed a shudder at the thought of something underway between them, Alwin a white-haired man of at least seventy, Dora a woman of average beauty, barely middle aged.

Ramona was already tired of this party, this party on Ammon

Lake, at Alden's estate where she had been several times before.

All was a summer dream, summer's last gasp, and amid the chorus of the crickets, lightning bugs could be seen glowing in the night outside the great hall's windows. Ramona supposed this was her life now — she had come to Galiope, and she would not leave. Parties, soirees — she expected them to continue, regardless of what happened in the war. The Empire looked to keep power in place, and in the west which they had conquered, her former husband Count Elfraine still reigned. So she had heard…

"What do the priests say, Alden?" said Fiona from a corner, teasingly.

"There is such a thing as too much good," Alden said, "just as there is such a thing as too much evil. All in moderation." He pecked Dahlia or Desdemona — Ramona could not tell them apart — on the cheek, and the other again.

All was a summer dream, but summer was ending. All a summer dream, but the Pan-Vardic Games were about over.

War drums… war. A resolution would soon be at hand.

Chapter Fifty-Five: Wand Against Wand

The audience had gathered, and as Bala stepped up to the podium with his wand at hand, he felt, for the first time, after the eleven battles he had participated in, a trace of anxiousness. His little hands were sweating as he embarked on the twelfth and final game, the championship, as his opponent appeared, a man much older than him.

Standing opposite him, at a podium several dozen yards away, he stood also with a wand of crystal. An eldritch gleam was in his dark eyes, and his pale lips quivered. When Bala beheld him, he thought he saw hatred.

"Begin!" cried Sestriel from the judges' box, and they did.

Bala's opponent raised his left hand and sent a volley of sparks; a dozen bursts of light soared in a semicircle to the delighted gasp of the audience, and they exploded in percussive surges before Bala's shield. A shield — as Aleksander had taught him.

This, the championship round, was what would win Bala the Victor's Crown. Everyone who had seen him had been amazed, six years old, a toddler, felling much greater foes than himself.

Bala responded, calling up percussive bolts of his own, withering rays of necromantic energy, purple and black coruscating beams. His opponent met them head on.

Another blast, almost breaking through Bala's shield, white and red — fire and flame. His little robe was singed, but the pain drove Bala forward, giving him energy anew.

He summoned another purple beam, and the man fell back, away from the podium.

"Bala, Victor!" said Sestriel.

Bala had won.

The crowd was cheering in amazement; Sestriel had grown hushed. And in the late summer sun, it dawned on Bala what he had done. He had prevailed over men much older, and much more experienced, than himself.

The Victor's Crown... and perhaps Aleksander would hear. The Victor's Crown... and perhaps his training could resume.

Chapter Fifty-Six: At The End

Gastreel was in a fog, and when he opened his eyes, he did not feel himself. Where was he? His mind wandered. His vision wobbled. He was in a bed… a room he did not recognize. There was a window, outside of it stone buildings. He was in Almania, he remembered, in Alzdorf. Names returned to him… the Great Hoff. Martin Durkheim. Friedrich, the Heer Meister.

He was on a diplomatic mission.

When he pushed the covers off himself his movement was rigid, and his muscles stretched in pain. When he set his feet on the ground, he felt there was no blood flow to them. Breathing itself was an intentional effort now, and when he stood up, he felt he had almost forgotten how to do it. His mind was clouded, his thinking foggy.

When the door to his room opened, a young elf with sandy blond hair and blue eyes stepped in. He was holding in his hand a quarterstaff of red wood.

"Gastreel!" he said.

How did this young man know his name?

"Who are you?" Gastreel said.

The young elf stared at him. "Wrinn," he said.

What was wrong? What was wrong with him? Wrinn Finnis, formerly a slave — they had come here on a diplomatic mission. Friedrich had said they'd give military aid if Galiope gave up its citizen, Ivan Xandrast.

"Wrinn, I'm sorry," Gastreel said. "I don't feel myself… I… I… have we heard back from Galiope yet?"

"We heard back weeks ago," Wrinn said. "They said no — Martin told you we should remain, continue to negotiate.

Remember?"

"No," Gastreel said, "no, I don't." When he thought of the time between now and he and Friedrich's conversation, there was only a long darkness — shadow, an abyssal sea.

There was a knock on the window. A bird was trying to get in. There was a letter clutched in its claws.

"Aleksander!" Gastreel cried.

He rushed toward the window and when he moved his legs, he felt he was moving stone. He felt he was at his last breath; he felt he soon would die.

Chapter Fifty-Seven: Sword and Sword

When Fortunato's challenger for the final match walked past the stands, he felt a lump in his throat.

It was Spyke, Spyke with his board, the man he'd gotten to know over these past few months, and whom he now considered a friend. Spyke, from Perremum, from a distant land, who boasted he was a relative of the current emperor — Spyke, a braggart but one who had the skills to back it up.

Fortunato smiled and hailed him. With Danenhir, lathed in Ink of Atälos, in hand, he made his approach. Spyke smiled in turn.

"Our final battle of the Sword!" called out Sestriel from the judges' booth. "Two remain… Spyke of Perremum, and Fortunato of Ríva."

The audience in the stands began to cheer wildly; some stood on two feet. And sword met board.

From one end of the arena to the other Spyke drove him, the board dripping Ink of Atälos. Fortunato was only barely holding on to Danenhir by the time the volley of blows ended.

Fortunato struck, and struck again, battling with all he had in him, but Spyke's footwork was masterful, his command of the battlefield was inviolable. Fortunato thought of Ambrass, he thought of Nicollo observing him from afar, he thought of everything that could put a fire within and drive him forward. He wanted to win above all else; he wanted to be victorious.

A battering blow sent him to the ground. He rolled to his left and hopped to his feet. He weaved right and struck, and sent Spyke tumbling away. Each blow by Spyke or Fortunato sent the audience in the stands into a cheering frenzy, a deafening roar that shook the earth, but as time went on, more and more the both of them were growing exhausted.

Their strikes were becoming feeble blows; their artful dodges were turning to clumsy fumbles. The Ink of Atälos on Danenhir was leaking in a stream, and Spyke's board was almost cleared of it, when he heard a voice ring out from the judges' booth.

"Gathered gentlemen," said Sestriel's voice, "we have a draw…"

A draw. Fortunato hadn't wanted a draw. But the battle had gone on for a quarter of an hour without any of them striking blows.

He turned to the crowd, scanned the faces more thoroughly than he ever had. He still could not see Ambrass's face. She would not see this victory, or as he saw it, defeat.

Spyke's dark skin was lathed in sweat. He smiled, baring yellowish teeth. "A battle well fought, Fortunato," he said. "I salute you…"

Fortunato had wanted victory; he hadn't wanted to share in the spoils.

But what spoils would there be? He hadn't seen Ambrass's face in the crowd.

~

On podiums they stood, the three victors of the battles of Sword, Wand, and Staff. Fortunato shared the space with Spyke, and together they stood.

The gathered judges were standing there in the light of the summer sun, Sestriel and others, eleven he counted, no, twelve. And he noticed something he hadn't before… in Sestriel's old hands was a new staff, one that was colored white.

"Bala, Victor," Sestriel said, "of the competition of the Wand. Of the three champions here, you cannot go without reward. The

Victor's Crown goes to only one, but two of three receive a prize, and you will not go home empty-handed. We rank your performance second of three. For your skill and might, you will receive a look into the Mirror of Antarim, by which you may glean visions of a future."

Bala frowned; it seemed he had wanted the Victor's Crown above all.

Sestriel looked to the third podium, inset with a picture of a staff. There a wizard stood in blue robes, young, perhaps Fortunato's age — the victor in the battles of magic.

"Ahron of Blue Robes, your performance was remarkable," Sestriel said, "but in the end we were most impressed not by the powers of the arcane, but by the grit and determination of two others... Spyke and Fortunato.

"The Sword prevails, and the Victor's Crown is awarded unto them."

A victory seemed hollow to Fortunato when he had to share it.

That, however, wasn't what he was thinking of.

The war would soon resume, and he hoped the aid that the council had gathered would be enough.

War drums, war... and Sestriel's staff.

Sestriel's staff... where had Fortunato seen it before?

Chapter Fifty-Eight: The Plot

Gastreel raised the window with his weak hands and allowed the bird to fly in. In the midst of the room, it flapped its wings, hovering, and deposited the letter onto the ground.

The letter was sealed in a wax seal, a mortar and pestle and skull — the sign of Aleksander Ivic, Bala's teacher. He stooped down at great effort, and let it unravel.

"Gastreel," the letter read, "I bring you grave news. Sestriel and the other members of the Wizards Council have turned against you. They long have. They have been plotting against you since you left the city. They have over you a spell of Degeneration. Try using your magic powers! Escape the spell before it is too late!"

Gastreel let the letter fall from his cold, deathlike hands. His entire body was rigid, not just his sense of the Weave. He tried to call up magic. He tried to summon up energy.

All that happened in return was a vision in his mind's eye, red lips, a curse. *Thou fool!*

Chapter Fifty-Nine: The Victor's Crown

Fortunato and Spyke were at the topmost floor of the Tower, and where Spyke seemed relatively interested, Fortunato was eager to get back to what mattered, the war.

Before them in the black chamber was a gold pedestal, on which was set a glass orb.

Sestriel and the eleven others were with them amid the austere yet grand surroundings.

"Fortunato, Spyke," said Sestriel, and as he spoke a glowing image of a crown appeared in his left palm, "you will now learn something that only winners of the Victor's Crown know. It is a prize, but it is also an obligation. When you accept the Victor's Crown you are committing to a lifetime of service, a lifetime of service to the wizards. You are pledging your sword to the All-Seeing Eye. You will be paid and well tended-to. You will not have to worry about sustenance ever again. But it is an obligation… an oath of service."

Fortunato stared at Sestriel a while, amazed at first, and then incensed.

"I would," said Spyke, "but my friend Fortunato has taught me about something that truly matters. A boy clothed in light in a mountain pass, six phantoms stricken to ash. I will serve him; I will not serve you."

Rage flashed in Sestriel's eyes. "The penalty for refusal is death," he said, and as the air in the chamber changed, Fortunato realized he recognized a face in the crowd, a woman's face — Ariya, whom he'd thought Gastreel had stricken dead in the snow.

He drew Danenhir. He would fight to his last breath.

Chapter Sixty: Unmasked

Gastreel cried out. He summoned all his strength. He cried, and he raised his fists, and struggled against the spell of Degeneration that had been at work in him for many months. That spell had lain into him; it had sunk its claws deep, and it had withered away not just his attachment to the weave but his physical body and his mind.

He cried out again, resisted the spell, as Wrinn Finnis looked on.

At last, he invoked the gods, and with a mighty shout, felt the weave course through him once more.

~

The shadowy face was before him, shadow and two red eyes. As he broke the spell and shattered it in twain, he saw there were other faces too, others — dark and crimson, among them Lydia and Elothiel. Shadow faded — red eyes turned to green and blue and brown. Faces turned to human colors, and Sestriel was standing in a dark space, his mouth agape and foaming.

There was the sound of shattering glass.

Chapter Sixty-One: All-Seeing No More

The glass orb exploded, and when it did a few wizards fainted, others fell back, and Sestriel was standing upright, motionless and stunned.

"What happened?" Fortunato said.

"Come," Spyke said. "Let's flee… let's fight, for Gallia, for the gods, for the Prince of the Dawn!"

Chapter Sixty-Two: The Mirror of Antarim

A nice wizard lady had taken Bala up a steep flight of stairs, and, guiding him by the hand, shown him through a magic door that dissipated into fiery wheels, to a chamber wherein there was a mirror. "Bala," said the woman, garbed in a white robe. "Look, and do not resist."

Bala stepped forward, and, adjusting his top hat, did just that.

In the room's faint light, at first, there was nothing, but as he stared into the mirror's cloudy glass, images seemed to appear, images that could have been faint shadows. He focused on those shadows, as shadows became shapes, shapes became figures, and darkness turned to color in his mind's eye.

~

There was a figure clothed in light, standing by the shores of the sea, in his hand a stringed instrument, and about him a snake coiled.

There were people in the snow, vampires like Bala fixing flags to flagpoles, battle standards — the insignia of a sun and tree.

There was Dada, his real Dada, on a sickbed, his body covered in spots, his eyes cloudy, his breath faint.

And there was a purple face, with yellow teeth like a donkey, and a pickle nose, an image that seemed to stink though there was no scent, but speaking in a beautiful woman's voice: "I am coming for you, Balor, King of the Elves."

Bala screamed and began to cry. He resisted at last, and the images had stopped. All he was left with was the feeling that his work over the months had been for naught, that he hadn't won the

Victor's Crown, that he hadn't impressed Aleksander after all.

All he wanted was his training to restart… that was all he wanted in the world.

Chapter Sixty-Three: Back to Business

Gastreel marched through the Great Hoff with fury, anger now with clarity. The spell of Degeneration was gone, and the weave was all about him. Wrinn followed a step behind.

His staff… Martin and Friedrich had taken his staff, and amid the dark spell in his cloudy thinking he hadn't acted on it. A moment longer, a little while later, and the spell would have been complete; Gastreel's weave would be gone, and he would be an easy target to kill, even by someone like Martin.

In the throne room, he saw them — Martin, Friedrich, Freya.

And when he appeared in his fullness, with strength returning to his bones, he saw fear in Martin and Freya's eyes, and alarm in Friedrich's.

"Lord Wizard!" Martin said. "How good it is to see you."

"Bring me my staff! At once!" said Gastreel. "Else, this will be the last day you see."

Martin gave a nervous smile. "Of course," he said, "at once."

He left the throne and walked off, down some dark corridor.

Friedrich strode forward, and as he did the coins in his coinpurse jingled. "Lord Wizard," he said, "is something wrong?"

"You know what is wrong, Friedrich," Gastreel said, "you of a forked tongue."

Wrinn stepped forward, bearing his quarterstaff, and from the light of some doorway a young woman appeared, one who'd been oft seen in Wrinn's presence, the elven maiden Rosalie.

"Aren't you going to continue our negotiations?" Friedrich said. "We want to get to yes."

"The spell is broken, Friedrich," said Gastreel. "There is no reason anymore to delay, or keep me here. You failed."

Friedrich gulped. In the corner, Rosalie sprinted away.

Friedrich placed a hand on the hilt of his sword. From the darkness Martin emerged, and one was with him, a wizard in red clothing and a red pointed hat, his mercenary, he of the red robes, Radobod.

In Radobod's hand was a staff of midnight black. But that was the only staff Gastreel saw.

In Martin's hands was a sword, Gastreel's sword, Maderias, and it looked a little worse for the wear. It had not been polished or sharpened in all these months, and Gastreel wondered if someone had used it, or dulled it down.

"Lord Wizard," said Martin, the grand duke, and no longer the timid sheep was he, but the crafty serpent. "Your sword. It has been in our safekeeping. You may have it back, as you have been promised."

"My staff," Gastreel intoned. "Where is my staff?"

"Your staff has been misplaced," said Martin. "I am sorry. We do not have it."

"Liar!" Gastreel thundered. "You take me for a fool!"

He turned to Radobod, in whose dark eyes the eldritch gleam of the weave was growing. Gastreel struck first, before a shield could be made, and the bolt of lightning and thunder pierced him, overwhelming him, stunning him and blackening him into death.

"A staff!" Gastreel cried. "Yours will do…"

He summoned Radobod's staff into his hand, and from Martin's paws summoned Maderias, his sword.

"Lord Wizard," Martin squeaked. "I–"

"Silence, worm!" Gastreel shouted. "I condemn you to death…"

His sword-strike was lathed in lightning, and lightning was dancing about the metal of Maderias when it pierced Martin's heart, sinking into his flesh like a hot knife through butter.

Freya howled and bolted away, into the darkness. Friedrich

swept his sword from his sheath and struck.

Wrinn joined the battle, and for many blows it seemed Friedrich might prevail. Then Wrinn delivered a mighty strike, and in that instant Gastreel pushed him back with a mighty gout of force. Friedrich stumbled back and fell, and his coin purse fell loose from his belt.

Coins spilled out, hundreds of gold coins, on the obverse the face of the emperor, on the reverse a temple. Imperial coins…

In all this time, the Almanians had been bought off. *What a fool I had been,* Gastreel thought. *No… the spell led me astray.*

Lightning was striking, and rain was pouring down. The night was deeply dark, and the stars could not be seen because of the clouds. In the Great Hoff's yard Wrinn forced his way into the stables, and procured Ivy, and procured Noble.

"Here," Wrinn said. "Our horses…"

"Wrinn," said Gastreel, "we go into danger. If peril falls upon me, flee. Take the Sage, protect him. That is your duty."

"Of course," Wrinn replied.

~

Gastreel was mounted on Ivy, trotting toward the gate. Wrinn had one hand on Noble's reins, and the other hand on the saddle. He was preparing to mount the horse when out of the doors of the Great Hoff another came running, lithe, slender, beautiful…

"Rosalie!"

She ran up to him in the pouring rain and blazing lightning. She laid her hands about his waist and kissed him firmly on the lips. "Wrinn!" she said. "I love you."

"I know you do."

"Let me come with you," she said. "Let me run away with you.

I don't care if we aren't married… you gave me this."

From her pocket she produced the daisy that had served as their engagement ring.

"No, no, Rosalie," Wrinn said. "Where I'm going you can't go. I go into danger. I may not survive. I won't put you in danger. It won't happen!

"But if I live, and you live, and the gods see fit, maybe we will see each other again."

He mounted Noble to Rosalie's agonized cries. He heard her weeping and wailing as he rode into the darkness, toward Alzdorf's gate.

Chapter Sixty-Four: Courier

It was night, and clouds were moving in, veiling and unveiling the moon, when there was a thunderous knock on the front door of Sunstone Manor. Ramona, upstairs reading, adjusted her fur-trimmed cloak that was keeping her warm on this cool night. She had been on a good chapter; she was learning with intent of the life of Ash's ancestor Cordeleon, and Cordeleon had just been crowned king.

She hurried down the grand staircase, to the great hall where Ash was playing with some whirly-topped gizmo that Chalmet had bought for him. She laid her hands on the knobs and swept the door open, to see a figure in the darkness, in the rain.

It was a city servant, one whose plain face Ramona thought she had seen before, in a blue robe and a blue cap. He was holding an envelope in his hand.

"Lady Nax," he said.

She still preferred "Countess Bensange."

"The council has asked of you something," he said, "Lord Alden more specifically. He asks that you deliver this package to a courier tonight, at Thelamar Fortress. It is imperative to the war effort."

"Wha– Why?" Ramona began.

Vespers had already rung – it had to be eight hours after noon.

"Alden asks that you come alone."

Thelamar was several hours' ride away – she'd not be there until midnight.

"You must be joking," said Ramona.

"I'm afraid not," the messenger replied. "Come alone… and tell no one of this."

Ramona took the envelope in her hands, and she could feel some foreign object within its paper folds. As rain continued to pour, and the doors shut, she was baffled.

A figure had been watching from the grand staircase – Chalmet.

~

"I suppose I must do this," Ramona said. "I took an oath…"

Chalmet in the flickering light of the hearth reached for the envelope, but Ramona resisted.

"The road there is lonely," Chalmet said. "There are highwaymen, bandits. Remember the tales of the Illothian Clan? Remember what happened to the Lady Esterley?"

"I cannot break my oath to the city," said Ramona. "And if they've asked of me this…"

"Let me come with you, my sweet."

"He said to go alone…"

"That's an unreasonable thing to ask," Chalmet said.

"Perhaps," Ramona replied. "Perhaps…"

~

With oiled cloaks they rode astride horses, doing what Alden and presumably the council willed. They left in the dark, in the rain and in the storm, down the lonely road, which by the time the journey began had grown muddy. Thelamar Fortress… it had long been abandoned, last used when Jerek the false Dark One's Hand had held court.

Chapter Sixty-Five: Telantis Awakened

Alzdorf was behind Gastreel and Wrinn, and they were venturing down the mountain roads, descending toward the flatlands. The Grand Duke had been killed, the Durkheim family had been dealt a mortal blow, and the craven behavior had put to shame their claim *Teli Telantari Indion.*

The feeble dominion of Martin was no Telantari Kingdom.

They did not have the glory of the Telantines in them, no – they who had been bought off by the Empire, they whose souls had been purchased by coins and promises of peace.

No, now Gastreel and Wrinn alone rode into war, empty handed but for one thing… the knowledge that the Telantines endured.

Reev Nax was descended from them, the great… on his father's and on his mother's side the Sage was *telantari.* So the prophecies had said…

Chapter Sixty-Six:
To Live or Die

The ground had ascended, and Ramona's horse was breathing roughly, and rain had turned to flakes of snow, when the ruined Thelamar Fortress appeared. The envelope was in her hand, and as she made the last few strides, at a time that was surely past midnight, Ramona envisioned what she'd say at council the next day. Perhaps, she'd demand a salary for partaking in the Council of War, though members were supposed to be of wealth, and money was meant to be of no consequence to them.

"Look!" Chalmet said.

And at the base of Thelamar Fortress, a tower whose top was faced like a skull, there was light – orange light cast against stone. Ramona followed that light in the night darkness, as the snow began to abate, the cloud cover to weaken, and the bluish moonlight cast all in an eerie glow.

~

As Ramona began to trot toward the light, across the snow-covered ground, she drew her oiled cloak a bit tighter, and was tempted to pray as a bit of anxiety assailed her, though what god would listen to her now, after the life she had led?

Chalmet was riding ahead of her. He had a sword clipped to his side, the sword Ash's father had given to his son, Oathblade.

The moonlight led her on. When she breathed, her breath was fog in the icy air. Up above, the mountains were dark shadows, titanic black shapes.

Chalmet gave a cry; his horse reared up on his hind legs. And Ramona saw it.

She drew near.

The light was coming from candles, black candles, thirteen in number, sitting on the body of a woman. That woman's lush red hair was falling to the ground in a cascade, part of it covering her breasts, but the rest of her could be seen, even her inmost parts.

It was Dahlia – or was it Desdemona? One of Alden's paramours… The Weird Sisters.

The other of the Weird Sisters approached from the shadows, hiding her nude body with a cloth. She was walking barefoot in the snow.

"What is this?" Ramona cried.

It all reminded her of what she had found in Jauchevin Ballens's house, the black candles thirteen in number. Jauchevin Ballens — the witch that the king in the west had executed, and whom she'd later found had been Elfraine's lover.

"I told you to come alone," said a voice, a voice she knew, but which she had never known in this way.

In the snow another emerged, male, Alden, also unclothed, barefoot amid the cold. His body was lithe and fit, and now bare to see. Ramona noted tattoos on his left bicep and his left groin, the symbol of two snakes biting each other.

"Alden," Ramona cried.

"I told you to come alone," he said. "It is no matter."

From the darkness there was a sword; Chalmet was pierced straight through, and fell dead from his horse. Another sword-blow, and his horse collapsed silently into the snow.

Ramona dismounted and prepared to run away, but Alden rushed forward and kicked her to the ground. Then she saw who had killed Chalmet.

~

If he was a man, he was the tallest of all men. If he was a man, or had ever been one, he walked with ghostly grace. The sword he wielded was dark in color and dripped with Chalmet's blood.

His cloak was so black it seemed to drain all light. And Ramona could not see his face for it was hidden by an iron mask.

Ramona cried out.

"Open the envelope," Alden said. "Open the envelope, if you know what's good for you…"

Ramona was transfixed, and as she looked at the being in the iron mask, she saw there were five others, mounted on creatures much larger than horses, whose wolf-like muzzles she could see, and whose eyes glowed red like candles in the dark.

"Open it!" Alden hissed.

And Ramona, weeping, looking to Chalmet's lifeless body in despair, used her shaking fingers to tear open the envelope, in which was what looked like a needle.

She let it drop to the snow.

"See?" Alden said. "All we want… a drop of blood."

There was something in the distance – a cauldron set on coals.

"A drop of Telantine blood, the missing ingredient in our brew," Alden said. "Hemlock and basilisks' venom, devils' honey and death cap. The water in which a murderer washed his hands – and a drop of Telantine blood. A poison brewed to kill the Sage."

"If I do it," Ramona cried, weeping, "will you let me alone…"

A darting shadow raced toward her, a shadow twice the height and thrice the girth of her horse. The tall being in the mask grabbed the creature by its collar, a collar forged of iron, and now the monstrous creature was bathed in light.

Like a dog, or like a wolf it was, a muzzle that could slay a horse in one bite. Its eyes were dead and featureless, yet glowed with a sulphureous hue.

"*Hungry*," the being in the iron mask said, his voice like a whisper, like the wind.

"We cannot let the appetite of Mephis spoil our plans," said Alden. He looked to the Weird Sister standing upright. She drew near, prancing across the snow.

"You have a task now, my sweet," Alden said, and was met in a lustful, passionate kiss. "A task," he said, "and the Master will reward you when he wins.

"Sate Mephis's hunger with your flesh… Do it, Dahlia."

And Dahlia laid down, and the being in the iron mask let free the collar. The monstrous beast lurched toward her, and Dahlia laughed in delight – a cry of joy at first, but pain and terror in the end – a wail, and Ramona looked away, unable to bear the sight, but her face was sprayed with blood and flesh.

The monstrous beast lunged at Ramona, but the being in the iron mask gave a shout, and it withdrew to the shadows. *"Glutton,"* the being whispered.

"If I do this," Ramona said, "will you let me alone? Will you allow me to live?"

"Yes," said Alden, but what was the promise of a worshipper of Seymus? What was the word of a man who served the Dark One?

She had no choice.

Ramona followed Alden to the cauldron, bubbling on coals, and took the small needle in her hands. She cut her index finger with the pointed tip and watched the liquid flare and glow, purple, red, at last black.

A poison to kill the Sage – they must have meant Reev. What had she done to her nephew? What had she done?

She looked back and saw that others were in the shadows, beside the devoured remnants of Dahlia, men and women, young and old, and Alden among them. They were kissing the iron mask of the tall being, giving unto him their worship and reverence.

Ramona was appalled… appalled and stricken. Young, old, men, women, dozens in sight, servants of the Dark One in the mortal world. Had they been her friends, neighbors? Among them were there members of the Council of War?

She looked to the body of Chalmet and despaired. "Let me live!" she cried with tears in her eyes. "Let me live!"

Chapter Sixty-Seven: The Answer Is No

The sky was red over Galiope, and Bala was in his booth at the Dragonpaw, dour.

He was looking out the window into City Square, when he saw a few dozen wizards on horses ride by. They were like jets of color soaring past, blue, brown, white, green, and most prominently orange.

Bala left his bowl of milk and hurried outside, into the cool air.

~

He'd made it only a few steps when he saw one he knew, and his heart surged in anticipation when he saw who it was, a man tall and thin, in black robes, carrying in his hands a feathered staff. A hawk was perched on his shoulder. He was riding on a gray horse.

"Mr. Aleksander!" Bala wailed. "Mr. Aleksander!"

The lanky, misshapen man looked in Bala's direction, and Bala waddled up to him.

"Mr. Aleksander!" he said, and their gazes met.

"Bala," he said softly, deeply, darkly.

"Did you hear I made second place in the games?" Bala said.

Aleksander seemed to be looking past him, not at him. His shoulders were slumped; he radiated grief.

"Can we start my training now?" Bala said.

"I… I am sorry, Bala," Aleksander said. "I am sorry, I cannot be your teacher."

"Not now?" Bala said.

Aleksander's eyes seemed to dim.

"Not ever?" Bala said.

"I am sorry," Aleksander said, "the wizards have again turned to folly. I am sorry I cannot be your teacher. I am sorry, Bala, that I made promises which I could not keep…"

He rode off into the red morning.

Chapter Sixty-Eight: For a Friend or Two

Reev, in the safe-house, knelt down to pray at dawn. The skies were red, and the wind that was blowing through his window was cool, with a hint of autumn on its edge.

He knelt down to pray at dawn, but he could not find the words to say; they seemed swallowed up in the early morning air. He could say and do nothing, and he had not heard from Gastreel, and war-drums were beating, and it seemed to Reev that Gallia's doom was sure.

There was a knock on the door.

He got up and adjusted his tunic. He would not endure another council meeting, no – such efforts seemed pointless.

He opened the door, expecting a plate of food, but instead there was another – no, two others.

It was Fortunato, his friend, and a man about Fortunato's age, swarthy, with dark hair. There was something at the man's back, a metal board with a sharp edge.

"Is this him?" said the swarthy man.

"Yes, it is, Spyke," Fortunato said. He looked to Reev's eyes.

"Reev," Fortunato said, "we are going to war. The Empire's forces are massing at the Eastern Leah… we are going to meet them in battle. Spyke wanted to know… do we have the Sage's blessing?"

Reev paused, and thought, and searched his heart, for the moving of the holy gods. He felt nothing, no inclination, only the feeling of danger, of imminent disaster that he had felt for months. "Yes," he said, for Fortunato's sake, and for Spyke's. "Yes, you do."

And he hoped that Fortunato and Spyke would go bravely and boldly into battle. He hoped they would prevail. But his greatest desire as he watched them disappear into the brush was that they survive, Fortunato, and Spyke too. He hoped they would do whatever was necessary for them to escape with their lives.

He shut the door, and when he thought to pray, he had words now – words, and desires.

Chapter Sixty-Nine:
The Battle of The Eastern Leah

In the wind wildflowers were dancing, and in the cooling air mist was rising, amid the green expanse called the Eastern Leah. Fortunato, on Tyra Jade, was riding while others were marching. Lord Eventide was marching, and Spyke was walking along, to his left and to his right, and behind him and about him were the allies which the Council of War had shrewdly summoned.

From the Wilderlands, Chieftain Bairbock had padded the Gallians' numbers, a thousand slingers and a thousand peasant-archers. The council's paeans to freedom and liberty had stirred him to action, from his fort in Dunning Marrow.

From Dorenzia came the landgrave Wilmar, with him a hundred knights fully armed and armored, and five-hundred peasant soldiers. In his aid, freely given, he had disobeyed his liege.

From the North Country came a thousand freedom fighters, warriors only in name, mercenaries from Hammond and Terrence and Dunway totaling several hundred, and from Kav came the most noble Vlad the Voivode, with him two-thousand Kavan Knights and eight-hundred peasant soldiers. The Kavan Knights' pointed helms shimmered in the sun, and the points of their spears glistened.

Combined with Gallia's native forces, about eight-thousand were marching to meet the Empire, here, on the Eastern Leah, where the fate of the North would be decided. Here, on the Eastern Leah, the forces of freedom and liberty would fight, and in all this time in the war, Fortunato of Ríva had never felt better.

Fortunato drew Danenhir, and when he drew Danenhir the

polished blade flashed in the sun, and when he drew Danenhir one appeared from among the mist like a ghost, a man astride a white horse, in armor.

"Niccolo," Fortunato said, and his voice carried across the vast fields.

Niccolo's cold blue eyes seemed incapable of glistening. Bright yet shark-like they were, as if there was no soul behind them.

"We have brought our allies," Fortunato said.

"So have we," Niccolo said.

From the mist the Imperial army arrived, a legion in its entirety, the soldiers in their metal breastplates and shining helms carrying red-and-gold eagle standards aloft. To their sides, and about them, Fortunato saw what allies they had brought. The Empire had not wasted time as the Pan-Vardic Games endured; they had done just what the Council of War had done, and with their infinite resources, they had done better.

On their left flank were auxiliaries, southrons – men dressed in scale-mail armor with spears and scimitars, and mounted horse-archers with turbans on their heads. On their right flank were auxiliaries from the conquered north – knights and men-at-arms, peasant soldiers bearing flags, a white ring against a purple field... the forces of the Black Count, whose betrayal had been instrumental in the king in the west's fall. To them were added on the periphery, jungle cats held by chains, hundreds of soldiers with round shields and spears, a force of bare-chested barbarians heaving great-axes in their hands, and many more Fortunato could not see.

Most fearsome, and terrifying to him, were things he could only see in the mist – shadowy shapes he knew, but which the Gallians surely didn't. Immense beasts, only shapes now but not for long, behind the visible soldiers – elephants, with towers on their backs. They were the size of castles.

"For the gods," Eventide said, turning to his men. He bore a great flail in his hands. "For the liberty of the Gallian people, and for the liberty of all. For the survival of the North. For the exile, and for all our people."

Gallian horns blew and the Gallians charged. Imperial trumpets sounded and the Imperial soldiers locked shields and extended their swords.

Eventide met them with a flail-strike, and Fortunato joined the battle. Would it be the last battle of his life?

~

The sun had burned away the mist, and heat was rising, and they were still fighting.

Eventide with his flail had struck many dead, but the battle at the Eastern Leah had come to a draw. Tyra Jade had endured many cuts and bruises, and she had whimpered and whined. Fortunato had been bashed and bruised, and sliced on the arm and on the leg, but three Imperials were dead by his hand, and that was no small thing. The thickness of the afternoon warmth was growing, casting all in a spell, and both sides were growing tired, when Fortunato instinctively drew backward.

Eventide was swinging that flail of his, mightily, at the Imperial lines, breaking their shields every time he did. He was invoking the gods, Heron and Alabaster, Amara and Maribel, when he was approached from behind by a Gallian soldier in quilted jack armor, carrying a spear.

Fortunato looked on, transfixed, as the Gallian soldier – one of their own – raced forward, and, heaving the spear in his hands, pierced Eventide, straight through the back.

Fortunato cried out, amazed, terrified, as Eventide sank bleeding to the ground. The Gallian traitor ran off, disappearing into the crowds of soldiers, and the crowds of soldiers did not take notice of him until he was long gone, but Fortunato had.

"Eventide!" a voice cried. "Eventide!"

"Eventide!" another wailed.

And the once steely hearts of the Gallian Army began to melt, and doom seemed writ all about them. The Imperial soldiers, once patient and stone-hearted, began to aggressively advance.

~

Elephants bowled the Gallian soldiers over with their tusks, and on their backs from their towers southron archers shot their bows. Tigers lunged at them with their teeth, and Imperial soldiers, maniples and cohorts, slowly but relentlessly culled their numbers.

Eventide… Eventide…

It was not honorable to flee. It was not honorable to run away. It was not the soldiers' way, or Fortunato's way. But he had a task, one more important than Gallia, one to which he felt he held the key. *Reev Nax, the Prince of the Dawn…*

How long would Fortunato endure this? How long would he fight?

~

By the time evening came, the Gallian Army had disintegrated, splitting into a dozen parts, having dealt the Empire a great deal of damage but no mortal blow. In the night, Spyke and Fortunato and about a hundred men found each other. Their thoughts were not of the war but of something else, a boy clothed in light, six phantoms burnt to ash in a mountain pass.

Chapter Seventy:
The Vote

Eventide had died – and Ramona didn't care.

Eventide had died, the army defeated handily – but that was the least of Ramona's concerns. The war was lost, and the city was in an uproar… doom and death, but Ramona hadn't a thought about it, for what she had seen was much worse than defeat in battle or the ruin of a nation.

She had seen Alden Grayhaupt for what he was.

The sun was rising, the day after the defeat in Eastern Leah, and Ramona was still in bed, not daring to leave, hoping against hope that what she had endured, in the night, had been a nightmare and nothing more. Yet the wound on her index finger was clearly visible, and the terror of her journey back home was a powerful bugbear.

She told Ash that Chalmet had quit.

Chalmet… poor Chalmet. He had insisted he come along. He had tried to protect her. In the end, the only thing he had done was have himself killed, and grieve Ramona's heart.

Through the doors of her bedroom, Guy appeared. "Milady," he said, "there is someone at the door."

"Tell them I'm not here," said Ramona.

"It is someone of the council," Guy said.

Ramona gave an exasperated gasp. She supposed she had to answer it now.

~

After hurrying into a black chemise, she rushed down the grand staircase, to the door which was hanging open slightly. She opened it, and there, before her, was terror and death.

There was a city servant, dressed in blue robes and a blue cap. But to his right was one she knew, one she wished she had never known, one whose sight caused her to fall back, and blood to swell to her head. She hung onto the doorknob and managed not to faint.

It was one of the Weird Sisters, Desdemona – the young woman who hadn't been eaten. Her lush red hair fell down her back, and on her face was a wicked smile. She was holding something in her hands.

"A mandatory council meeting," said Desdemona, "at *tridium*. I think it is in your best interest, Lady Nax, if you vote in the affirmative to Alden's proposition.

"Also, I think this is yours…"

And she handed Ramona what she was holding, Ash's father's sword, Oathblade, speckled with blood spatter… Chalmet's blood. And she fainted in truth.

~

She came to, panting. She busied herself about the house. She cleaned Oathblade in water from the well, and hung it up back where it belonged, on the mantle above the hearth. She drank water, and she drank water mixed with wine. She found she couldn't eat. She was too afraid.

She was in the dining hall when Ash appeared. "Go to your room!" she howled. "Lock your doors! Do not go in or out!"

The force of her voice seemed to drive Ash away, and he scurried off like a mouse frightened in the dark.

She heard it – the bells ringing *tridium*.

~

Anxious faces were in the city, people hurrying about their

business, the faces of a people doomed. Ramona overheard as she walked people talking.

"They're a mile away!" said a peddler.

"They've taken Estenberry and Southkirk!" said a young man in the street.

At last, she arrived in Middletown, surrounded by guards, her hands covered in cold sweat, her breathing faint, her head lightheaded and dizzy. The doors to the Townhall opened, and she entered unto the chamber.

~

Alden and eighteen other faces greeted her. Rivien, the Lord of Horse, was nowhere to be seen, nor was the Lady Fiona. The Lady Llewyn of Leyshaw was standing by her lectern, ashen-faced.

A priest was standing in the center of the Townhall, a priest in a brown frock, brown speckled with gray. As Ramona arrived, the last of all, he began to give his invocation.

"Master hear us," he said, "and prevail. Give to us the power of the holy gods, and bring to us success and victory. So let it be…"

"So let it be," some said and some didn't, and Ramona remained silent, for she did not know what master this priest was speaking of.

Alden spoke. "Men and women of the council," he said, "twin tragedies greet us. The Lord Eventide has fallen in battle, and the Lady Fiona has taken ill and died. In life they were one; their hearts were bound. Their destinies were tied together. How fitting that at the same time they go to the grave."

Ramona would have loved to talk to the mortician who cared for Fiona's body, and now, she was suspicious of Eventide's death. Yet she was fully cowed, and she knew not only she but also Ash was in danger.

"Men and women of the council," Alden said, "the defeat at

the Eastern Leah is a terrible loss, but not one that can't be overcome with strength and wisdom. In a time of such emergency, there is precedent – "

"Where is Lord Rivien?" intoned the Lady Llewyn of Leyshaw.

"He is sick," Alden said, and he lifted a piece of parchment paper, "but he gave us this letter. He wishes to give me, Alden Grayhaupt, emergency powers until this war is ended. There is precedent – there is precedent…"

There were scattered mumblings.

"You wish to be a king?" said the Lady Llewyn of Leyshaw.

"Only until the war is ended," Alden said. "The Empire is at our doorstep, and the council though wise is full of bickering. Decisions must be made at one instant or another. In war, one is often better than nineteen."

The Lady Llewyn of Leyshaw mumbled something.

But the air in the council was one of desperation, the defeat and imminent danger threatening to overcome all. The Empire at their doorstep… Eventide fallen, and Fiona dead. Terror oft caused rash decisions, and caused the weak to flock into the arms of the strong.

Alden, not strong, but crafty…

"As the Lord Rivien is incapacitated," said the Lord Alden, "and Eventide dead, I am the premier member of the council. The task of emergency powers falls to me. Let us take a vote."

The clerk stepped forward. "Yeas, raise your hands."

They all raised their hands, eighteen. Ramona thought of Ash, stricken dead. She thought of what happened to Chalmet happening to him. She raised her own hand weakly, and the clerk shouted, "The motion is carried… all the powers of the council are given unto Alden, until such time as the war is ended…"

Chapter Seventy-One:
A Weapon, Formed

Reev was in the safe-house by the window one lonely afternoon, under the blue sky. He was thinking of Gastreel, and above all of Wrinn. He was dreaming of leaving, dreaming of another place… a better country. He was thinking of Nenré in her veils of white.

The door to the safe-house opened. A guard walked in.

"Mr. Nax," said the guard, "the safe-house has been discovered. If you will, I ask that you come with us."

Reev hadn't heard at all from the outside world; he'd been shut in, not going in or out, and hadn't been summoned to the council in many days. He was surprised his location had been discovered, unless another had revealed it.

He clipped Doomblade to his belt and dusted off his tunic. He found he was hungry, and a bit tired in the late afternoon.

In the warmth of the early autumn air, he departed, surrounded by guards. The city in the distance looked different now, a place not of light and hope but of shadow. He walked, and as he did he began to utter prayers… prayers that they'd soon depart, that Gastreel would come home and spirit him away.

~

Through Godsgate they walked, and Reev found it odd that they were entering the city. The safe-house having been discovered, he would have thought another rural location would be best to hide him away. But perhaps, there was another more anonymous place amid the urban sprawl of Galiope.

Through Cathedral District he walked, and as he passed a

quaint stone church, he could hear a dirge playing amid the pews. People were staring at him, monks, nuns, priests, lay-people, as he marched down High Street flanked by guards.

They walked across the Bridge-Oe'r-Galios, the waters of the Galios River sparkling in the early autumn sun, when he began to get a terrible feeling.

The coin of his necklace was glistening in the sun – he began to get restless. He stopped his walk, said, "I want to go back!"

But the guards, for the first time he remembered, did not obey him.

"I want to go back!" he said.

And he moved in that direction, south, but a guard grabbed him with his gauntleted hands, and began to drag him down the street.

"What is this?" Reev cried. "What is this?"

He was dragged, resisting, through the crowds, as Cathedral District became Middletown and Middletown became a squalid urban sprawl. He was dragged, resisting with all he had in him, into the midst of an empty City Square, totally bereft of people.

The guards tossed him to the tile ground. They began to clear the area. And Reev, in the early autumn light, stood up stunned, as from a side street a man came running, a man carrying a dagger dripping black liquid.

The man was upon him an instant.

The first blow struck the coin of his necklace. The second blow grazed his neck. The third blow pierced his groin, and Reev staggered backward, breathless, ill.

His vision was turning cloudy, darkening quickly. His muscles were growing rigid and paralyzed.

Xan came running – yes, Xan — and with his butterfly blade beheaded Reev's assassin before he could run away.

Another step – another staggering step.

Sickness… and all went black.

Chapter Seventy-Two: Mighty Men

Days had passed, days and nights, and they blended together, for in the daylight and the evening Gastreel and Wrinn rode, and they hardly slept.

In the spare hours Gastreel managed to shut his eyes, he thought of Reev – his task, his true task, the cause against Seymus. Where was Reev? Did he yet draw breath? Fortunato… had he fallen to the Empire?

In the North Country, he heard from travelers along the road that the Gallian Army had suffered a stunning defeat at the hands of the Empire, a devastating loss — and that Eventide had perished in battle. As they drew near Hammond and Terrence, he heard from passersby that the Lord Alden had seized emergency powers, and was guiding the war effort by an iron fist.

Gastreel knew they rode into danger. It was late afternoon, turning to dusk, and he and Wrinn were two days, perhaps three, outside Galiope. They had come to a tavern by the road, one Gastreel recognized, The Tabard. And before him, in the dusky light, was a panoply of color.

White, gold, he saw, starry and garbed in moons… wizards, all of them bearing staffs, and at the head of them Sestriel the Orange, gripping Gastreel's staff in his hands — the Staff of the Archwizard.

Ivy reared up onto her hind legs. Sestriel's eyes gleamed, and in them appeared a green hue.

"Gastreel," the Orange Wizard said, "we thought you would use this road. *Thou fool…*"

"Run, Wrinn! Fly!" Gastreel said, and Wrinn galloped away, for he knew his purpose, *adari*, the Sage's helper.

Gastreel's eyes were fixed on his opponent… no, his

opponents.

He peered into Sestriel's eyes. "Sestriel," he said. "You have my staff... you took it from my possession. Who gave it you?"

Sestriel snarled. "As was agreed... the Empire in their astuteness has made a deal with us, the wise. I shall be made Archwizard – we shall help them. And in the coming centuries, the Empire has agreed to respect the boundaries of the tower and the city which they will soon control. Your position as Archwizard was made by falsity and force, and is invalid — as we, those gathered here, have agreed. Eventide forced you onto the council. Eventide — curse his memory."

"The council cannot rule by eleven," said Gastreel. "It is the Council of the Twelve."

"Ariya has donned the Green, and will take your place," said Sestriel. "All gathered here agree... and you have been declared a renegade. The penalty is death."

Gastreel dismounted from Ivy, clucked and sent her away. He gripped his newfound staff in his hand, the staff that had once belonged to Radobod.

Carefully, quietly, he drew up a shield, for he knew that soon a volley of acid awaited him, a volley from Sestriel, an oxymancer.

He backed off as Ivy trotted away.

"Gastreel, fool," said Sestriel, "you destroyed the All-Seeing Orb. Death is what you will get, but you deserve something far worse. Death — it is too good for you."

Gastreel took a new step back. He drew in a cold breath.

He had destroyed the All-Seeing Orb, an ancient artifact, and no longer could the wizards call themselves the All-Seeing Eye, but now the Arcane Eye again, instead. Gastreel had dealt them a blow, and their prestige would not recover. The fault lay with them; they had used the All-Seeing Orb to strengthen their spell of Degeneration.

"You have betrayed the city you swore to protect," Gastreel

said, "and delivered them into the hands of their greatest foe."

"The city," Sestriel uttered, "they betrayed us, the true wizards, long, long ago."

"Twelve against one," Gastreel said, "only then will it be a fair fight. I suppose you learned Syrion's lesson."

Sestriel snarled; his eyes bulged with wrath. In an instant, he had reached into his pocket and had hurled a percussion ball, a glowing orb that would knock Gastreel unconscious – a sphere of light pulsing toward him. Gastreel countered it and the weapon burst into a fiery flash, dropping to the ground as a burnt-out metal ball.

Lightning struck and fire rained, twelve against one — spears of frost and columns of swirling air, battering Gastreel's shield, withering it to within an inch of him. And Sestriel pulled from the pockets of his orange robe a small object, glittering gold.

A simulacrum…

Gastreel swallowed a scream.

Sestriel twisted the simulacrum with a snarl and Gastreel went flying upward, as if the ground were the sky and the clouds above were Varda's surface. He fell upwards, the air turning colder and colder, thinner and thinner — wind whipping in the high places — until Sestriel and the gathered wizards were tiny dots, and he could see the River Galios as if it were a painted map in his hands.

Far below, Sestriel twisted the simulacrum again, and Gastreel went falling — and he could not answer it. He plummeted to the ground from the unfathomable height, toward a certain death… as he was joined by another.

It was Aleksander riding in on his gray horse, Aleksander, a feathered staff in his hands, and as Gastreel neared the ground, Aleksander thrust forth his fist and the simulacrum went flying away. Gastreel's fall was halted, and he landed with a bruising thud. He hopped to his feet and called down a bolt of lightning, splitting against Sestriel's shield.

The wizards' interests now divided, between Aleksander and Gastreel, Sestriel fired off a volley of acid, and his acid was met. A few flecks burned Gastreel's wrist.

And Sestriel, eyes pulsing with wrath, drew a wand from his belt, even as Aleksander was overcome, and by spears of fire and lances of wind, fell dead from his horse.

The wand burst with energy, green and blue, and struck Gastreel head-on. He felt his muscles weaken and his breath grow faint.

Another wand was drawn, and the burnt-out wand was discarded. That wand glowed bright green — *telemancy* — and Gastreel gasped, fumbled with his staff… too weakened to resist.

~

When Gastreel opened his eyes, he was somewhere else, a farm on the east side of the Dragonteeth — a farmhouse, a silo, a farmer in the distance harvesting his wheat.

"Curses!" Sestriel howled, and he drew another wand of *telemancy*, and again Gastreel was too weakened to resist.

Green, brilliant white — and in an instant Gastreel was in a new place, a place of terrifying brightness.

~

Gastreel couldn't breathe. The air was thin and so cold his skin at once began to burn. White, white everywhere — snow up to his waist, and he looked down, and saw that he was at the top of one of the Dragonteeth's peaks. He was weakening, and he couldn't breathe, and he began to faint. His eyes fixed on Sestriel ahead of him — Sestriel, drawing a wand from his hand, a wand of *telemancy*. He intended to leave Gastreel to die here, here — high on the Dragonteeth's peaks, left in an icy tomb.

With all the strength that remained in him, which was little, Gastreel sent a gout of force. The wand fell from Sestriel's hands, and in Sestriel's eyes the wrath had become something beyond murderous. Dark and terrible were those eyes, a looking-glass into the Void, holes through which Gastreel could see the Abyss.

Sestriel reached for his wand in the snow, and as he did, as Gastreel began to succumb to the elements, as he began to lose all feeling in his feet and in his toes, as his breath — already faint — was slowly waning away… he thought of something.

It was the ultimate crime against the wizards, the ultimate crime against the All-Seeing… no, the Arcane Eye. It was the ultimate sacrilege, and one which would dishonor the wizard order forever.

He focused in on Sestriel's staff. As Sestriel called up the magic from the wand once more, Gastreel reached weakly with his hands. Everything in him, every bit of energy that remained… all of him, and the Staff of the Archwizard burst in two, shattering into wooden shards, splinters of wood and bits of crystal, magic… and the most precious artifact of the wizards was gone.

The wand in Sestriel's hand discharged without effect. Sestriel, standing in the snow, stunned by his staff's breaking, lay motionless, and quickly froze.

The cold was withering away Gastreel's strength. All breath was gone from him. He cared no longer. Here he would die… into the embrace of the gods he would fall.

~

"No!" There was a figure of light. A flash of light and no controlling darkness to answer it. A figure was in the light, a figure outlined amid the brightness, seeming to sit in a chair.

"No!" the voice said. "That time is not yet. You must deliver the Sage into our hands… Do not die, do not perish. If you do, the Dark One will prevail."

~

In the snow, weakened, his breath a shallow pain, Gastreel staggered, looking to the peak, to the valleys far below. He staggered ahead, to Sestriel's frozen corpse, to Sestriel's robe, which he felt, and there was something… some sort of padding.

In his weak, delirious state he tore open Sestriel's robe. Beneath the orange was something, a vest… a cloak.

The aegis cloak Gastreel laid about his shoulders, and when he wore it he could breathe a bit better, and when he wore it, the cold though it stung him did not seem to burn. An aegis cloak, and Gastreel took all the remaining wands from his enemy's belt.

He fired them, one at a time. Three remained in total…. A blast of fire, a spear of cold, a withering sphere. No wand of *telemancy* remained. Someway, somehow, he would have to descend the mountains — he, a sixty-five-year-old man, he a wizard and not a god.

"For the gods," he uttered, "for the Prince of the Dawn…"

Chapter Seventy-Three:
In the Square He Lies

In the time that Reev had been stricken with the dagger, they of the city had made bets, whether he were dead or comatose. Some uttered prayers to the gods for him, and others gave gifts in secret, that the Prince of the Dawn was dead. Ramona, for her part, had kept indoors, too terrified to leave, a city now under the tyranny of Alden… a city, and a nation, now ruled by a worshipper of Seymus.

The doors were locked, the windows closed, and at all hours she'd check on Ash and make sure he was safe and secure. Guards she had posted in the front yard, before the gate and even upstairs. By night she'd dream of Desdemona breaking through her windows.

And yet… yet, in the silent moments, when she fought through her guilt, she wished to visit that City Square, where Reev was lying. If any god would hear her, she wished to pray for his health, that he might survive.

One morning she was walking through the great hall, and Ash was standing amid it, with a bundle of flowers in his hands.

"Where did you get those?" she said, more harshly than was warranted. Every moment was a waking terror; anything could provoke an outburst.

"The garden," Ash said.

"Why?"

Ash peered into her eyes. "When Reev died, some in City Square have taken to leaving flowers on the ground before him… marking their prayers."

"And will you do that for your cousin?" Ramona said.

"If I do," Ash said, "I think you should come too."

But it was her blood, that drop of blood, that had completed the poison, if Ramona's nightmarish experience had been true. Had she, not, in some sense, killed her nephew… if he was dead in truth, and not only poisoned?

"Come with me," Ash said. "Come with me, Mother."

And she did, though she knew not why. She took no guards. With Ash at her side, she ventured through the streets, the two of them alone.

~

At City Square, Reev lay lifeless, without motion on the ground. Before him, lurking, was that criminal Ivan Xandrast, bearing a two-sided sword in his hands.

"That's Ivan," Ash said, softly. "If anyone draws near to Reev, he strikes them dead. Not even the town watch will approach him…"

Had Ash been here before?

Ash tossed a few flowers on the ground. The whole City Square was scattered with them. He handed a few flowers to Ramona, and Ramona took it, and did the same.

"Gods heal him," Ash said.

"Gods heal him," Ramona said in turn.

What had come over her boy? He seemed changed. And yet… and yet… Ramona thought she would come back here. Every morning and every evening she'd travel here, throwing flower petals on the ground, and saying a prayer for him.

"Reev," she said softly, "wake up, if you can."

Chapter Seventy-Four: For Dada

"What's going to happen to Mr. Reev?" Bala asked Glenda in the morning light.

Glenda's eyes were fixed outside the windows of the Dragonpaw, where Mr. Reev was motionless on the ground. She said nothing; she remained silent.

Bala was worried; at night he cried and at day he would fidget with his fingers. His training had been canceled, but that was the last thing he thought of now. And he couldn't go outside and shake Mr. Reev awake, because when he did Mr. Xan would give a scary shout, and rattle that two-sided sword.

Glenda went about her business. All in the inn continued as normal, the kitchen staff clanging their pots and pans, making breakfast, lunch and dinner… beer and wine poured, and a steady stream of guests. But wasn't there more to life than that? Wasn't there?

As Glenda walked about the inn, Bala could see she was holding something in her hands, something small.

Chapter Seventy-Five: Mission Failed?

When Wrinn reached City Square, and heard all that had gone on, he didn't take no for an answer. On Noble he pushed past the crowd, galloping up ahead, across the tiles which were strangely covered in flowers, to Reev's lifeless body.

And when he saw that body, his heart seized up; he felt he couldn't breathe.

Ivan Xandrast was walking toward him, Ivan the former warlock, and he was rattling his butterfly blade as he drew near. Anger replaced Wrinn's calm, consummate anger, and he had a thought of striking down Ivan Xandrast, as he had done once before.

"Wrinn," he said, "don't come any nearer."

Ivan Xandrast, in the shadows of the morning, made for an intimidating specimen. But Wrinn wouldn't show any fear.

"Back away," Ivan Xandrast said. "If you wish, leave flower petals on the ground, and pray."

Maybe Wrinn would.

Chapter Seventy-Six:
Two For the Dawn

In the trees of the South Weald, Fortunato watched and waited, with Spyke at his side. Cloaked in the greenness and the forest's vast expanse, he surveilled the farm fields beyond.

In the gold light of autumn, there were Imperials marching freely through the landscape, infantry bearing the red and gold standards and the titanic forms of elephants wandering through the fields of wheat.

The borders of Gallia were gone, erased, and the Empire had seized it without resistance. They had taken it all without a fight, but Galiope's walls would hold, wouldn't they?

"Time to give up," Spyke said. "Time… for what?"

"Time for what?" Fortunato said. "I think I know… I do."

~

An outrider met them at evening, an outrider in full plate, wearing a spangenhelm.

"General…" The warrior's helmet gleamed in the light. "Southkirk has surrendered. Estenberry has fallen, after siege. Cardunnon and Leyshaw are suing for peace."

"The war is lost," Fortunato said, not a thing for the General of the Army to say. "Galiope…"

"Galiope holds firm," said the warrior, "for now."

"And the Sage?" said Spyke.

"Reev Nax," the warrior said, "I suppose he is not the promised one after all. He is dead…"

That night, Spyke and Fortunato rode alone, at full speed, toward the city.

Chapter Seventy-Seven: At the Square, In the City

The crowds in City Square were gathering. Every day, more and more citizens threw flower petals, and the chorus of prayers grew. On the morning Fortunato joined them, dropping rose petals beside the edges of the square, the sun seemed to grow in brightness. There was a flash… and motion.

Chapter Seventy-Eight: It Is Not Agreed To

Reev was floating amid the stars, and about his head a crown of stars circled. Before him was light — and voices. A sun, brighter than any he'd seen, and larger, was casting a sphere of rock in shadow.

The voices echoed, inscrutable.

"It has been agreed," said a voice, he thought.

"It has been agreed…"

"The Enemy has said…"

"Water, in which a murderer hath washed his hands…"

"And in that we must consent…"

"No, wrong…"

The swirling voices echoed, a hundred, a million.

"Not a murderer. It was in self-defense that Illothian was slain…"

A voice, stronger than before, booming, echoing: "The council hath sat… the agreement was not fulfilled.

"The Sage shall live! He shall not get such a chance again!"

~

When Reev woke from the dream, the air in his lungs was the purest breath he'd ever taken, the moving of his arms and legs the smoothest as he had remembered. And when he stood up, in City Square, there were terrified shouts and screams, and many in the crowds around began to flee.

Some wailed, some wept… and Ivan Xandrast was lurking over him. Fortunato was running ahead, joined by Wrinn a moment later. And he saw Ramona, and he saw Ash, amid the onlookers.

"Fortunato!" Reev said. "Wrinn!"

And he was glad of Ivan Xandrast's presence, too.

Wrinn met him in an embrace and began to weep. Fortunato's eyes began to well with tears.

"So all hope is not lost," Fortunato said.

"I've had the strangest dream," Reev replied.

"Where will we go?" Reev said, thinking of the Empire's forces, thinking of the war-ravaged landscape.

"Where is Gastreel?" Reev said.

And Wrinn placed a hand on his shoulder, saying nothing, as if he didn't want to tell.

"We are leaving the city," Fortunato said. "To the land of the elves we go…"

"How will we get there?" Reev said. "The Elf Lands are thousands of miles away, and it will soon be winter."

"We will," Fortunato said, "because we must."

Reev thought he had heard such a motto from Fortunato's lips before.

Chapter Seventy-Nine: From Danger, To Danger

Gastreel arrived with the Empire.

Godsgate was closing, and soldiers hurrying to the battlements, when Gastreel hauled his frozen, battered body into the city.

The tips of his fingers had been frostbitten; even with the aegis cloak, the cold had almost killed him. The threat of avalanches he had braved, and rokahn camps, as he descended rocky peaks and snow that at time had reached his neck, and at other times covered him. His knees ached, and the cold of those mountains had not left him, even after days in the warm autumn air. He had seen death; he had endured beyond what he had thought he had been able to bear. Yet he was still here, still in the mortal world somehow — still somehow drawing breath.

His walk was at times a stumble, but as the siege began, his thoughts were on other things. Galiope, as a city, was now an island in a sea of Imperial control. The wizard order had been shattered by Gastreel's own hand, and now… now… the greatest task lay ahead, one he did not know how to accomplish.

"Reev!" he began to call after him in vain.

"Fortunato!" he said, delirious from the long days in the cold.

He found them at last in the Dragonpaw Inn, preparing to leave… Fortunato and Ivan Xandrast, Wrinn and one he had not known before, a man with a swarthy complexion and a board strapped to his back. Reev — Reev… at the sight of him his heart could rest.

They were cramming their packs with goods, with road-bread, with salt-pork… all that was needed of a long journey.

Sitting in a booth, nearby, was Reev's aunt Ramona, and his

cousin… what was his name? Ash…

They were leaving — as was wise. "Fortunato," Gastreel said, "hail."

Fortunato turned to him, still stuffing food and equipment in his pack. "Green Wizard," he said, "we are going to the Elf Lands."

Where else was there safe haven? Where else was there to go? Where else was there wisdom, the knowledge of the ages stored… guidance for their mission?

It would be a grave risk… perilous. The steppe, which they would have to travel, was so cold in winter that it could kill. Snow, ice, the threat of rokahn raids… along the ancient road they could go, but it would take weeks, months… and survival was not guaranteed.

Yet… yet… "It is wise to do so," Gastreel said. "The Elf Lands, where the Shadow has not fallen. Far from the Dark One's prying ears and eyes. Far from the powers of evil. One problem, though."

"And what is that?" Fortunato said.

"The city is surrounded."

The horns began to blow, Gallian war horns and Imperial trumpets, and as they stood amid the inn there was the sound of falling stone, boulders thrown from catapults. Galiope, Galiope… it could be no more.

"No way in; no way out," Gastreel said.

"Garrick's Gate," Fortunato said.

"The city — all of it — is surrounded," Gastreel replied.

Ramona stirred from her booth. "Green Wizard," she said, "if you will… I have an idea."

Glenda was listening from the shadows.

"In the Townhall in Lion's Square, there is a secret passageway. If you take it to its furthermost extent, you will exit out a cave in the Dunshire Hills."

What better way was there to escape? What better way was there to go?

"Your horses will not fit," Ramona said. "You will have to flee by foot…"

"Glenda," Wrinn said to the Dragonpaw's innkeeper, "take care of Noble while we're gone."

While we're gone… they would not be coming back.

"Hurry! Gather your things," Gastreel said. "We must leave at once."

"Wait," Fortunato said. "There is one last thing for me to do."

Chapter Eighty: Goodbye Galiope

In Selwyn's Parish he searched for her.

In Selwyn's Parish Fortunato scoured the streets, as stones fell from the sky and the collapse of buildings could be heard far-off. In the early autumn light, on this day of doom, he searched for his love.

But Selwyn's Parish seemed empty; the windows of its lean-to tenements and slums were mostly dark. In its market squares and piazzas, its stone churches and its astrologias and observatories, there were few people it seemed, and no gypsies. He saw no sign of her, she whom he hoped to meet one last time, she whom he still loved.

"Ambrass!" he shouted in vain. "Ambrass!"

Down streets he walked, despair growing stronger and stronger with each step, until at last he heard "They've broken through Godsgate!" and he sprinted back to the Dragonpaw alone.

~

"The Companions," said Gastreel in the Dragonpaw Inn, "that is what we are called. Reev Nax, Wrinn, Ivan Xandrast — "

"Xan," he insisted.

"Xan… Fortunato."

"And Spyke," Fortunato said, his pack about his shoulders. "Spyke is coming with us."

Gastreel eyed the newcomer warily.

"Do you not trust him?" Fortunato said.

"I trust anyone you trust, Fortunato," Gastreel said. "Hurry! Let's go!"

Glenda's eyes were watering. Her lips were trembling. The somberness of the moment endured, until at last, through a door, Bala came stumbling, Bala in his top hat. "What about me?" he said. "Can't I come along?"

"No, no," Gastreel said. "We go into danger. You cannot go where we go. You are safe, here, under Glenda's care."

Safe… but the Empire would soon control the city, and as they stood idly in the main hall, there was a chorus of Imperial trumpets, and audible shouts.

"Hurry!" Ramona said. "There is no time…"

Ambrass… Ambrass was on Fortunato's mind as the six of them departed, six against the Dark One. Six against Seymus, being led out of the Dragonpaw Inn's doors, into the heat of the early autumn sun.

~

They rushed through the streets, running, as there were wild cries in the distance, and stones cast from catapults continued to fall.

Rumors spread, shouted in earshot. The Lord Alden had hanged himself from the ramparts of Horn Keep. One dangled with him, a young woman red of hair.

"Desdemona, one of the Weird Sisters!" a peddler was shouting on a street corner. "But no one knows where her sister is…"

Fires were starting in the city, and the Imperial trumpets blowing were like a chorus. The sky as smoke wafted up was taking on the colors of ochre, and Fortunato's heart was racing in his chest.

At last, Lion's Square — and in Lion's Square were revelers, dancing about. They seemed to be unaware of the siege, unaware of the imminent destruction. Beside them were great kegs of cider, and from those kegs they were variously drinking from cups or guzzling from the tap. In red and gold they were dressed, some in leaf outfits, others with wreaths of apples on their heads.

"What is this?" Gastreel said.

They were singing and dancing as all fell apart around them, apparently the only ones in the city unaware of imminent doom.

Avelonas, Orchard Lord
We raise our glass to thee
Under autumn sky we sing
The blessed Apple Tree!

The Apple Festival, in ordinary circumstances, would be underway now. But the city now was falling.

Gastreel and the six against Seymus, Fortunato among them, stared at the revelers in stunned amazement. There was not a trace of fear on their faces. They were dancing and they were drinking, carried away by spirits and song.

"Fools!" Ramona shouted. "Come with me — hurry!"

They raced to the doors of the Townhall, and Ramona laid her hands on the knobs. She yanked on them, and met resistance.

"Locked!" she said, and panic dawned in those eyes of hers. "Locked…"

"I have a key," Xan replied. "I have the Skeleton Key."

Hounded

Harona 2, 1153 Y.E.
22nd of Oré, 1469 of the Age of Humanity

Sergio, once the leader of the Empire's 19th cohort and now Legate Nicollo's personal adjutant, burst down a narrow street and found himself looking into a small city square.

There he saw the one he'd been asked to find, the one he'd been ordered to deliver into Niccolo's hands.

He was there, the boy — with a coin necklace about his neck. The emperor had heard about this boy, who had traveled under the mountain and who had worn about his chest a coin of the True Empire. The emperor wished to bring this boy to Imperial City, to the emperor's palace, and to know him.

But others were there — others.

Drunken revelers dancing about, and six people nearby the boy. The seven of them were entering through the open doors of Galiope's Townhall, running into the darkness one by one.

One he saw — his childhood friend, Fortunato of Ríva. Fortunato had spared Sergio's life.

A favor for a favor.

Sergio could earn the Grass Crown some other way.

He turned to the men behind him. "The boy is not here… Turn around. Search elsewhere."

They fanned out, away, into Galiope's rabbit warren of streets. The boy was slipping away now, by Sergio's hand, by memories of Fortunato's mercy.

A favor for a favor.

He wished Fortunato, his childhood friend, luck.

***

In the Townhall, Ramona pointed frantically. She pushed aside a statue and pressed an indentation on the wall. The wall expanded, bearing a dark space.

"Gods be with you," she said, as the six against Seymus entered into the cavernous depths.

"Gods be with you," said Ramona, Reev's aunt, as Fortunato and others entered the musty tunnel, and sprinted away under the city streets, toward a destination far in the distance.

They hurried for what seemed like hours in the dark, in the cool must of the subterranean air. Fear was rising in Fortunato, but also relief — and grief.

What had happened to Ambrass? Where had she gone?

Their feet were sore, their breathing growing faint, their tunics stained with sweat, when a bit of illumination appeared, and after a quick sprint, fresh air.

Beyond the cave they ran, into the light of the sun. They were out in the open, in a war zone. Now, the greatest challenge would come.

Chapter Eighty-One: More Than A Dream

The wagons of the gypsies were gathered south of Godsgate, bright green and red, gold and orange, fiery yellow and inky purple. There were hundreds of them in the vast space, and Gaius and Ambrass were in one of their own, Gaius and Ambrass and their expected child. The hearts of the gathered gypsies were filled with hate and grief. The Gallians had treated them well, but the Imperials never had, and never would.

"Where will we go, Gaius?" Ambrass said to her husband. She could feel their baby kicking within her. "Where will we go?"

"To Khandara, some say," Gaius answered her. "Others say, to Vharat."

Vharat, the gypsies' mythical homeland, where they were driven from long ago. Vharat… a place where honey flowed like rivers, and wine was on the leaves of the trees like dew. A place, mystical, the yearning desire they all had nurtured since they began to wander long ago.

"The Imperials," Ambrass said, "I hate them."

Gaius was nodding off to sleep.

And to their side was motion — through the window, a face.

Gold hair greeted Ambrass, green eyes, a tunic and trousers and a tomboyish gait. Earrings in ears that came to slight points, a fine figure, and the yearning for the mystical Vharat was replaced with something else, a yearning for something else, something real.

She lowered the window and fought tears, as Gaius snored.

"Ambrass," said Glenda, Glenda her former employer, whom she'd now never see again. "Ambrass…"

Glenda's eyes were welling with tears.

"Ambrass," she said. "I thought you should have this."

From her hand she gave Ambrass something, an object that struck her heart, that stole her breath, an object that caused her eyes to well with tears, and her whole self to shudder.

The inward calm she had forced within began to spiral undone, as she saw the small bit of fabric, green, stained ever so slightly with mud.

It was the piece of Fortunato's cloak she had held to her chest during lonely nights, the piece of Fortunato's cloak she had left behind with intention.

"No, no," Ambrass began to say, but her words were swallowed up in tears, and nothing emerged from her lips.

"No, no," she said, but as the horses stirred to life and the wagon began to move, on its way to mystical Vharat, she took the piece of Fortunato's cloak, and, weeping, held it to her chest.

Chapter Eighty-Two: Hunted

Where was she?

Where was the one that Fortunato loved?

He had not found her.

Fortunato, one of the six against Seymus, was moving through the lands north of Galiope, a wild and desolate country. They were biding their time, and it was their first day, their first many hours' hike.

They were following Gastreel's recollection, trying to find the Ancient Way which would lead them to the land of the elves. But as the morning turned to afternoon, and the afternoon turned to late afternoon, the sun's light flashed on something — Imperial soldiers, up ahead.

There was a battalion ahead through the brush, searching the wilds, scanning with their eyes and listening with their ears. Through the green grass an elephant was treading.

Gastreel made a motion to stop, and to wait.

At last, the Imperials passed them by.

~

Where was she?

Where was the one Fortunato loved?

The next day, Gastreel and the others had even less luck. They had traveled scarcely an hour before an Imperial platoon crossed their paths, now just yards away, and they spent much of the day hiding in the bushes.

When they had gone, Reev said, "The Imperials are fearsome… but they do not worship Seymus. They do not fashion secret groves.

Why do we fear them?"

Gastreel replied, "They cannot be trusted. For their ends are their own, and are not ours. Their god is not Seymus, but themselves. As for them, some light is in them — but if you fell into their hands, they would try to twist you for their own ends. They would try to use your powers in a cause not our own."

~

Where was she?

Where was the one Fortunato loved?

The third day they made no progress. They remained in the woods all day, hiding, as Imperials passed them by, left and right, soldiers in breastplates, auxiliaries of the north and south, elephants and horses and white chargers.

"Where is the Ancient Way?" Reev said.

Gastreel replied, "We will find it... we will find it, somehow."

Chapter Eighty-Three: As Was Written

Two Days Ago…

Bala had followed Mr. Fortunato and Mr. Gastreel and Mr. Reev as quickly as he could go. He had sprinted through the tunnel in the dark, but his little legs couldn't catch up with their grown-up feet. He had followed them out of the cave, into hills, through a desolate and wild country where there were no roads to be seen. At last, their flagging forms were slipping away, and sometime in the evening disappeared entirely into the green. The sun was setting, the light turning to gold and to red. Darkness was setting in, and fear was filling Bala's heart.

He began to call after Mr. Reev, "Dada! Dada!"

And as the sun finally sunk beneath the hills, there was motion… ahead of him a shape, rising, growing, taller than him, taller than Fortunato, then half as tall as the trees.

A creature was there before him, a woman clothed in rags, her skin a bright purple, her nose shaped like a pickle and covered in warts. Her eyes were yellow, her teeth square like a donkey's. Flies and fleas buzzed around her, and in her outsized hands she gripped a walking stick.

"Who are you?" Bala cried.

"I am named Yaga," she said, "but you may call me Granny."

"What?" Bala shrieked.

"Hail, Balor, King of the Elves!" said Yaga, and two other hags joined her, one green, one blue.

"Jenny, and Anise," Yaga explained.

Jenny, of blue skin, was holding something in her hands, a callow staff of wood.

"Don't you want to finish your training?" Yaga said.

"Yes," Bala said. "Yes, I do!"

Anise, of green skin, approached, and placed on Bala's head a wooden crown.

"Hail, Balor, king... a magician," said Yaga, "and soon a conqueror of the earth."

~

Into the woods, Bala was led, deep into the woods, to a cottage by a glen. There he had a feast of whatever he wished.

"Sweet cakes," he said, "and milk, for dinner."

That night in the dark, the training began, summoning, calling, banishing and purging. And for the next two days on, and long into the future, Balor grew in wisdom, and power, and might.

Chapter Eighty-Four:
By Ancient Ways

Where was she?

Where was she?

It was days after the journey began, after many narrow escapes, and it was a wonder Fortunato and the five others had gotten away with their lives. Before them was what they wanted, or so they had thought — the trailhead to the Ancient Way, but Imperials were patrolling it, and were even taking tolls.

"We cannot escape them," said Spyke, from the shadows.

"No," Gastreel whispered, "no, it seems not.

"And the Ancient Way is not well tended to. Nor are humans welcome to travel through elven realms. It seems… it seems…"

"Lord Wizard," Xan began.

"Do not call me that, anymore," Gastreel said.

"Lord Gastreel," Xan said, "I know little of the affairs of wizards, but there is a legend I heard… a great gate that they use to vault across long distances, by which they can travel to anywhere in Varda. What was it called? The Port of *Terron*…"

"It is called Tedron's Gate," Gastreel said, "and it has not been used in centuries. None know if it still operable."

"Is it not worth a try?" Xan replied.

Silence greeted Xan — silence, and the stirring of the Imperials beyond the bushes. They crept away, and Gastreel's silence was assent. In the growing dark they followed him, and as they did Tyra Jade — a black shadow — joined them. As they ventured on, it became evident that the Imperials were searching for something, or someone, and the close brushes with the Imperials, it was becoming clear, were not a coincidence.

~

The Imperials spotted them as they were drawing near the mountains, and in a scramble, they darted into the deep brush. Night was falling, the stars were shining — the air was cold, and they had come to Tedron's Gate.

In the distance were signal fires, far away in the fields below Imperials galloping on horse. In the darkness they ran, the seven against Seymus, the companions who fought against him and his servants in the mortal world. They ran, they sprinted, six plus one — Tyra Jade, and as darkness fell there was a howl, a howl that caused Fortunato's heart to thunder, and the hairs on his skin to waver.

Darkness, fear, and speed, and the first howl was matched by five others. Six, against seven. Seven, and the Empire was following, too.

Gastreel rushed through the cave, into the dark, and there it was — what looked like a hollow gate of stone, marked on its sides with runes.

Gastreel raised his staff — his staff, a new one, no longer white but black. He began to call out in a language that Fortunato did not know. The air grew colder; there was a crispness to it, but the gate remained dead and inert.

Horns and then three howls. Silence, and three howls followed.

Gastreel cried again, and raised his staff, and again Tedron's gate remained lifeless.

"Gods hear me! Gods help me!" Gastreel cried, and thrusted forth his fist, but Tedron's Gate was dead and dull.

An Imperial horseman was in view — darkness had fallen... and Gastreel lifted his hands, and gave the mightiest shout of all. Scars ripped into existence across his forearm. Gashes opened on his cheeks and on his mouth. He seemed to shrink back, his body to wither in size — and the cave blazed with light.

Within the hollow gate was a blazing green fire, and the Imperial horseman stopped, stunned by its brightness.

"Run in!" Gastreel cried. "Think of 'Danarion'…"

Gastreel ran in first, then Xan, then Spyke. Reev followed, then Wrinn.

Fortunato hopped astride Tyra Jade, and in the night darkness, as Imperial soldiers appeared, there were six shadows, six beasts, six iron masks.

Fortunato sprinted on Tyra Jade through the light, and as Tyra leapt, and green light surrounded them, he felt the presence of six others, inhuman, alien, void.

Chapter Eighty-Five:
Seven Against Six

Where was she?

Where was she?

Fortunato on Tyra Jade was in a new place.

The air was cool and crisp. The sun had not yet set, where they were.

Green grass could be seen all about, grass in which danced wildflowers blue and violet.

In the distance was a massive mound, a tell. Danari Hill.

The five others were in scattered places. Reev and Gastreel were in view.

"The gate is faulty," Fortunato said, astride Tyra Jade. "It took us not to Danarion, but to *Don Danari*... Danari Hill."

But Fortunato knew the way. He had been here once before. He had seen the tell before, in the distance, during his sojourns in the Elf Lands.

Danarion, the capital, was a hundred miles away. Danarion was where they would go, the seat of the King, their destination... the City of Light which legend said could never fall.

"The air is so fresh," Wrinn said. "It almost smells sweet. Cold... and yet refreshing in its coldness. Not frigid."

"Do you feel like you belong in this place, Wrinn?" Gastreel said.

Wrinn's jubilant face was confirmation.

It was evening, and though they had escaped the Imperials, the six presences Fortunato had felt were ones he knew. If the six Servants of Seymus found them, they would overpower them quickly... Gastreel was no match for them. They'd quickly kill them all, and take Reev back to their master.

"Danarion," Fortunato said, "a hundred miles away. Let's get moving!"

~

Where was she? Where was she?

They had marched into the night, until the late hours, and in the new moon there was no celestial orb to guide them. They had marched until they had been able to march no longer, and collapsed in piles in the grass.

They awoke, at dawn, to a new world.

Amid the green grass were farms, and villages built on tells… in the distance mountains standing alone, peaks that rose titan-like from the ground and had no sister — their bases marked by pines and their peaks crowned in snow. There were fields of golden wheat, and farmers tending to them. There were vineyards, and servants plucking the grapes, for the harvest season was at hand.

There was air, fresh, dry and cool, a sun that seemed kinder than anywhere else Fortunato had been. There was light and an air of serenity, in this place where only elves could go, where the darkness could not touch.

As they ventured through the grass in view of the scattered peaks, and at last began to traverse a road, Fortunato began to notice birds perched in the trees, purple and blue, gold and green, some with bills or white beaks or violet plumes. Whenever the seven companions drew near, they'd fly off south.

There seemed to be a new gait to Reev's step, and he was walking with new energy. There seemed to be something new kindled in Wrinn's soul, for whenever Fortunato looked at him there was a smile on his face.

For twenty miles they traveled, and the sun began to set.

They had procured their bedrolls, and were beginning to nibble at their road bread.

Reev approached Fortunato and sat down beside.

~

Where was she? Where was she?

Reev asked, "What day is it?"

"The new moon, yesterday," Fortunato said, "that makes it the 29th day of Oré by elven reckoning. Or, in our terms, the ninth of Harona."

"My birthday," Reev said.

"Your birthday…" Fortunato said. "No cake, no present. But maybe you'll find a gift in the City of Light."

"Seventeen years old," Reev said. "I'm a man, now."

"Yes, you are," Fortunato said. The gold of Reev's coin necklace seemed to sparkle as sunset turned to twilight and twilight turned to night.

Chapter Eighty-Six:
To the Stars

The wagons were making their way through the Great Weald. Gaius, as ever, was snoring. In the back of the wagon, Ambrass reached into her breast pocket, and did something she had not oft dared to do in Gaius's presence. She grasped the piece of Fortunato's cloak.

Through the wagon she climbed, toward where the driver was sitting. Here Gaius had no chance of seeing her, beyond the curtain.

She looked to the piece of fabric and clutched it to her heart. Softly, she wept.

The night was deeply dark. The stars were bright beacons.

The stars — a certain band of them seemed to be moving most prominently in the sky.

"Oh, love," she said softly, and she cared not whether the driver could hear her. "Oh, on that night on the battlements there seemed to be a dark fever. And darkness prevailed... oh, love."

Clutching the fabric to her heart as the landscape passed her by, she thought of him, whom she had loved, whom she still loved. Nocturne, Gaius, they were nothing. No, no, there was another. All day she hid the fabric in her pocket. She clutched it when she spoke to Gaius. She set it to her heart when she looked away. She clutched the fabric when she relented, and she thought of him when to Gaius she made loveless love.

She looked to the starry band. "I will see you soon," she said.

Chapter Eighty-Seven: By Starlight

Where was she? Where was she?

Reev sitting beside Fortunato was peering southwards to their destination. "When will we get to Danarion?" he said.

~

"Soon; I will see you soon," said Ambrass to the starry band. The trees in the Great Weald loomed high above her.

"Will I?" Ambrass said, looking up to the sky.

~

"Soon," Fortunato said, "I will see you soon…"

Reev looked at him quizzically.

"Ah, I mean," Fortunato said, "we will get to Danarion soon."

~

"I love you," said Ambrass to the starry band.

"I love you," she said, and then a third time. "I love you…"

~

"I — " Something was on the tip of Fortunato's tongue, something ready to escape. Something… but the night was dark, and peril was on his mind.

"I — " he began.

Where was she? She was gone…

Chapter Eighty-Eight: Six Against Seven

Reev felt the pain anew flaring in his left forearm, and began to arise. Danger he sensed, peril — here, in the Elf Lands, in this place of light.

Gastreel was sleeping. Fortunato was off in the distance. "Wake up!" he began to cry. "Wake up!"

And he saw in his mind's eye six iron masks, six snarling maws, six dark blades ready to poison and to injure… he sensed minds not of this world, intent on capturing him and dragging him screaming to their master.

"Awake! Awake!" he cried, and began to sprint away without them.

~

They, much stronger and faster, the six others against Seymus, quickly caught up to Reev, sprinting southwards, away. Tyra Jade's dark form was racing through the night, and she was beginning to whimper and to whine.

They were all running, all, in the darkness, fleeing a peril it seemed only Reev could sense. They were over a hill, between two tells, when he looked back and saw six dark forms rapidly approaching. The light of the slivered crescent moon gleamed on their masks.

But over the hill, darkness was met with light. Over the hill, beyond, the light halted the darkness, and the six Servants of Seymus fled away.

There before the seven, riding on horses, was an army, lit by sorcerers' staffs. Elves, countless thousands, stretching into the distance, left and right and beyond — elves, and at the head of them a woman in a white veil whose very body seemed to emanate light.

"Nenré!" Fortunato cried.

"Welcome," said she, "to my father's kingdom. We rode with all haste to you, when my father's birds alerted us to your presence. Welcome, Fortunato. Welcome, Wrinn, and Gastreel, and others. Welcome, Sage, our hope. Here, darkness dares not tread."

Reev looked back, to the six Servants of Seymus, now fleeing — not even they could overcome an army so vast.

Faces he saw, faces he thought he knew — beside Nenré, a man with long hair, so fair it was almost white.

"Welcome," said she. "We will now take you to the royal city. Peace you will find, and comfort for your bones — Sage, you who will soon crush Seymus under your feet."

THE END

Continued in Book Five, *The City of Light*...

Glossary

Times and Dates

Vardic Calendar	Julian Calendar Equivalent
1. Albos	January
2. Kaldsil	February
3. Primrane	March
4. Tidusca	April
5. Brenua	May
6. Aurelios	June
7. Odens	July
8. Sextil	August
9. Harona	September
10. Brightleaf	October
11. Anthanos	November
12. Candlebright	December

Elven Calendar (Lunisolar)	Julian Calendar Equivalent
5. Gilné	Jan. – Feb.
6. Sindjé	Feb. – Mar.
7. Sorjé	Mar. – Apr.
8. Ríal	Apr. – May
9. Vlesti	May – Jun.
10. Kelvé	Jun. – Jul.
11. Kaudé	Jul. – Aug.
12. Oré	Aug. – Sept.
1. Yanenré	Sept. – Oct.

2.	Estion	Oct. – Nov
3.	Dorion	Nov. – Dec.
4.	Dandathon	Dec. – Jan.

Bell Hours

Term	Time
Lauds	6:00 AM
Prima	9:00 AM
Merida	Noon
Tridium	3:00 PM
Vespers	6:00 PM
Compline	10:00 PM

ZARUBE PHRASES

Abollondon: Hellion; the thing of hell.
Mordblood: Daemon-blood.

ELVEN PHRASES

Teli Telantari Indion: "Great Telantine Kingdom."
An: "Go!"

TERMS

Aegis Cloak: A cloak, specially crafted by wizards, which provides protection from fire, ice, and lightning.

Alonar: An Elvish term roughly corresponding to Gallia and certain surrounding lands.

Apple Festival: A festival of Galiope with ancient roots, celebrating the apple harvest and featuring the drinking of cider and the eating of apple confections.

Archwizard: The highest-ranked wizard. His duties include presiding over meetings of the Council of the Twelve and overseeing the maintenance of the Tower of Pythor.

Astrologias: Observatories meant for the conducting of astrology and astrological rituals.

Bell people: Prehistoric ancestors of the people of the Northern World, named for the bells which are often found in tombs and lying with them in peat bogs.

Black wolves: Large, intelligent wolves of the Dragonteeth Mountains. They are often captured and forced into the service of rokahn. They are one of the three divisions of Great Wolves, along with White Wolves and Brown Wolves.

Cathedral District: A large district of Galiope just north of the main gate, Godsgate. It is home to the city's churches and cathedrals.

Council of the Twelve, the: The ruling body of wizards, consisting of the foremost members of the twelve orders -- Green Robes, Blue Robes, Gold Robes and so on -- and presided over by the Archwizard. They meet in the Tower of Pythor once or sometimes twice a year within the walls of the city of Galiope. Most of the Ruling Wizards live apart from the city, but many have a home in Galiope.

Dark One, the: A name for Seymus, the enemy of the gods, the king of the Abollaren or demons.

Doomblade: One of the original *estirion* blades, first called *Pelladrimas* ("Flame of Fire") and wielded by the elven warrior prince Camlon in the First Shadow War. Through many names and owners it eventually made its way into the hands of the human Simeon Nax.

Dragonteeth Mountains: Large snow-capped mountains, stretching from Gallia in the east to the ocean in the west, forming the border of the Northern World and the lands of the elves.

Empire, the: A vast state composed of seven provinces, ruled by an emperor and an Imperial Council. It is considered the foremost military power in the world.

Galiope: A large city of the Northern World, called by those that love it the Queen of the North.

Gallia: A region east of Zarubain and west of Kardir, a place of mixed forest and farmland. Its greatest city is Galiope.

Gallian League: A league of towns in Gallia which bands together in times of war.

Godsgate: The south-facing main gate of Galiope, serving as the major exit and entry point.

Grass Crown, the: The Imperial military's highest honor.

Gypsies: A wandering folk who traditionally roamed the world in colorful wagons. In recent years, they were welcomed by the Gallian government and allowed to settle in Galiope.

Illothian Clan: A band of robbers, said by some to be of honorable cause. They killed the Lady Esterley, a Gallian aristocrat and member of the Council of War. Alden Grayhaupt personally led a band of soldiers to neutralize the threat, to the great consternation of Gallia's poor.

Imperial: To those outside the Empire, a citizen of the Empire. To those within the Empire, a man or woman originating in the coastal provinces associated with its founding.

Imperial City: The largest city in the known world, the capital of the Empire.

Market District: A large district of Galiope, north of Middletown, known for its shops, mansions and financial institutions.

Middletown: A district in Galiope just north of the River Galios. It is home to many shops and market squares.

Oxymancer: A sorcerer with powers over acid.

Perremum: A small city in the Imperial east.

Riverside: A district of Galiope abutting the River Galios. It was once home to rich and affluent noblemen, but in recent decades, elves of the Umen tribe (Wood Elves) have begun to populate the district.

Rokahn: Humanoid creatures known to dwell in the Dragonteeth Mountains, considered creatures of shadow. When their population swells, they will often raid the lowlands for food. Breeds include kehrad, toltar, and the standard species simply known as rokahn.

Selwyn's Parish: A large district of Galiope named after Saint Selwyn, an ancient Gallian renowned for his piety. Decades ago, a fire swept through the district, destroying most of the buildings; around the same time, the gypsies arrived in Gallia and were welcomed. They rebuilt and settled the district.

Servants of Seymus: Six beings in service of the Dark One. They wear iron masks and are clothed in black.

Secret groves: Woods, marked sacred, which the prehistoric Bell people and ancient Gallians were known to make. They were consecrated to various spirits and marked by fetishes and the blood of animals.

Solarias: An elf of ancient days, born in the early years of the Second Era, who received a message of the gods and paid the ultimate price.

Stew: A brothel.

Tell: A mound, consisting of the remains of consecutive ancient settlements.

Telemancy: Magic of teleportation and disruption. Telemancers can project themselves far distances, or scatter the bodies of their opponents into various parts.

Vampire: In Elvish, *druen* -- a tribe of elves cursed in ancient times with a thirst for blood.

Wodenscross Court: The richest district of the city of Galiope, built on a high flattop hill. Its large mansions are passed down and usually remain within families; they are never for sale.

Wizards: Powerful magic weavers of the Northern World. They are governed by a council and have their own nation-state within the walls of Galiope.

Wizard's staff: An implement of magic that wizards use. Without it, their skill at magic weaving is weakened. The first task a wizard who has achieved full rank undertakes is the fashioning of a staff. They are constructed of crystal and certain types of wood.

APPENDIX 4: THE FOE OF ËARNO

It is called:

In the language of the Bell people… *Orm Huluk,* or "God of Worms"
In the language of the Dweorg… *Hashba Hashba,* or "Great Enemy"
In the language of the elves… *Lormon Abollé,* or "Vermin of Hell"

The foe of Ëarno… The creature that laid Ëarno low. It slumbered in the caverns deep beneath the Dragonteeth Mountains. The dwarfs of Ëarno knew of its existence and had been warned, but their greed for gold and gems could not be sated. They continued to mine, until at last it was awakened. It — offspring of the ancient wurm Lindorm whom the god Alabaster was said to have personally wrestled into the subterranean depths and killed — devoured the miners in the caverns deep, but its hunger only grew.

It sent dreams and nightmares to those who lived above the surface. It caused the last king of Ëarno, Shai Ha-Thu, to offer it daily sacrifices of young Dweorg, and demanded that he build a temple for it in the midst of what is now the Vale of Ahorne.

The Dweorg worship would not sate their false and ravenous god. Shai Ha-Thu was eaten and devoured, together with his court, and the above-ground cities were, by it, turned to ruins. Those who should have escaped remained transfixed by their murderous god, continuing to offer it sacrifices until all of them were gone.

Then, seeing its source of food was no more, it slithered into the Dim Roads, the passages under the mountains, where it oft slept, and over the centuries slumbered.

Yet it knew that judgment was promised it, and all Lindorm's offspring.

About the Author

Cursed at birth with a wild imagination, Andrew Cooper spent his youth dreaming of worlds more exciting than Earth.

He is a graduate of the Odyssey Writing Workshop. His stories have appeared in Morpheus Tales, Fear and Trembling, Residential Aliens and Mindflights, among others.

He is also a graduate of the Creative Writing program at Western Michigan University.

Visit **www.aj-cooper.com** to sign up for the newsletter and stay up-to-date on new releases.

Find him on **x/Twitter** @ajcooperwriter.

www.ingramcontent.com/pod-product-compliance
Lightning Source LLC
Chambersburg PA
CBHW050756190726

48285CB00005B/1681